Way Down Dark

Book One of the Australia Trilogy

J.P. Smythe

HODDER

First published in Great Britain in 2015 by
Hodder & Stoughton
An Hachette UK company

First published in paperback in 2016

1

Copyright © JP Smythe 2015

The right of JP Smythe to be identified as the Author of the Work has been asserted
by him in accordance with the Copyright, Designs and Patents Act 1988.

All rights reserved. No part of this publication may be reproduced, stored in a
retrieval system, or transmitted, in any form or by any means without the prior
written permission of the publisher, nor be otherwise circulated in any form of
binding or cover other than that in which it is published and without a similar
condition being imposed on the subsequent purchaser.

All characters in this publication are fictitious and any resemblance to real persons,
living or dead is purely coincidental.

A CIP catalogue record for this title is available from the British Library

Paperback ISBN 978 1 444 796339

Printed and bound by Clays Ltd, St Ives plc

Hodder & Stoughton policy is to use papers that are natural, renewable and
recyclable products and made from wood grown in sustainable forests. The logging
and manufacturing processes are expected to conform to the environmental
regulations of the country of origin.

Hodder & Stoughton Ltd
Carmelite House
50 Victoria Embankment
London EC4Y 0DZ

www.hodder.co.uk

For A, J, K, T and W – because knowing you
made me want to be better at this.

And for C – because of absolutely everything else.

how the story goes. The people scrambled into the ships. They

PROLOGUE

The story goes that Earth was much older than the scientists thought. We had assumed that we had billions of years left; that we would be totally prepared if the worst happened. Maybe that made us complacent. We thought that we understood what we were doing to the planet. We thought we had time to fix it.

The first problem was overpopulation: too many people on the planet and not enough room for them. Then there wasn't enough fuel, there wasn't enough power, and we were wasting what little we had left. The planet got full around the same time as it started cracking and shaking. The weather changed, becoming warmer and colder at different times, extremes of everything and we couldn't adapt fast enough. The scientists knew that we were doomed.

The people of Earth scrambled for anything to save themselves. They built these ships in a rush – as many as they could manage, that's how the story goes – and they loaded them up with people and sent them up into the sky.

I've imagined that so many times: all of these ships crowding in the skies. Not everybody could be saved, that's

1

how the story goes. The people sent up in the ships – they were the lucky ones.

The ships were launched into the deepest parts of space, trying to find new homes. They didn't find anywhere, so we're still here.

Even when life here is at its worst, I know being on Australia means we have a chance. We still might find a place to belong, to set up and make into home. Things might still get better. And until then, being here is better than nothing.

It has to be.

PART

ONE

PART

ONE

ONE

After I helped to kill my mother, I had to burn her body. She and Agatha had been dreaming up the plan for months, when I wasn't looking: when I was asleep, or working. They spoke in whispers, but they had always done that, ever since I was little. I'd given up trying to understand them. And then, in her last few days, she told me everything. She said that it was to give me a chance to talk it through with them, to understand exactly what needed to be done. I think that was a lie; I think she believed that she would need to persuade me. But when she told me what I had to do – she was lying in her bed, barely anything more than skin and bones, Agatha at her side, cradling her hand – I didn't balk. It was what she wanted. She was in so much pain, and this was the only way that I could help her.

'As soon as I'm gone,' she said, 'they'll come for you. This is all I can do to protect you now.' I was young, that was her thinking. I was young; and Agatha was old, and soon she would be gone as well. That was the way of the ship: it took everybody in the end. All you did was survive until it was your time. My mother's survival had been incredible, really. It was because she had a reputation. Her reputation meant that I was always left alone, because so many others on the ship were scared of her. Only when she became sick did that change. Not that anybody knew what was wrong with her for sure, but there were rumours. Rumours are nearly worse than the truth, because they get out of control. People started looking at me differently, pushing their luck, sizing me up. They wanted to see just how weak she now was, and how weak I was. The gangs started coming nearer to our berth, sniffing the air and staying quiet to hear if she was still alive, and they would skulk and wait and brace their bodies against walls, their knives in their hands, ready to make their move. Power is everything on Australia. Power is how they rule; it's how they take territory, make parts of the ship their own. But, somehow, our section of the ship stayed free. Somehow – and part of me wants to lay the responsibility at my mother's feet, though I know it can't all have been her doing – we stayed out of it. By the time that she died, three sections – half of the ship – belonged to the gangs. But three sections had stayed free.

The night that my mother died, it was almost like everyone on Australia knew. She had spent ten days and nights in bed by that point, and she coughed so loudly that it echoed. During those ten days, people came to pay tribute: the Pale Women; the Bells; all the guilds of the free people: the tailors and the merchants and the smiths. I couldn't be with her while they visited. I didn't want to be. I stayed outside, and I watched them parade in, one by one. She coughed gratitude at them, and they shook their heads as they left.

She had done a lot for the ship. Her friends – all free people, not associated with any of the gangs – thanked her. They all cried. I had never seen so many people cry, because sorrow is such a weakness. Crying's when they get you.

And then they were all finished – this was on the last day, when we knew that it was her last day, because that feeling is like the air itself, a weight of it that stays over your head the entire time. Then it was just the three of us: me, my mother and Agatha.

'Can I have some time alone with her?' Agatha asked me, and I gave it to her, because I couldn't deny them that. They had known each other longer than I had; they were each other's family, had been since they were young. I was nervous; I knew what was coming, what I was going to have to do. I stood outside the rugs and curtains that made up the walls of our berth, and watched the rest of the ship. From our home on the fiftieth floor I could see everything else. Five other sections, all surrounding ours. The ship itself a hexagon of walkways and homes and shafts, over ninety floors high. And in the middle – suspended from the roof of the ship, attached by gantries to our floor, and by a jutting arm that linked it to the water system – was the arboretum, a walled box full of grass and trees and plants and bushes. Usually, I would be in there, working, picking fruit. (Not everybody has a job here, but those of us who want to contribute do what we can.) Vines grow up the arboretum walls, covering the sides. Maybe when we left Earth it was totally clear, but now, from pretty much anywhere on the ship – outside, looking in – it looks like a jungle.

And beneath the arboretum, fifty stories below, was the

Pit: a place so dark as to suggest that there was no end to it, just emptiness below us all. We all knew what was down there – clothes, trash, broken pieces of the ship itself, even her inhabitants rotting in a stinking mulch of decomposition – but we rarely (never, if we could help it) visited its depths. Stories were made up about the Pit, because that's the way of everything here (stories about ghosts who rise during the night, cloaked in the darkness, come to cause havoc), but those stories weren't real. What was real was the smell of the Pit, pervading everything. Usually you can get used to smells. Not that one. I never looked down there if I could help it, especially not on that day. Instead I concentrated on looking at the rest of the ship, because if I had tried to do anything, I felt as if I would have broken. There would be no work today. The arboretum wouldn't notice I wasn't there.

It felt like hours before Agatha came out and tapped me on the shoulder, waking me from my numbness, slumped against the walls of our berth. I knew what was coming.

'She wants you,' she said, and that meant that it was time.

Alone with my mother, I said my goodbyes. She told me things. She gave me rules: that I was to stay away from the lowest depths of the ship; avoid the gangs because they couldn't be trusted; eat healthily, because malnutrition could get me just as brutally as the gangs would. She smiled when she said it, because these were things she'd told me before, over and over. She knew – almost expected – that I wouldn't listen to her, but she told me anyway. And then she made me make promises to her, last-ditch attempts to influence me when she was gone. To stay out of trouble; to be selfish and think of myself first and foremost, even when it meant potentially hurting others ('Even Agatha,' she said, sadly); and then, finally, to not die.

'I can't promise that,' I said. 'Everybody dies.'

'Before your time,' she said. She coughed, and I saw fresh blood line her fingertips as she wiped her mouth. 'Don't die before your time.' And I thought, who's to say when my time is? How can anybody know how they're meant to die? But I didn't ask her that. That hardly seemed the point. It was easier to nod and agree to what she asked.

She coughed and clawed at her skin in her agony, and she spat the words out as though they were hurting more than her disease was, going over what I already knew; what I had been dreading. I had to be there when she died. I couldn't allow her to die of her sickness; I had to control the situation. And when she was dead, I had to burn her. The ship understands ritual, because rituals suggest control and control suggests power. The gangs choose their leaders through displays of power over life. They have rituals where they flex their muscles and their weapons, and somebody dies so that another can take their place.

My mother wanted me to have that power. If the gangs believed that I had killed her, they would respect me. They would fear me, just as they had feared her. Didn't matter that I knew it was a lie: as long as the rest of Australia believed it, maybe it would hold.

And then there was her ghost. I had to make them believe in her ghost.

She handed me a knife. I had never seen it before: it had been made for her, by one of the forgers. She commissioned it for this, letting it be known among the free people that it was special. It didn't matter what the knife looked like; what mattered was that people talked about it. And then she spoke to me, her voice a thin whisper that sounded almost nothing like the woman that I had known for the past sixteen years, telling me that it was time.

We both cried, but I tried to hold back as much as I could. Deep down, I knew that she was in more pain than I was. I helped her move from the bed to the floor. She lay there in the middle of our berth, arms by her side. She looked so small. She pressed the knife hilt into my palm, and she closed my fingers around it for me, and she held my hands tightly. 'In case anybody sees us,' she said. She would do this; I would just be there, helping her to find the strength. I don't know if I would have been able to do it if she didn't show me how.

I bent down to kiss her goodbye. Her lips were so dry. That's the last thing I really remember about her; how they felt like she was almost already gone.

For a second, I was somewhere else. For a second, none of it was real. We weren't on Australia, our ship, the dark and noisy home of our ancestors, ruined by time and violence; and my mother wasn't dying from a tumour that she had no hope of fighting; and I had a childhood like people used to have, never too terrified to sleep or breathe. The stories that we were told, about the time before – before Australia, when the Earth was still whole and people could live there – they were the truth. This was just a story. I could breathe in and smell the air. I could feel the grass between my toes, even as I felt the knife penetrate. Even as I felt warm blood, felt her chest rise and fall too quickly; and then as it slowed, until the last time, it just didn't rise at all.

When I finally opened my eyes she was dead, the blade in her chest, right through where her cancer was. I don't know how it happened. I don't remember it.

'It's done,' I said, loud enough for Agatha to hear. My voice cracked as I spoke, and I knew that I would have to fix that. I couldn't let weakness in again. There could be no tears, no shaking. I had to be as strong as my mother had been; I had to wear the power that she had created for me; her armour, now mine.

Agatha came in, pulling back the curtains for the rest of the ship to see the body; the rest of the ritual. She lit candles and placed them around us, and she took the knife from me – prising it from my fingers, exactly the opposite of my mother's last action – and laid it on top of my mother's body. 'We don't have much time,' she told me.

'Okay,' I said. I wanted to be weak again. I wanted to hold my mother and have what had been done be undone. But that would never happen. She asked me to do the ritual, my final act for her, and I made a promise. I wouldn't break that promise.

Days before, I had been told to go down to the markets, to make a trade for fuel. But the free tradesmen are canny and ruthless, and I got very little for what I had to pay for it. I was sure my mother would have managed to get twice as much. I only had enough for one attempt: a jar of thick glue that we were to spread over her body. That felt like the worst part. She was already cold. I had been near to enough bodies in my life to know that I was wrong; that she would be warm for hours. But then, my fingers on her skin, she felt so cold she could almost have been dead for days.

'This has to be down to you,' Agatha said. She handed me a match, crudely whittled, the head a thick black crust, and she made sure that the curtains were pinned back as wide as they could be. I could see lights in the darkness twinkling from distant parts of the ship, below, above and through the glass walls and trees of the arboretum; and eyes glinting in candlelight, as people watched what I was doing. It seemed like everybody knew what was coming. I wiped my hands of the fuel, I took a breath that hurt, and I struck the match on the rough metal of the exposed grated flooring of our home. It flickered, and it took.

I said goodbye and dropped the match onto her body, and she burned like I have never seen fire burn before.

In the days that followed, the others around where we lived would talk about it: about the smell; the crackle; the noise that I made, as her body turned to ash, burning so hot and so bright that it hurt to even look at it. But I heard none of that. Agatha and I stepped back, away from the body, and we watched; and I thought about what my mother had done for me; and I thought about how I was silhouetted against the flames for the rest of Australia to see. They all knew what had happened, and what I had done.

Now it was just a matter of waiting to see how they reacted.

* * *

It didn't take long to find out. My mother was still burning when I saw another flame spark up, three sections over – deep in Low territory. They were coming.

'I don't think that they'll make a move now,' Agatha told me. 'They're just sizing you up. They want to see that she's dead with their own eyes.' Ten, twenty, maybe more: even in the darkness I could see them swarming to the ends of their gantries, watching. But only a few approached, crossing the gangways that connected the different sections of the ship. 'Just don't let them see that you're afraid,' Agatha murmured.

'I'm not,' I said. And I wasn't. Right then, I felt nothing at all. I watched them circle the ship, clambering and climbing like cockroaches, the flame that was consuming my mother's body lighting their way. They were carrying torches, bringing their fire to meet mine. As they came closer, I saw them better. The sick runt of a man who led them was the ruler of the Lows – their king – and he was known only by his title: Rex, a word passed down from before. With him were two female Lows, both of them eyes-down, teeth gritted. All of them covered in their blood tattoos, the flames of their torches reflecting on the slick-ness of their skin. As they came closer, they called to me, their voices bouncing off the walls, the cruel rasp of their breathing preceding them. Their leader was watching me, his eyes glittering in the dying firelight. One of the Lows accompanying him avoided looking at me, but the other raised her head and stared directly into my eyes. Her gaze was like a challenge.

'You need to be here by yourself,' Agatha told me. 'They

won't fear you if they think you're hiding behind me.' She turned and slunk off into the darkness. She would be watching, I know; she had to be. But right then, that barely seemed to offer me any comfort.

'Riadne's daughter!' the Lows shouted, all three of them in some twisted harmony. 'Riadne's daughter!' They didn't know my name. They only knew me in the context of her. As they came closer, stalking along the gangway towards my home – as my mother's body burned its last – I told them my name.

'Riadne is dead,' I said, as loud as I could manage. 'My name is Chan.' Saying my mother's name hurt. It was the first time I'd said it since she died, and already it felt like she wasn't real any more; like she was just a dream that I remembered, vaguely, hours after waking. The Lows stepped onto our section, and I looked along the gantry – for Agatha, for anybody willing to help me to ward them off – but there was nobody. I was alone.

'Your part of the ship is ours now, yes?' the leader said, coughing the last word, wheezing to draw breath back in. On his skin was a tattoo: his title, his name, scored across his chest. The letters were somehow almost delicate, at odds with the damaged, scarred rest of him. 'And you? You are ours as well?'

'No,' I said, 'none of this is yours.' I held up my hands, covered to the elbows in my mother's drying, browning blood. I heard my mother's voice come through me: the voice that she used when she spoke to people who she wanted to fear her, a put-on falsehood of rage. She had power, everybody knew that. She was feared, and she was respected. She had earned that. I had to persuade them that I was just like her, that I had taken her power. And her ghost, I reminded myself. That wasn't real, but they were superstitious. I could persuade them.

'If you come closer, I will kill you,' I said. I believed that I would, as well; or I would try. But my words weren't about starting a fight. Really, I was just trying to make sure that I wouldn't have to.

'You've never killed a man.' Rex licked his lips, his tongue stumped at the end, fixed by a crude patchwork of stitches. The scars on his body were so numerous that I couldn't have counted them had I wanted to. Pieces of him were missing: fingers, lumps of flesh, an ear. That was how he had become their king: by clawing, scratching, fighting his way to the top and surviving all challenges. Power follows death. He was powerful, and he bore the traces of death about him.

'I killed Riadne,' I said. 'I burned her, so that she'll protect me. I have her power, and still she watches over me.' I said it with false confidence; I didn't believe the lie, but he had to. I had to sell it.

And then he laughed at me, this roar that came from nowhere, but I could see behind it. He was nervous. He believed in the facts: I had killed her, and I had burned her. That much couldn't be disputed, thanks to the blood on my hands, the embered corpse on the floor. The two female Lows with him stared at me: one of them was afraid, or getting there, but the other? There was nothing in her eyes at all. No fear, not of me, not of anything. She didn't believe in the story that I was telling. Their leader, though, he wondered. His head tilted in curiosity. He stepped toward me, moving his head from left to right, as if it was loose upon his shoulders, and he slid in close. He didn't see my hands, because he was fixated on my face, on my mouth. He didn't see that I had lifted the blade from my mother's body, that I was holding it in my hand, my fingers tightly closed around the hilt, slick with still-warm blood from my mother's body and the fire that had consumed her.

'That is where she died,' he said, when he was close enough that I could smell him – the dirt on his skin, the sickly metallic stink of old blood – and he looked over my shoulder at my berth. 'Nothing less than she deserved,' he said. 'But now, she's gone. Ghosts are stories for little children. You don't really believe in them.'

That was when Agatha dropped the smoke pellet from above. It plumed as it fell, and I will admit that, in that second, it felt supernatural; as if it was magic, almost – my mother's ghost, there to protect me. The leader panicked, rushing to me, as if that would end this faster. He was quick, but I was quicker. My mother and Agatha had trained me my whole life to protect myself, and I wasn't about to stop now.

I jabbed upwards with my mother's knife. I jammed it into his neck and he howled in agony, coughing, blood gurgling into his mouth, tumbling around, throwing the smoke in all directions. It happened so fast that the others didn't have time to react. I didn't even know that I was going to stab him there before the knife was in his throat, my hand covered in his blood. He staggered backwards, out of the smoke, away from my berth, clutching at his neck as the blood gulped out. 'Bitch,' he gasped, his eyes wide, his voice shaking. I don't know if the choking smoke or the wound I had inflicted affected him more, but suddenly he was scared of me.

Actually afraid.

He stumbled away, falling to the gantry floor and then pulling himself up, clinging to one of the other Lows. He motioned to the side, telling them to go back the way that they had come. One of the women – the one who hadn't met my eyes – stroked him, soothing him, trying to tend to him until he swatted her away as they retreated. The other, though, she didn't stay at his side. She didn't support him as he walked. She stared at me as she had from the beginning. She was looking me over through the now-clearing smoke, searching for weaknesses. Her body was a mesh of scars as well, but they were different from Rex's: they weren't all from fighting or torture. There were delicate cuts all down her shoulders, across her chest and neck, her legs. Across her belly, a puckered scar curved from one side to the other, like a grimace.

'You're strong, little liar,' she said. Her voice was thick and dark, a gravelled rasp that emerged from deep within her throat. 'Not at all what I expected.'

Then she turned and ran – a sprint, a furious dash past the other berths and onto the gangway between sections, to catch up with the other Lows – and when she reached them she leapt, launching herself into the air, landing on the leader's back and throwing her arm around his neck. My mother's blade: it was still there, dug in, jutting half out of his flesh. I had missed it. I didn't notice.

My mother's blade, gone. But she – the Low – didn't care what it might have meant to me. She grabbed it by the hilt and pushed it further in. She pushed it in and then pulled it out, driving it into Rex, over and over. Her hand moved so much faster than mine. After a few blows he dropped to his knees, his hands beating at her as she clung on. She didn't stop. The other female howled, but she didn't pause. When the leader was on his knees, she dismounted from his back and slashed at the other female, cutting her, making her step back until she lost her footing and fell backwards off the gangway, making no sound as she plummeted into the darkness.

The leader died there on the gangway. As he went – again, I do not know how long it took, only that it was quick – his killer took up my mother's blade and began to carve something into her chest. I watched her face as she worked the sacrificial knife. Her hand shook, through the pain, I'm sure; but she carried on, determined to get the job done. When she was finished she turned, showing herself off to the rest of the ship, and she beat at her chest with her arm, making the wound bleed more, forcing the welts to open wider.

She revealed herself to us, and we all saw it: the letters *REX*, etched into her skin, hard and deep. She had killed the last leader and now was carving his name – his title – onto herself. His power was now hers. I watched her return to the Lows' half of the ship, howling and calling her own arrival; and I watched as the other Lows crept toward her in worship, bowing their heads as she passed them.

The night that I took my mother's power, the Lows gained a new leader.

* * *

18

When the commotion died down, something resembling a more conventional night set in. The lights dimmed, heralding the sounds of people all over the ship: the calls of the vendors and traders fifteen floors down; the prayers of the Pale Women from the top floor of the ship, carrying through the motionless air; the grunts and moans of the Bells as they fought each other for pride or food or whatever it was that they were fighting over; the Lows, laughing and drinking and preparing for more carnage in the morning; and the whirring thrum of the engines that reverberated through us all. I closed the curtains and sat by my mother's ashes, and I finally cried, so quietly that the noise was lost amongst the chaos of night-time aboard the Australia.

TWO

Today, the arboretum is in full harvest. This is when I love working here most. It's so hot that you can only stand to be inside for a short while at a time, and most people, sweating and on the verge of fainting, give up. They aren't used to these temperatures. But my mother was sensible, and when I was a child she moved us to a berth closer to the engines. The noise is the same as anywhere else on the ship – you can't escape the turbines, which sound like the loudest rumble you've ever heard, constantly behind everything else – but you don't need to make fires when it gets really cold, because the engine is always there. So I've learnt to live with the heat. That means I can work in the arboretum even when it gets too much for everybody else. It's then that I have it to myself.

In the hundreds of years that we've been on Australia, nearly all of those things that were once beautiful on the ship have gone. Still, the arboretum has survived. It's central, which is something. Nobody owns it, and nobody has fought wars over it. Everybody on the ship needs it, because without it, we're pretty much screwed. All of us – Lows,

Pale Women, Bells, free people – have the same basic needs. We understand that the arboretum gives us our oxygen, which allows us to breathe; that the water purifiers work through it, giving us clean water to drink from; and that it gives us crops – the only fresh foods in the whole of Australia. That's before we even get to the bugs that the protein machines turn into food for us: they thrive there. It's an ecosystem, is the word. Everything works in conjunction with everything else.

I love fruit; my mother loved fruit; and, from how she told it, her mother did as well. I work the pear trees today, because I'm small and I can climb. I think I get the same things out of it as they did, as well. It's not just the food aspect; it's having time to yourself, time to think. You climb a tree – if you're lucky to get to work on one of the taller ones – and you're suddenly somewhere else.

Nowhere else on Australia feels like this. Here, there is grass on the floor, vines on the walls, and trees and plants and crops growing in small patches. In the early days of our being up here, the story goes that they grew the vines around the mesh on the walls on purpose, so that you could stand here in the centre of the arboretum and be surrounded by nothing but green. Back on Earth, there were places like this everywhere – vast areas of land populated by trees, rivers, vegetation, flora and fauna. So our arboretum is like that, only not as large, and man-made.

Through it all runs the river. We use the river for everything. It feeds the trees and the crops, sure, and we drink from it, but we also use it to wash our clothes. And at the end of it, before it goes into the system again, you can even go in and bathe, if you want. You wouldn't want any-body to end up drinking from that end, so nobody bathes at the mouth, the clunking bit of metal that the river pours out from; but at the end, where it drains off and goes back into the water to be recycled, that part is always busy, people wading into it to wash their bodies and their clothes. We used to have running water in the berths, that's what we're told, but that stopped a long time ago. Some of us still care about cleanliness. If others don't care about stink, that's their business. Maybe if you live on the lower floors, there's no point. Maybe the smell of everything – of the Pit – is absorbed into your skin anyway, to taint you forever. But I love how it feels so good to be clean. I can't get enough of it.

Pears taste wonderful. This is the best part of working here: the unspoken rule that you can keep the fallen, dam-aged fruit for yourself. Today I eat one, and it's perfect. It tastes almost powdery in my mouth, and so sweet. Better than what usually passes for food here. Some of the old protein machines still work, turning bugs into these lumps of grey jellied biscuit. We eat those for health reasons. Some people make stews, and maybe the taste isn't so bad then. It's at least tolerable.

When I'm done, and I've weighed in the rest of the day's harvest – nearly fifty pears, hand-picked (which is as good a day's work as I've had here in a while), and a further seven damaged pieces of the fruit for me to keep for myself – I see Agatha at the berry bushes, and I go over to her. We don't talk much these days. Since my mother died – it's been nearly a full year now, or as close to a year as I can guess it's been – she's kept her distance. I remind her too much, I think. I've tried to understand that, but it hurts.

'You look tired,' she says, but that's not an invitation for me to tell her my woes. She doesn't want some long story, because she's been alive so long that she's heard it all before. She wants me to nod because I agree with her. Yes, she wants, this is tiring. Being here. Being alive.

She's more tired than I am, anyway. I have no idea how old she is. I haven't asked, and she wouldn't tell anyway. She's older than my mother by some way, that's for sure. When my mother was a child, Agatha rescued her once. She went missing, one playtime, and Agatha had to go and get her back. That's how they met. Agatha told me the story, when my mother was sick. Told me a lot of a stories. Not everything – she's guarded, and she acts like her secrets are somehow more secretive or important than anybody else's – but we all have secrets. And I get it. It's easier to not tell others your secrets. Easier to take them to your grave, where nobody can use them against you.

Agatha has hair that flows halfway down her back, long ago turned white. She has never shaved it, not since I have known her – not like most of the rest of us. Somehow she manages to keep the lice away. Everybody on Australia is a little afraid of her, I think; maybe the lice are scared as well. Her hair covers most of one side of her face, draped down over her left eye. She has a scar there, dug in through her brow and down, straight across the puffed-up eyelid. The hair hides it. That's not like anybody else here either. For the gangs, scars are like a sign that you've survived. People show them off. But not Agatha. Agatha's bottom lip is entirely scar as well, it seems, and it moves like rope when she speaks, slack and then taut. She doesn't make any attempt to hide that one. Harder to, I suppose.

I hand her one of my damaged pears, and she nods thanks. She pulls a knife from her pack, slices a piece off one and eats it, and her crumbled rope lip folds itself down as she chews. It looks odd: like her face is starting to crumple in on itself with every bite.

You get used to that.

Before my mother died, when she was lying in her bed, in her last few days, Agatha would talk about what she remembered from when she was growing up. She told me about how her childhood was trial by fire; that she lived wild, or as wild as you can here; and how she doesn't remember her parents. She lived with people who were abandoned by a lot of the rest of the ship, the elderly and infirm and rejected. I think that she lived with the Pale Women for a while, even. She's still got a lot of time for them.

There comes a point here when you join a cult or you don't, and she nearly did. She never tells me why she didn't, but they were good to her; I know that much. She finds it easier to talk about my mother than about herself. But today she doesn't want to talk at all, which is fine. She wants to stand here under the tree and eat her pear; and when she's done, she nods a second time – thanks, again – she returns to her own picking; and I go home.

Everything on Australia revolves around stories. They're all we have to entertain us; and all we've got to keep the little bits of who we were before we left Earth alive. We're told them from the moment that we're born, and we keep them alive until the day that we die. We create them, and we destroy them. The stories keep us safe, and they keep us scared. Sometimes, it seems like you need one to feed the other.

When I was young, my mother told me endless stories. She told me about her parents, her grandparents, the whole legacy of our entire family, going back as far as she had been told. She said, all the time, that she didn't know how much of it was true, but that didn't seem to matter to her. I loved those stories: lying underneath the single bunk in our berth, eyes forced shut, knowing that my mother's voice would carry me through until I was asleep. She told me about what happened when we left Earth, and how we came to be here, drifting for what seems like forever. She just didn't want to forget the good stuff in the past, the stuff that was probably worth fighting for. Same with the lessons that she gave me. She thought that it was important that I took parts of the old times with me: reading, writing, counting. And physical stuff, as well. She taught me how to run: how to control my breathing, focus my eyes to see where I was going, how to not trip over my own feet. With Agatha, they taught me to fight, to defend myself – with my hands and feet, and with knives, if it came to that. There are a lot of knives on Australia.

My mother wanted me to be able to defend myself. She knew that, one day, I would have to. She told me stories about when she had been forced to fight, knowing that I might find myself in those same situations; and then she told me how she escaped. That was the lesson. Then, when my mother was dying, Agatha took over the storytelling. She was forced to. But that was fine by me. She had new stories. And it's always good to get another perspective on the things that you think you already know.

When I get home, satchel full of pears, I lie on my bed and listen to the ship. It's endless, the noise: not just from the engines, but from everybody else who lives here. There's not as many of us as there once were. I know this because not every berth is full any more. Maybe it's harder to survive here than it once was.

I'm tired. It's hard to block the sounds of the ship out. Harder to block out what's inside your head; the thinking about what might have been. Agatha used to say, when I asked her about the time before we left Earth, that it was pointless worrying about what came before. You can't miss what you never knew, she would say. But I can, I think. I can miss silence, even if I've never really heard what it's like.

I kick off my shoes, and feel one of them pull apart as I nudge it off with my other foot. Looking down, I watch as it falls in fragments to the floor. Just what I need! I pick up the pieces and hold them together, to see if I can stitch them into a whole again, but the rubber is worn away and the cloth is frayed almost beyond belief. I should be grateful they held up until now, really. They could have gone when I was climbing a tree, and I don't fancy knowing what sort of cuts my feet would have ended up with then. The shoes have been patched too many times already. They've outlived themselves. Time to get new ones.

There's only one place to get shoes on the Australia: down

on the thirty-first floor. That's deep in Shopkeeper territory. The Shopkeepers have a few floors of the ship, and they're somewhat neutral between all the gangs. You give them money if there's something that you want, and there's always something that you want. They make food, and they make medicines, and they make clothes; and on the floor below, there's a few that make weapons. Bartleby is a shoemaker who my mother used to do business with. He's fair, she used to say. Fair and as honest as any of them; so he's who I'll see. I take my satchel up, bundle the pears back into it – no idea if seven pears equals the shoes that I need, but this is what I've got – and leave my berth, barefoot.

'Goodbye,' I say out loud, to my mother's ghost. She doesn't answer back, because she isn't real. But it doesn't hurt that I act like she is.

Every floor on the Australia is the same. It's hard to get your bearings at first. It can take years to get the floorplan in your head. Each section has the same number of floors, and almost every floor has the same number of berths. The same thick black iron gantries in front of the berths; the same thick black iron railings on the edge of each gantry; the same thick black iron floor, grates and plates of stiff metal. The ship is a hexagon, and we all look out at each other across the Pit. The only thing breaking that space is the arboretum.

In another life, maybe the design was intended as something social: all of us facing each other, able to see what everybody else is doing at all times. In reality, it's hard to know where you are. There are few landmarks that we haven't made ourselves. Once, there were signs, but they're long gone. I live in section IV, level 50. The floors directly above mine have a chunk taken out of them, for the engines. There's no way to see into my berth from above. But the floors below? That's a different matter. To get to them, you use the stairwells.

I watch my step as I go down the stairwells; as I climb over the jagged remains of the steps that were once here, and the doors that once sat at the top and bottom of each set. It's dangerous, because people still come and work on the metal for scraps that they can use, leaving each new edge sharp. The stairs are gone, so moving between floors generally means dropping – and that means a climb up when you want to return – but it's faster than walking around to one of the few ladders that people have bothered to build, to replace the stairs. I never use the ladders. I like the straight shot down. I sit on the edge and let go, and I brace my knees. Something about it feels more efficient than climbing. If you can take the fall, it's almost always better.

As you get further down the ship, the floors start to smell of sulphur: a thick stench that's nearly pleasant, if you spend enough time with it. You get used to it, that's what the people who live here say. You stop noticing it. This is where the purification systems are, for the water and the oxygen (even though that one barely seems to work any more), but they don't make it any easier to breathe. You have to hold your breath for stretches, because otherwise, in spots, the stench will make you gag.

You have to cross the fortieth floor to get to the next

pathway down, because the stairwell here is blocked up. This is a walk I know well. I pass families who have no choice but to live on this floor, and I greet them all. My mother always said that it never hurt to let others see that you're friendly. Can't hurt, and it doesn't.

One of the people I greet shouts out at me. He always does this. 'You want to buy a weapon? I've got a weapon right here for you!' His friends laugh. There's no malice: he's just an old man with nothing but time on his hands. I tell him where to stick his weapon, and raise my middle finger at him. 'Come here and show me!' he says.

'You'd love that,' I reply, and he nods. 'Filthy bastard,' I say. I'm still smiling.

'How did you know my name?' he replies, and his friends fall about laughing. They're on stools and crates in one of the berths, huddled around a small pot of something boiling in the middle of them: something nasty, judging by the smell. I get to the next stairwell and jump down to floor 38, which was once the medical floor. It runs the entire length of the ship, in every single section. It's hard to see any remnants of its original purpose, though. Supposedly, the mattresses were more comfortable than those we have in our berths, so they were ransacked, and the metal frames were salvaged, just like everything else. There's no medicine any more, either. We had machines that used to synthesise drugs, but apparently they were hacked up and pulled apart, the fittings taken, the guts wrenched out for parts. Or maybe for no reason other than to cause havoc for those people who actually needed the stuff. So now we have herbs and liniments that we create ourselves from plants – and prayers – but nothing that actually does any real good. (And, when I am saddest, I wonder if anything in those machines could have helped my mother; and if, therefore, there's somebody real I can blame for her sickness. That's pointless, I know, and a waste of time, but it helps to try to find a place to lay the blame.) I wonder what Australia must have been like when our ancestors first boarded: because on some parts of this floor you can still see the white tile underneath the dirt.

Even though I want to get my new shoes quickly, I stop. I don't know why exactly, but I like this floor. There's nothing here – no partitions, no berths, no grates or gates or anything to make living here actually doable. I like being here, though, because of how quiet it is. It's not like noise from everywhere else doesn't travel, but it's more muted, and you never see anybody else. There's nothing here for them, which somehow leaves something for me: the quiet. I watch my step, because there are glass slivers on the floor still. Nothing big enough to do any immediate damage, because that stuff all got taken for weapons or whatever, but if you catch a splinter and can't get it out, that's just as likely to kill you. Infection sets in and, soon as you know it, you're having that foot amputated. As good as a death sentence, that, if you don't have somebody to help you out. Those people never last long here. So I tread carefully, head down, eyes on the ground, trying to catch glimmers of light reflecting off anything that could stick in me. Stupid, really. Eyes down is no way to live on Australia. I know that.

I hear the breathing before I see the Pale Women – a group of them. They never travel alone, it seems. And when

I look up, and they light their candles in front of their faces, I suddenly realise how close to them I am. Feet away – nothing more. But they never come down here. They stay on their floor. That's the rule.

'Hello,' I say. I start to back away, but I stay friendly. They are no threat to me, I know that. But this – their being here – breaks all the rules.

Used to be, Agatha says, that way, way back, the Pale Women tried to save people on the ship. They went around butting in when fights broke out, doing what they could to help. But then they abandoned the rest of the ship, choosing to stay on the top floor and never leave. Agatha knows more about it than I do. They call their floor Limbo. I don't know what it means: it's a word from one of their *Testaments*.

One of them steps forward. She tries to speak, but the words don't come, so she licks her lips, which are chapped and dry (I can see that much in the flickering candlelight), and then tries again. 'You're lost,' she says. They have hoods on, covering their whole heads nearly. Her chin, I can see, is a mess of scars.

'I'm not,' I reply. 'I know exactly where I am.'

'Child,' she says, and it's the first time I've been called that in an age, 'we're worried about you.'

'Well, don't be,' I reply. 'I'm fine.'

'Will you take this?' She holds something out, her hand darting out from underneath her cloak, and her motioning makes me jump. Usually, somebody producing something that fast means a weapon. This? It's a bundle of papers, nothing more. I can see a scrawl of handwriting across it.

'I'm fine,' I say.

'You think that you have a choice?' It's threatening. I've never had any trouble from them, and I don't want to start now.

'Okay,' I say. I step forward, and she does, and I reach out as far as my arm will extend to take the thing from her fingers. As she lets go, I see that chunks of her hand are missing: the tips of two fingers, the nails from another. I look away, up at the other Women. I can see them all clearly now, all dressed the same; and another person behind them, head bowed, outfit slightly different. More covered, darker, more ragged. Not a woman: a boy. He's younger than the woman. Around his neck is a thick white collar, tight to his flesh, digging in. I can't be sure, but the edge looks lined with something sharp – metal or glass. His skin is scarred where it's cut into him, a ring around his throat. It looks punishing.

'Reading these will change your life,' the first woman says, and the other two murmur their agreements with her. 'This is the true story of Australia, of life before Australia, and of why we are here.'

'I'm sure,' I say. I can't even count the number of supposedly true stories of Australia that I've been told in my lifetime, and how disappointing each one is. No stories ever have a happy ending, I know that, but there's some promise when people talk about what came before. I don't tell her that though. I can't predict how she'll act. That's the worst: when you just can't tell.

I step backwards again – another of the ship's unspoken rules, *never turn your back on somebody you don't know*

– and make it to the stairwell. I wave to them, in the distance. Seems like the right thing to do. It isn't until I lower myself to the floor below that I feel the sting in my foot, and every muscle in my leg twitches to stop me putting any weight onto it. I crane my neck and bring my foot up and there's the end of a needle, jutting from the fleshiest part of my foot, right in the middle. If it had gone near the ball or the heel, there's every chance it wouldn't have made it past the skin, which is so much tougher in those places. That skin is so thick it's almost like bark. But, no, just my luck: right where it's softest. I pull the needle out, but something snaps. These things are so bloody fragile. I squeeze the hole, feeling for the bits of sharpness in the wound, and then pluck the final piece of the needle out. My foot is really bleeding now.

Shit.

I step, but it hurts. More need for the shoes than ever, now. I walk on my toes, tiptoeing forward on them, slower and more delicate than before. This was stupid. I should have wrapped up my feet. I'll never learn. Feels like I've been told that a thousand times before. I think about the jobs in the books that my mother used to read to me. One was a ballerina. This is how they stood. They could manage it, so I can.

I drop down the stairwell to the next floor, as gently as I can, and again, and again, and then I'm on the thirty-first and suddenly Australia becomes a different place. What was quiet and sad is suddenly vibrant; Shopkeepers everywhere, their calls and cackles loud as they try and pimp whatever they've got to whoever happens to be passing.

You don't come here unless you've got a hankering, but it's always busy. Everybody wants something. And there's still so much colour! It's almost too much to take. Where the rest of the ship is all blacks and greys and reds, the Shopkeepers have these clothes that they've made themselves, dyed and bright (or as bright as they can get them), patched and stitched. They have converted their homes into stalls along the entire length of this floor, right up to the edge of the Lows' half of the ship; fabric coverings dragged out and tarpaulins stretched across the gantries to make warm, colourful caverns. They play music, they shout, they laugh. They hang whatever they're selling on the sides of the walls, or they arrange it on their beds and on tables.

Outside some berths, there are trays of food fresh out of ovens. I focus on the buns and twirled pastries, made from what they've bought and then recycled. But they're sold at such steep prices that I have only ever tasted anything like them a handful of times, and even then only a quarter . . . a fifth of one. That was years ago, when I was far younger than I am now. I can't even remember the taste, not exactly, but still sometimes wake up craving it, even to this day.

'Go on,' one of the sellers says to me, as I pass and gaze. He is tall, his skin a sickly shade of pale yellow, and his teeth glimmer, polished glass set into the enamel. 'You're Riadne's daughter. She loved these treats. You love them too.' He knows who I am, which is good. My mother's reputation holds, which is nice. It won't help me haggle, though. 'Taste it, right?'

'No,' I say. Doesn't matter how tempted I might be. I've

got enough for shoes. I'd enjoy the bun for a second, but shoes? They'll last a lot longer. 'Another time. I'll save up for them,' I tell him. I inhale, because that smell . . . It's almost intoxicating.

'You sure you'll have the time?' he asks. 'Maybe the end is already here.' He smiles, as if he knows something. But this is typical: there are always rumours that the end is coming, and some people believe them. Especially since the Lows fell under their new leadership: they're worse than ever before. That's what it feels like, and that's what the rumours suggest. True or not, this seller is enterprising. He's benefitting from panic.

'If it is, I'll never know what I've missed out on,' I say. He shrugs and looks away, to find the next – hopefully more gullible – customer, and I tiptoe off, down towards the clothiers. What they have, they make from fragments of what's been before. Everything we wear is recycled, like the air, like the water, but how they get their materials is different. They scavenge. We've come to accept it: that they go to the Pit at the bottom of the ship, take what they need from the bodies and then clean it, dye it, re-cut it. They turn the scraps into something new, and you'd never even know where they originally came from. Rumour has it, even the dyes that they use come from down there. Rumour has it that they harvest skin with tattoos and recycle the colour from them, draining it out of the dead skin, soaking it out and breaking it down. I don't know if that's true, but it feels like it could be. I've seen them pressing clothes, driving colour out of anything that they can to get the ink that they need. When it comes to it, skin is the same as clothes: if you don't need it any more, you take what you can from it, I guess.

At the furthest end of this section, nudged up against the barricades to protect against the Lows, are the shoemakers. There are three of them, all jostling for space, tables set up outside their berths. But as I get closer I see that there's a crowd here. They're shouting for something, crowds of people fighting over something. My foot stings more and more, every step that I take. I could really do without the hassle of having to fight through people to get the shoes that I want. I know that much.

I can't get close enough. I'm at the back, behind other Shopkeepers. I catch glimpses through the crowd of what's going on, though. There's a Bell up there, his hand wrapped around the neck of one of the shoemakers: Bartleby. Bartleby is bald and small, the shattered remains of spectacles clinging to his nose and ears. He looks terrified. What's he done? He must have done something. The Bells are stupid and violent, but they don't do anything unless they're provoked.

'Please!' I hear him shouting, 'It wasn't me!' That's not good enough for the Bell holding him up, who pulls back his fist and slams it into the side of Bartleby's head.

'Don't lie,' the Bell says. His hands are the size of Bartleby's face. Hardly seems a fair fight, but nobody's stepping up.

'What did he do?' I ask one of the Shopkeepers in front of me. The woman doesn't look back, but stretches up onto her toes to let her see better.

'Nicked something from them. Gave them a bad trade.'

'Bartleby?'

'He's the same as anybody. Saw an opportunity, took it.' My mother liked Bartleby. She trusted him, as much as she trusted anybody. I feel around behind me, to my satchel. I've got my knife here: a small scalpel blade that I tell myself I carry to help me in the arboretum with stubborn branches, but that I really carry for protection. I could put myself into this. I'm fast – faster than the Bell, that's for sure. Bartleby's face crumples under the Bell's fist and he drools out teeth and blood from his mouth; insists, once again, that he didn't do anything, that the trade was fair. I'm amazed he's even conscious, but he must be forcing himself; he must know what will happen if he doesn't persuade them that he's telling the truth. There aren't any half-measures on Australia.

'Please,' Bartleby says. He's yammering desperately, and as he talks he accidentally spits blood out from between his shattered teeth. It spatters the Bell's face. I take my hand off my satchel, off the outline of my knife. This is over.

The Bell roars with anger, and Bartleby is hurled over the edge, over the railing that divides the gantry from the Pit. There's no sound as he falls, and no sound as he lands. It's soft down there. The crowd cheers – they don't even know what they're cheering for, just that this fight (such as it was) has ended – and then they swarm. They tear into Bartleby's shop, taking whatever they want. I'm too far back. The Bells at the front destroy his possessions, hurling his table down after him. And then the sated crowd, bit by bit, disperses: some carrying shoes, blankets, whatever else Bartleby owned. When they're gone, it's like his berth never had anybody there in the first place. It's empty, apart from some fragments of rags left over the doorway, and there are scuff marks on the floor: the only signs of life. There are globs of bright red blood spattering the gantry, and I step over them carefully. You never know what you could catch.

It's sad, seeing the berth like this. I always liked him. He used to say, whenever I came down here, that he remembered me when I was a child; that he always liked me. That's one less person who'll be kind to me for no reason, now. But there are still two shoemakers left, and I still need shoes. I watch them both putting what they grabbed from Bartleby's stock on their tables. We're a ship full of scavengers, and I can't blame them for taking what he had.

I think that if I'd been able to, I'd have taken my shoes for free.

When the scavenging is done, one of the other shoemakers notices me. His first customer to hawk the new stock to. He waves at me, beckons me over. He smiles, not a single tooth in his skull, but he bares his gums as if he's got every single one. I can see that his tongue has been snipped, leaving a half-tongue that, in the darkness of his mouth, seems like it's barely even there. There's no telling what happened; that's a common injury here.

'John,' he says, 'I'm John. Call me John.' The words stumble as they come out of his mouth, a mess of chewy sounds. 'You want shoes, yes?' The final S hisses at me. 'Because I've got the right ones. Look, right here.' He holds up a pair of thick black plastic lumps, not even close to as pliable as I'd need them to be. There would be no climbing in those things, and they would make one hell of a noise.

'I need something else,' I say. 'Anything smaller?' He tilts his head. 'I climb trees,' I say, as an explanation, and he laughs at that.

'Yes, yes,' he says. I hate the sound of him talking. It's awful, and makes me picture his empty mouth even as I try not to look. That's unfair, I know. Maybe he was injured through no fault of his own. Maybe. But usually, injuries like that are a sign of having made a mistake; saying the wrong thing to the wrong person, and being punished for it. I'm quick to judge people, but more often than not it's the right thing to do.

He brings another pair out from underneath the table, and I can tell before I've even touched them that they're perfect. They're thin, and the rubber around the sole is almost beautiful, carved and neat. Rubber warps, and it rots. These? I don't even know how he's got them – that's how new they look. I reach over to hold them, and he swats my hand away.

'Nuh-uh,' he says, 'you come back here. Try, try.' He steps back and reveals a stool, and I step towards it. My foot is sore, and he sees that I'm not stepping on it. 'Cut?' he asks.

'I stepped on something,' I say. He shakes his head.

'Okay,' he says, and pulls a thick wodge of tattered material from a pocket and hands it to me as I sit down. 'Your foot,' he says, and he indicates that I should wrap the material around it. It's filthy, but he's protecting his merchandise.

'It's fine,' I say, 'I'll just take them. How much?'

He sucks in air through the hole where his teeth should be. 'No,' he says, and he kneels in front of me and picks up my foot, stroking it with his fingers. He has no fingernails,

I notice. Not a single one, not even the indications of stumps where they might have been pulled. My skin crawls as he touches me. He slips the shoe onto my foot. It fits, because of course it does. And it's so comfortable! My toenails touch the end, but that's my problem. Toenails can be cut. I place my foot gently down on the ground, and he slips the other shoe onto me, and I stand. I want them, I know that much. I really want them.

'How much?' I ask again.

'What are they worth to you?'

'I have pears,' I say. I take three out first and put them on the table.

'No, no, no.' He shakes his head and closes his eyes.

'Fine,' I say. I tip the rest out. I really need these shoes. Along with the pears, I've got some scraps of metal that I've salvaged over the past few weeks, and the booklet that the Pale Women gave to me. My knife I keep hidden. He doesn't need to know about that.

He looks the collection of items over, and he laughs. 'No good to me!' he says, picking up a pear. 'No good at all. Soft food for me! Softer, softer!'

'You can cut them up,' I say, 'or stew them. They're delicious.'

'Not enough anyway. More than this many fruits.' It takes me a second to work that last word out. Nothing about how his mouth is now is made to say it.

'They're all I've got,' I say.

'So,' he replies, holding up the first pair of shoes, which look even bulkier, even less practical from where I'm now standing, 'this is what you get.'

'I want the other ones,' I tell him. I reach to take my pears back but they're already gone, and I didn't see where: somewhere in the dark of his stall. Wherever they are, I won't see them again. 'Give them back,' I tell him. 'They were mine.' He looks down, and he makes a fake-sad face: he pulls his bottom lip over the top, his face almost folding in on itself. The inside of his mouth is rotting, and only now do I notice the smell. He raises his hand and makes a gesture, and he undoes his trousers, letting them drop to his feet. This is how I get the good shoes, he is telling me. He laughs at his suggested method of payment, as if it's some shared joke we have together; and then I see that he's got a knife of his own, suddenly out, in his left hand. He thinks that this is how this ends.

He's wrong.

'Good girl,' he says. He walks around his stall, dropping the tarpaulin fabrics over the table, hiding us from the view of the rest of the ship. He doesn't see me slide my own knife out from my satchel; and he doesn't see it hidden in my palm as he takes my hand and pulls me towards him. The noise of the rest of the Shopkeepers hides his screams as I deal with him, leaving him cradling himself in a puddle of his own blood.

'I hope you don't get an infection,' I say. I pull the bandage from my shoe and throw it to him. 'That'll stop the bleeding.' And I walk out of there, wearing my new shoes. I take the other pair – not as good, but good enough – as I go. I know somebody who'll appreciate exactly how sturdy they are.

* * *

41

I climb up and go to the arboretum in the middle of the ship, that giant silver dish full of greenery and vegetation. As I walk across, I see Agatha resting by the river. I wave to her, and she waves back. No smile, though. I can't remember how long it's been since she smiled at me. She's been uncomfortable with me since the night Mother died, and that hurts. We had to do what we did, and I can't help that I remind her of that; or that I remind her of my mother. We used to be so close, but now? Now she's excellent at walking away from conversations that she doesn't like. So now I just try to keep her around for as long as I can. Maybe, someday, I'll break through to her and we'll be close again.

She's sitting by the water, washing her face, lifting her palms to her skin and splashing it over herself.

'It's hot,' I say.

'It really is.'

'You're done for the day?'

'Too tired. Just too tired.' She leans back as I sit down next to her. 'I'm too old for this.' She looks at my feet as I slip the shoes off and place them next to me. 'New shoes?' she asks. It's a rhetorical question. She taught me that word. I pull the others from my satchel and hand them over to her.

'A present,' I say. 'I thought that they might come in handy.' She weighs them in her hand, and then sets them down next to mine.

'Thank you,' she says. I dangle my feet into the water, and then rub my hands over them; and then I dig my fingernail into the tiny cut that the needle made, forcing it bigger and making it bleed, a thin red trail in the water that runs downstream and to the processors.

That night, in bed, I read the book that the Pale Women gave to me. It's a copy of their three books, the three *Testaments* that they treat as their holy scripture. The first is terrible: it's full of a hateful God, in a world that I barely recognise. The second: that's a good story (or, at least, the fragments of one), about a man who tried to heal the world and then died. The third is the tale of the nine floors of something called *The Inferno*. On the top floor is Limbo: the same thing that the Pale Women call the floor that they live on. It's not the whole thing, that's clear: the stories are short, and end as soon as they begin. And it's too dry. I keep it though. Something to read is better than nothing.

After that, it's time for my night-time rituals. There are things that I feel I have to do to my berth to ensure that I'm as safe as possible while I sleep. I hang the leftover metal scraps I've salvaged from the curtains at the front of the berth, so that they'll clank and clang if somebody tries to come in. I arrange my pillow so that I can keep my knife underneath it, my hand resting on it, just in case. I have my shoes ready to step into; and I sleep in enough clothes that, if I'm forced to run, I won't be caught short. And I say goodnight to my mother. I have said goodnight to my mother every single night of my life; I don't stop just because she's dead.

Doesn't hurt to keep that story going, either: that she's haunting the berth, protecting me, somehow. You'd have to be slightly naive to believe it, but given the majority of people here, that's definitely in my favour.

And then the lights go dim. Every day, fifteen hours they're bright, then nine hours they're dim. That's how we know day from night; how we know when it's time to go to sleep. It's also how the worst parts of the ship know to come alive. In the darkness, I listen to the sounds around me; mostly, from where I'm sleeping, below the generators, that's the sound of the ship. Somehow, hearing it is almost soothing; knowing that it's there. It never changes. Maybe it's louder some days, quieter on others, but it's always the same sort of noises. It's a constant: predictable. I appreciate that.

AGATHA

You want to hear a story? Then I will tell you a story.

I was seventeen, really only a few months older than you are now. The ship was a very different place then, because the gangs were not like this. There was death, of course — there has always been death, and there's no way for that to change, not with the balance being the way that it is — but it was somehow more chaotic. There was less structure. If that sounds as though I like the way things are now, I don't; but now, you know who to fear. That makes it easier, maybe. Back then (thirty-five years ago, if I haven't lost track) anybody could be the one who would stab you in the back. There were no safe havens, none at all.

Your mother was ten, and she was a pain in your grandmother's side: a thorn that your grandmother couldn't pick out. Your mother was wild, always went wandering where she shouldn't. This is when I met her for the first time: when she went missing, and I was tasked with finding her.

Back then, I worked for whoever would pay me. It wasn't like now, as I say. The arboretum was closed off to outsiders, still controlled by the family who ran it when this all

45

began; and I never fancied seaming or sewing. I never had
the patience for it. Your mother had been missing for two
days when your grandfather came to me, showed me a
drawing of her and offered me a stipend at his stall. He sold
leathers, real skin leathers: he was quite the craftsman. I
was angry and selfish, and I wanted more than I probably
deserved. But that didn't stop him, because I had a reputation. Not like the Lows do now, nothing like that; but a
reputation nonetheless. I knew how to look after myself. So
we haggled, your grandfather and I, and I went up in price
– up and up. I stopped when he began to sweat. I knew I
had him, then.

I knew your grandfather, of course. He was the best
leather craftsman on the ship. Everybody knew him. And
your grandmother, she had her own reputation. Stories
about her told us that she was a witch. She could make
smoke come from her fingers. She learned the craft from
her mother, and her mother before that, all the way back
before our ancestors even got onto this ship. Everyone was
scared of her. So your father was respected all the more. So
to have their respect? That would mean a lot for me. It
would get me things. Didn't take long before I stopped
pushing and I took the job.

Your mother had been playing some stupid game, some
imaginary treasure hunt or other, and they last saw her
amongst the traders as she passed through their stalls.
That night she hadn't returned, so they worried. They
searched as much as they could, going to the ends of the
ship – so they thought – but they couldn't find her. So they

went to their berth and they stayed there, in case she returned. They tried to sleep, but you know how it is: hard at the best of times. Your grandfather apparently couldn't even shut his eyes. That's what he said to me when they found me, at the end of the second day, as they returned home again. Another night of no sleep ahead of him. I was taking advantage of their situation – of your mother's stupidity – but back then, I didn't care about these things. I cared about the leather. I took gloves first, as a down payment, and wore those as I went. My hands were softer than they are now. Look, you see? These scars? They were from those days.

I started at the top. This was during the night, when so much of the ship was trying to sleep. I woke people, to ask what they had seen, if they had seen anything at all. Of course, your grandfather had already been there, past all of them. Nobody knew anything, or nobody told him anything: one or the other. For with their respect came fear. More than likely, people were terrified of getting involved. No sense in being a part of something that (with your grandmother's reputation being what it was) could have turned very nasty indeed. So when he gave up, I took up the search.

The Pale Women were the first that I visited, highest up in the ship, just as they are now. They scared me even then, you know. They're hard to understand, even harder to predict. The Lows? They're savages. Vicious, nasty, the basest parts of us run wild. The Bells? They're idiots. Lunks. Driven by impulse rather than anything resembling logic. But the Pale Women are something else. They have faith, which makes them tricky. Back then, more than now, they tried to save us. They walked the ship, trying to convert whoever would listen to them. They had their books – their three Testaments – *and they thought that faith was enough. It's never enough.*

I met with them first. Their envoy then was Sister Calliope, who was reasonable enough. I knew her from the Shopkeeper floors, because that was where she preached, reading passages aloud while everybody else pushed fabric and food. I asked if she had seen you, but she hadn't. That's something you're guaranteed from them, thanks to those bloody commandments: they won't lie to you. They might have their own agenda, just like everybody else on the ship, but at least they're honest.

I worked my way down the floors, through the sick and infirm – none of them had a clue who your mother was. Hard enough to get them to look at her picture, that's true. But still, I had to believe them. I wasn't being paid to find her. I was being paid to look, so that's what I did.

Your grandparents watched me the whole time. I knew it – I could see them, sometimes, peering out across the darkness, keeping an eye on me. Not that I blame them. In their position, I would have watched me too. They watched as I worked my way through the markets; some of the vendors peered at the photo, knowing who she was, trying to work out when they had last seen her. Was it yesterday? None of them could be sure. Almost everybody knew everybody else, because how could you not? There's not nearly enough of us here for anybody to be a stranger. So they knew her – some by name, some by face – but nobody had seen her that day.

I went to the Bells, who all protested and wouldn't make eye contact. One, in particular, was shifty with me. Wouldn't even look at the picture. Your grandparents watched me kick him, hit him, drag him to the markets – he was far bigger than I was, but stupid, and that helped – and then beat him some more. He had seen her. He was the break-through: she had been there the night before, trying to convince them of something. He said that she made smoke from her fingertips; that she told them she was a witch. One of them had hit her, lashing out, scared of her. Your grand-parents' reputation ran to her, of course it did. They said that they came from a line of darkness: Riadne must have been the same. When he had lost most of his teeth, he finally told me where she had gone afterwards. Down, to the Lows.

I can't remember when we started calling them that, you know. My memory isn't what it was. The Lows, before they were so united, were just the people that you didn't mess with. Before, the Lows referred to where they lived, not who they were. The people who lived on the bottom floors of their section, they were the ones you avoided; the ones who used to look at you in ways that made your gut churn and your head swim. Over time, the people in the Lows became the Lows. The Bells was some joke that got out of hand. I'm not even sure that they were a gang before we laughed them into being. 'Heads as empty as . . .', that was the idea. Nothing in there but an idiot tongue that occa-sionally made noise ring out. But, as I say, they were harmless. The Lows? I traded with them when I had to, but stayed away the rest of the time. It's not like you would go for a walk in Low territory and hope to come out unflayed.

But I had made a deal to find your mother. I thought, at that point, that I would only find her body, and even I didn't want to be the one who delivered that back to your grandparents. But better dead than never found. If somebody you love goes missing here, all you can do is imagine what might have happened to them. Chances are, your imagination will conjure up worse things than the truth.

I climbed down into the Lows' territory, as I had done before. Back then, they only inhabited one of the ship's sections. Now, they've got three; half of the ship is in their hands. But then, they were a nuisance. We didn't see their strength growing. Had we, I don't know what we would have done. Probably nothing. That's the way on Australia: ignore it until you can't anymore.

I went into the Low territory as if I had something to trade, head held high. They knew I could take care of myself, so the ones on the outskirts – the weakest, furthest from their Rex – they let me pass. Snarled and postured at me, sure, but they let me through. I was amazed at how quickly they had abandoned so much of our language, our customs. Our morals. It's as if they willfully forgot those last remnants of who we were before Australia. Or maybe they regressed, went back further. I don't know. But I got a few floors in before one of them had the nerve to ask me why I was there.

'I'm here to trade,' I told her.

'What you got?' And of course I didn't have anything, because anything that I could have traded had already gone. Then I remembered: the gloves. Your grandfather's handiwork meant that they were practical and beautiful in equal

measure, delicate stitching that held up under incredible amounts of pressure. We never asked where the leather came from, but we all knew. Everything on the ship is re-cycled; nothing can be wasted. He made miracles with the material he had access to. Climbing through the ship – admittedly, there was less to climb, because there were still quite a few stairwells intact back then – was so much easier with the gloves on. But I was there on a mission, and I knew that if I found your mother's body, your grandfather would give me another pair. If I brought her back, dead or alive, he would give me pretty much anything that I asked for. So I held them up.

'Good leather,' I told her, 'and I want to give them to your king. In tribute.' I wasn't sure that it would work – they were just as likely to try and take the gloves off me, there and then, which would have led to blood – but they relented and let me through.

I made my way down to the fifth floor, where the leader was. He was a nasty piece of work, that one. Leaders tended to last a year or so, nothing more, but he had four years under his belt. Perhaps he's the reason that the Lows grew so quickly. When I think on that, I think about how this could have ended. Maybe I could have saved more people on the ship by doing something different. But, your mother . . .

He smiled when I showed him the picture. It stretched across his face, bending his flesh, making the scars around his lips stretch into an exaggeration of a grin.

'That girl,' he said, 'I have her.' As simple as that.

'Alive?' I asked. I wasn't expecting his admission.

'You want?'

'Yes,' I said.

'You can't have.' Everything about him was broken. I remember stories about back home, back on Earth, about how we were in the oldest days: like animals, scrabbling in the mud, beating each other with the bones left over after our hunts. He spoke like he wasn't even raised by humans: the words the same as anybody else would use, but hollow, like there was nothing behind them. They might as well have been nothing more than noises. 'She's mine.'

'She's not yours,' I said. 'I want to trade for her.' He held out his hands and I peeled the gloves off. 'They're leather,' I said, 'and very strong. Good gloves. The best.'

It wasn't enough. I knew that. I had never bought a person on the ship, but I knew that they went for a lot more than a pair of well-made gloves. 'There's more where that comes from,' I told him. 'So much more. You give me the girl, I'll get you many pairs of gloves. Boots, as well.' He stayed quiet, turning my gloves over in his hands. He pulled at them, tugging them larger, and then forced his big fingers into them, one by one. The soft skin stretched over his own skin – it didn't tear, even though his hands were much bigger than mine, and I thanked your grandfather's skills for that – and then he flexed them, and he watched his fingers as he did it.

I looked around. She wouldn't be far, I knew that. I looked, and I listened, and I heard something coming from below. Mewling, I thought. Your mother was ten; she would have been terrified. What they would have done to her . . . What might already have been done to her. I didn't know.

'No good,' their leader said. 'No deal.' I was worried: the situation was just as likely to end badly for me as for your mother. The room was swarming with Lows. You've never been to their section of the ship – thank God – but it's not like the threat of them when they wander into our territory. It's far closer. Like a change in the atmosphere. I couldn't take them, not that many.

'Get out,' he said, 'or I kill you,' and he waved his hand. It's a miracle he let me leave. His minions escorted me, leaving me at the edge of their section. I climbed up the ship through the other sections, all the while knowing that your grandparents were watching me returning empty-handed. When I got back to them, their eyes told me everything I needed to know. They were done, despairing. They assumed the worst. When I said that your mother was still alive, that changed. Your grandfather pulled a weapon from his bunk, a knife he'd carved himself. Huge thing. I told him to wait: that it wouldn't help, and he would just get himself killed. We needed a plan, I said. I don't know why I helped them, then: I had done my part. But they cared, Chan. They wanted your mother back more than anything else in the world. Seeing your grandfather's face when I said that he would die in saving her . . . He didn't care.

It was your grandmother who decided what we should do. She wasn't a fighter, and never had been. She'd had no need for it. All the stories about your family and their witchcraft, Chan: they came from her, and her mother before her, and back, and back. I didn't believe them, but only just. Some of the stories were persuasive. That's when she told me how she did what she did; the tricks that she knew. She told me how her witchcraft worked, and she gave me some of the pellets that she crafted. They were how she made smoke come from her fingers: a trick, a lie – nothing more. They were made from parts of the soil, of sugars that we otherwise used for cooking, with a piece of rope. I had never seen anything like them before. She said that the smoke would confuse them; that using the pellets would allow me to pass into Low territory and get your mother before they even knew that I was there. I would have to go to the bottom of the ship, of course – to the Pit, which I sincerely hope you never have to visit. But I agreed. It was important to me by then. Your grandmother gave me the pellets, and your grandfather his knife. I promised them that I would return with you, and I could see in their eyes that they believed me. They had faith in me.

The plan was this: I would climb straight down to the Pit, then cross it to sneak into the Lows' section. It was a stupid idea, which was why I thought it might work. No one ever goes down into the Pit. They would never see me coming.

I went that evening. The bottom of the ship was a sad, lonely place. No lights; all of them were broken because that served those who lived down there better. The floors closest to the Pit have always been where the true degenerates live, because we wouldn't allow them up here. They tried – lying about what they were, their . . . tastes – but we knew. So we made them stay down there, and they stayed. And I went down, slipping through their floors, and to the Pit.

Chan, I can't even describe travelling through that. Pushing through the remnants of those we'd lost: their clothes, their bones, their blood. Nothing can prepare you for it. But nobody was watching me, and when I climbed out on the Lows' side, they didn't see me. There were no guards, nobody to set off alarms. Just some older Lows, fast asleep, but I made it past them. I knew from my visit earlier that your mother was being kept one floor up. It almost seemed too easy.

Of course, I was a fool. I was young and stupid and full of myself. When I reached the berth where your mother was being kept – her and three other children, all just as terrified, all mewling because their throats were sore from the crying that they had been doing – the Lows attacked. I was untying the ropes that held the metal cage front to the berth and they ambushed me. Flames lit up all around us, and in their glow I could see their leader smiling. He had known that I would come for them.

They rushed me, and I fell to my knees, huddled into a ball. They kicked at me and I made the right noises, to let them think that they were winning; that I was done. In truth, I was fumbling with the pellets that your grandmother had given me. As I felt my ribs cracking under the Lows' feet, I shouted at your mother to cover her eyes, and I slammed my hand down onto the gantry. The pellet exploded and the room filled, a cloud of thick grey powder swarming over everything. The Lows coughed and sputtered and panicked, and I had my chance. I have never been in so much pain as when I stood, then; and when I tried to breathe, to gasp for air, I took in only a lungful of that cloud. But that didn't stop me. I grabbed your mother and bundled her into my arms, holding her close to my body, and I ran. I kicked and fought my way out, clutching her to me, and I slashed with your grandfather's knife, and I escaped. Still, to this day, I'm not sure exactly how. When I try to picture it, all I remember is the smoke. I don't know how we got off that floor, away from them; or how I got your mother back to her parents. All I remember is putting her down as we approached, and their tears as she ran towards them. How grateful they were.

I left them. I went back to my life. I went back to whatever I was doing before. And then, a week later, your grandmother tracked me down.

'She's been asking for you,' she said. 'Riadne wants to thank you in person.'

How could I refuse that?

THREE

At the very beginning, none of the gangs had names. The Lows, for example, weren't called that. They were just people, until they became something more structured. They lived at the bottom of the ship, so the name got bandied around by those who were afraid of them, and over time it just stuck. Apparently, the worst of the worst banded together, and they decided to try and run the ship the way that they saw fit. Evil likes evil, Agatha used to say, when I asked about them. I'm sure that I asked about them a lot. It's natural to want to know more about what you're afraid of. Originally they took a part of the ship, section II, and turned it into their own private hell. And, over time, that hell grew.

Some people – the Pale Women, mostly, but some others with their own faiths (whatever they might be) – think that this ship is a hell anyway. That, in time, it will be revealed that we died in whatever happened to the Earth, and that this is our punishment. I don't believe that. I think that we'll get somewhere, eventually. We have to.

The Lows assimilated anybody who wanted to side with

them. I couldn't understand why anybody would want to, but Agatha said that it was because they offered protection, of a sort. She said that, after a while, everybody they took in began to dress the same, and act the same. After a while, they sort of lost who they were before. They lost who they were and became something else. Seeing them now, it seems like conformity came pretty naturally to those that they took. They survived, for one. You put up a fight, there's a good chance you'd be dead already.

I'm good at waking up when there's something wrong. Noises, people in the berth, even just a change in the atmosphere – I'm good at sensing that, my brain kicking me out of my dreams. Now, I wake up after only a couple of hours of sleep. They're coming. There's something in their breathing that's distinctive, individual to the Lows. They inhale in these abrupt little gasps, short bursts of sucking in air, and they cough their breath out. They always wheeze. It's because of where they live. There are six oxygen generators – one in each section – but where we've tried to maintain ours, they've abandoned theirs, leaving the air to choke its way out in darkened plumes. And they live so close to the Pit, which is nearly as bad. The fumes from it – the gases – must affect them. It's still breathable, just; doesn't matter what it does to them. And for the rest of the ship, the side effects are useful, because thanks to their screwed-up breathing, you can always hear them coming. I hear them, and it wakes me: that nasty cough, rattling to signify that they're close.

They're closer than they should be, as well. There are

unspoken rules about their territory. They've taken half the ship now, and that's theirs. Nothing we can do about it. Others have tried, over the years – about five years back, the Bells attempted to take another section for their own, and failed; and that was only one of who-knows-how-many attempts. And still the Lows grow. And yet, this part of Australia is ours, not theirs. It belongs to those of us still trying to survive.

The trespassing Lows are somewhere directly below me. Cough, cough, that's all I can hear; and then, also, crying: a man, a child's voice. I strain to listen. I was wrong: two children's voices.

I sit on the edge of my bunk and pull my new shoes on, and I rub my head, the back of my neck. I'm aching, which isn't a good start. Sometimes – doesn't matter how much sleep you've had – you can wake up and feel amazing, like you can take the whole ship on. And other times you're stuck with a pain in your skull, and a feeling that all you want to do is lie on your back and not move an inch. My hair is growing out, I realise as I run my hand over the stubble. I need to shave my head again, before the lice get me.

The crying gets louder; and the coughing keeps collapsing into laughter, which then turns to coughing again. A cycle.

Somebody get involved, I think. Somebody else please get involved.

I pull my knife out from underneath my pillow, and I lift up one of the boards that I've got covering the floor. Through the thick iron grating underneath, I can see right through. Two Lows – nothing special about them. Furs and skins and thick red tattoos on their faces, their hair shaven blunt and fast to their heads. Their targets are the man who lives below me and his sons. I don't know what the Lows are doing here, and I don't care. They shouldn't be here.

One of the Lows is holding the man's youngest child. I don't know where their mother is. She's never apart from them. I like her. We say hello, and sometimes I give her fruit that I can't eat before it goes rotten, and she turns it into whatever she can, things that she can preserve and eat over time. I love the smell that comes from their berth when she's cooking.

She's probably dead already, I know. That's how the Lows work. They pick you apart, and they separate you from everyone else, and eventually you go the same way as everybody else.

The man is sobbing. I've never seen him like this. He's one of the people in charge of the arboretum, and he's strong. He's a good fighter as well. One time I saw him kill a Bell who was trying to steal from somebody, and he did it pretty efficiently. He's not a man who's easy to scare. But to see him now, you'd never be able to tell that.

'Please,' he begs, 'please let them go, please let them go. Take me instead.' He's on his knees, shuffling forward, his hands held out. There's no use in begging, I know. Hell, he knows that. But he's overwhelmed. That's what comes from having people to care for. My mother's made me promise to be selfish for exactly this reason. 'You'll be okay,' he says to his son, the one being held by the Low, and he sounds like he believes it. I wonder if he actually does. The other boy is behind him, cowering. If they tried – if they let the Lows have the one child – they might be able to escape. I'm impressed that the father hasn't tried to run already. He could, he totally could. He could take his other son, find somewhere safe. That's what most people in his situation would do. They'd cut their losses and start again.

That's what I'd do.

I put the panel back on the floor. They can't be helped now, and this is not my fight. Mother's rules, and her voice in my head as if her ghost is actually here with me, whispering into my ear: *Stay out of trouble. Be selfish. Don't die.*

I remember Agatha's story about finding my mother. I hear the child crying. I hear the Lows wheezing.

Be selfish.

I promised her I would be, but then . . . I need to sleep. And I can't sleep with that noise happening. I can't sleep unless I know how this ends.

Screw it. I have to do something.

I leave my berth and run to the closest stairwell, and I jump down to the forty-ninth floor. I could try and distract the Lows, give the man a chance to grab his boys and run. They might make it. Or, I could pile in, fight them. Maybe that would give the father the confidence to join in, and maybe we could beat them. I wait, hiding in the shadows, watching them. I'm breathing hard, so I try and control that. Don't want them to hear me; that would ruin any chance I have of taking them by surprise.

I don't know what the best choice is. I can't tell.

I don't get the chance to decide. It all happens in an instant. The Low who's holding the boy laughs, and throws the child over the side of the balcony. The kid screams as he goes, and the father rushes forward, charging the Low. There's a sickly crunch, a blade going through flesh – through bone – and then the father stops crying. I see him fall forward, his face smacking the gantry floor, his eyes already empty. That just leaves the other boy, and he screams in one terrifyingly loud burst before falling suddenly silent. I can't see what happens to him, and I don't go any closer. They're done.

I was too slow.

I shut my eyes for a second and try to calm down, holding my breath until my heart stops hammering; and when I open my eyes I'm calm. I climb back up to the fiftieth floor and I'm in my berth, on my bunk, listening. Usually you can hear your neighbours moving, talking, having sex. But now no one is making a sound, and the ship's engines, the sounds that are all there always, they fade into the background, fade away completely.

The silence that's left is so deep it's overwhelming.

It's morning. Agatha listens to me talk about what happened and doesn't say a word. She isn't one for interrupting. When I'm finished telling her about the family I didn't manage to save, she sits down on the grass. In her hands, there's a basket of berries. We've been picking them together. I don't like picking berries – it's time-consuming, and there's no peace, swarms of people around the bushes – but I wanted to speak with her. From the minute I woke up this morning – and I'm amazed that I managed to get back to sleep after what happened – I didn't want to be alone. She scoops a handful of the berries out and examines them for damage, finding an overripe one and popping it into her mouth. She hands another to me.

'They were gone when you went to sleep?'

'The Lows?' Stupid question, I think, as the words leave my mouth. That's another thing she hates. Of course that's what she meant. 'They were gone, yes. No sign of them.'

'Had they taken anything?'

'Didn't look like it. I don't know what they had before, but their stuff all seemed to be there.' Everything was as neat as I'd ever seen it. The mother's name was Courtney. I remember standing in that berth and taking the containers of stewed fruit from her when she was done, and thanking her. I can't remember her children's names. She must have told me them. Must have. And now, as quickly as they're gone, I've forgotten them.

'They attacked others last night,' she says. 'A few different people.' She lies back and stretches out her knees. They click as she unbends them, something in her bones and muscles grinding away inside her. I wonder if they hurt, or if she's used to it now. 'Maybe they're looking to expand. This happens.' She waves her words away, as if they don't matter. 'It's a cycle: this has happened before, and it will happen again. We're powerless, so there's no sense in fighting it. You should move.'

'I tried to help,' I say. 'I went down there, and I was . . .' I don't know how to finish that. *I dawdled. I stood back. I let it happen.*

'You shouldn't have done anything,' she tells me. She doesn't look at me when she says it, though. 'These things will happen, and the best you can do is to stay away from them.' She sits up. 'We should get back to work. Life doesn't stop just because we do.' And then she's up on her feet and she's back at the bushes, plucking the berries out and dropping them into her basket. She doesn't wait for me to join her.

The day goes slowly, as it always does; and I can't stop thinking about the missing Courtney and her dead husband and sons, and how there might have been something that I could do. I wonder what Agatha would have done in that situation.

I wonder what my mother would have done.

At night, I try to sleep, but the ship is shouting. It seems louder than usual, the noise of the Lows echoing through the gulf in the middle of the ship. All around me, people are worried. I don't know how this happens: something in the air, I suspect, that sets everybody on edge. I'm scared, and I don't mind admitting that. There was a time when I thought that it was enough to have my mother and Agatha here with me; that they would protect me and I didn't need to worry about shutting my eyes. Now I sleep so lightly that any-thing – the slightest rustle, the faintest patter of feet on metal floor – can wake me up. Tonight, there's no way that sleep's coming in the first place. It's chasing ahead of me and I can see it, but it's out of reach. I squeeze my eyes shut, but that makes them water. It makes everything worse.

So I picture the things that have made me feel safest. My mother's face: her eyes, which were so dark that they were nearly black; her hair, the same as mine, tight dark knots constantly fighting to grow out of coarse stubble; and the touch of her soft skin on my face when she held me and told me that this would all be alright. That was her mantra, a song that she used to sing, like a hymn, passed down. *Everything's gonna be alright. Every little thing's gonna be alright.*

I sing it to myself, under my breath, so quiet that only I can hear it. It's a lie, I know. As the noise from the Lows' half of the ship gets louder and louder, it's suddenly harder to believe that song than it's ever been.

'Chan?' Somebody says my name, and that makes me sit bolt upright, my hand darting to my pillow, to my knife. 'Chan, are you awake?'

'Yes,' I say, and the cloth drape serving as a door to my berth is pulled back with a musical tinkle from the metal scraps I've hung. It's Bess, the woman who lives in the berth next to mine. She's holding her son in front of her and his eyes are a bitter red mess of tears, snot covering his chin.

'We're scared,' she says, 'can we come and sit with you?' I shuffle to one side of the bunk and pat the space I've left behind.

'Of course,' I say. Peter shuffles forward and I help him onto the mattress. He's only three, maybe. If he's older he doesn't seem it. 'Don't cry,' I tell him, as if that will help. I've never been much good with kids.

'He's fine,' Bess says, 'he just can't sleep. He always gets like this.' She strokes his head, smoothing his stubbled hair down, his cheeks damp with tears. She holds him to her chest and looks out through the gap she's left in the curtains. 'They're bad tonight.'

'Yes,' I say.

'But we can't do anything.'

'No,' I agree. Then we sit there, in silence. We all shut our eyes, all three of us. This reminds me of the past. That's comforting, in itself.

Screaming. Not from Bess or Peter, but coming from further away. Still, it's close enough, and it's so full of fear that it sinks into the air around us and won't fade. I've still got my knife in my hand, and I slip my feet into my shoes and wrap a cloak around me. I think about the children the Lows killed last night and how scared they were; and how I didn't do anything. I can't do that again. I won't do it again.

'Stay here,' I tell Bess, 'you'll be safe here,' and I leave my berth and look around for the source of the noise. You can see the Lows' half of the ship from here: below the arboretum, their bottom floors peering out from underneath it, a constant reminder. Over there, their torches are lit, and fires burn, and I can see them, beating at their chests, rallying each other. They're clustered, somewhere down below. I can just see them, through the darkness: a pack of them, cheering something. One of them is speaking to the rest.

Then the scream comes again, and louder, from the next section over, on the same floor as mine. Not Low territory. My territory.

Last night I dawdled. This, I can do something about.

I run down the gantry, towards the noise. It keeps going, which helps, like a beacon, calling for me. It's them. It must be them.

I don't stop running, flashing by the people cowering in

their berths, under blankets, behind curtains and makeshift doors, their shades pulled tight. I see glimpses of their eyes peering out as I run, watching me. They're keeping their heads down. That's sensible. I should take a leaf from their books, I know, but I'm in this now.

Stay out of trouble, my mother's voice says. *Be selfish. Don't die.*

'I'll be fine,' I tell her, but I'm not even sure that I believe it myself.

The screaming woman is on her own, in a berth that's on the far end of section IV, as close as you can get to living near the Lows and still being free. I recognise her: she works in the arboretum as well. She's older than me, and she's got something wrong with her left arm, which usually just hangs by her side as she works the soil. She's holding a knife in her good hand now, her arm outstretched, swinging it wildly at the Lows who surround her. Her clothes are torn and there's the twitching body of a Low woman lying at her feet. There's blood arced across her, across her berth: so much mess that it can only have been an accident that she managed to kill the Low. If you know what you're doing, it's always neater. But there are still three others and they're circling her, laughing their strange half-coughs at her. There's no time to stop and take stock, to catch my breath. I can't let last night happen again.

As they move towards her, so do I. My knife is smaller than theirs, but it's sharp and I know how to use it well. Agatha gave it to me, to protect myself. She used to use it herself. It's good to know that it saved her life. The Lows are so focused on the girl that they don't see me coming. I slice the little tendon at the back of the ankle of the one nearest to me. He collapses to the ground, as if there's never been a single muscle in his body holding him up, screaming his pain aloud. The other two turn, and they look back at me, their expressions almost comically confused.

'Let her go,' I say.

And they do. All of a sudden, I'm much more interesting to them. One of them – the one who isn't holding a weapon – swings at me and his fist connects with my chin. It's a sloppy punch, totally untrained, no real weight behind it, but that doesn't mean it doesn't hurt. My head snaps up and I can feel my chin reddening, bruising, almost immediately. He tries again, and this time I duck. I step back, to get some distance between us. Behind them, the girl whimpers.

'Run,' I say to her, but she stays still. The other Low has a mace of some sort, a thick wrought-iron stick with what looks like shards of glass fastened to its head, and she rushes forward, swinging it wildly. I'm smaller than her, and faster as well, and I hop backwards, avoiding her. She swings again and this time the side of the bar hits my leg. It hurts a stupid amount, but I can't think about that. You get caught in the pain, and it's all over. I manage to stumble forward and slash out, and I catch her belly, cutting through the vest that she's wearing and puncturing her skin in a thin, sharp line. She gasps and staggers backwards. It's an opportunity. I back up more, leading them out onto the gangway, away from the girl's berth. They follow slowly, wheezing their intentions at me with threatening breaths, their eyes fixed on mine.

Two of them. I can take two of them.

The one without a weapon runs at me and I meet him, ducking down at the last second to try and use his momentum to trip him, knock him over. Agatha taught me to defend myself when I was younger, just as she once taught my mother, and this was her first tip: someone bigger comes at you, you use their own weight against them. I push him up and over me, and he thuds to the floor, right on the edge of the stairwell gap that leads to section V. Damn. Any closer and he'd have been over and down into the Pit, and this fight would have been one-on-one. My leg stings and my chin aches. The one with the weapon swings it. The mace clips my hand, hard enough to make me lose my grip. I drop my knife, which bounces on the floor; and then over the edge and into the darkness below.

Damn, damn, damn.

Don't die, my mother's voice repeats, inside my head. I turn and leap across the stairwell gap, and I don't miss a step. It only buys me a second. I keep running, but they're right behind me. My feet clang on the metal flooring and theirs follow, their footsteps like echoes of mine; and I can see their shadows flickering as they pass dimmed night-time lights, first ahead of me and then falling behind as we run past the individual lights. Four berths away from mine, and then three, two, and then I'm throwing aside my curtains, and I'm here. Bess and her son sit up on my bunk, rubbing their eyes.

'I'm sorry,' I say to them, 'but you'll have to hide. Under the bunk.' They move, but too slowly. 'Now!' I shout, and that kicks them into action. They're scared of me, I think.

They've probably never seen me like this. I'm not sure that I've ever actually been like this. I can hear the Lows outside, stopped, talking about what to do. They know about me, and they know who I am. They know the reputation that my mother had, the power. I have to channel that. They have to be afraid of me.

They have to believe that I am willing to kill them.

'Riadne's daughter?' one of them says. I don't answer. I scrabble around on the floor, trying to find a jagged edge; and when one catches on my fingertips, I press my palm to it and I push down, breaking the skin, and I drag my hand across to make a proper cut, nothing that will hurt too much in the morning, but enough to draw blood. I flex my hand, over and over, making it flow, and I smear it onto my face. This is all for show. My mother used to do this, I think. Warpaint, she called it. I want them to see how like her I am. When it's done I rifle through my mother's things, the stuff that she left. I find her smoke pellets. She used to use these to scare people away; and Agatha used them when she died, in exactly the same way. Maybe they'll work again now.

The Lows pull back the curtains, and they see me standing there, eyes closed, head bowed, my face covered in my own blood. They watch me: I can feel their gaze on my head, looking all around me. I'm terrified, but I can't let on. They can't see me crossing my fingers, praying that this works. They step forward: time for them to meet her ghost, and to see just how afraid of me they should be.

I slam one of the pellets to the ground, and it takes a second – a second where I think that this is all over, that I'm screwed, that they'll be in here and on me and I'm dead – but then it coughs out the smoke in these towering plumes around my body. Through the smoke, I speak. 'Leave,' I say. I channel her voice, lowering mine. I speak almost from my throat. 'Leave, or I will kill you.' I can't see them through the smoke now, but I hear their footsteps stop, their breathing quieten. They're scared, or wary at the least. They're trying to work out if they can take me; or if the rumours are true, and if I'm protected by something other than just my tiny knife.

They're trying to work out if I'm worth it.

I'm not. They leave, backing away from my berth, and I follow, striding slowly through the smoke, letting everyone see me. They skulk off down the gantry, looking back over their shoulders. I hear their footsteps getting fainter, and then they haul themselves down off the edge. I go back to my berth, indicating to Bess to stay down, below the level of the smoke, and then I creep to the edge of the gantry, to the railing. I put my hands onto the cold black metal and hold on, and I lean over, craning my neck to see them return to the girl's berth. I can't see inside. I don't know if she's still there, still alive. They throw her things over the side, but there's no noise from her; and then they throw the bodies of their fallen after them, and I watch them fall until they're just glints in the darkness at the bottom, joining my knife and god knows how many other bodies.

I breathe then. I didn't know that I was holding my breath, or how long I'd held it for, but my lungs almost ache when I start again. As the smoke dissipates I shut the curtains to my berth and I wipe my blood off my face, and I hold myself to stop myself shaking. Bess tries to say something to me, but I can't listen to her, not right now.

I feel like I'm a child again, wanting to hide behind my mother's legs while she protects me; but now she isn't here to tell me that it's all going to be better again.

It's not enough that life is scary. We invent other things to be terrified of; to scare the children into staying in line. *There are things worse than Lows*, we say. The story of the Bell who went insane, who killed an entire section of the ship in the early days; the story of the Nightman, who comes and takes children who wander off while their parents are asleep; the story about when the Pale Women supposedly poisoned the water in the arboretum, killing off all the fish and water bugs. All of them carry their own warnings, but there's nothing worse than the Lows. They're here, and they're not stories. And we're right to be scared.

After a night spent with Bess and Peter – all three of us drifting in and out of half-sleep, waking each other with our snoring – work seems like a relief. Being back in the arboretum, amongst the plants and the grass and the trees, is calming.

I ache like I've never ached before: my chin is tight when I try to speak, and my leg hurts so badly that I'm walking with a limp. I look at myself in the river, kneeling on the bank and peering into the water. The flesh is a plum colour underneath my jaw, and the skin is slightly broken (the punch was harder than I thought, evidently), but I'm fine. I wash my face, and that makes it feel slightly better. It always does, without fail. My leg is worse, but not nearly as bad as it could have been: a nasty graze, that's all. I wash and dress it. It will heal.

Around me, everybody is talking about the Lows, everybody has a story about what they did last night. The girl I saved wasn't a one-off: Lows were everywhere last night. Every story ends the same: that they killed or injured somebody, threw their things into the Pit. I listen to snippets of conversation about how they spilled over the edges of their sections, out into section IV or section VI, how they attacked somebody, ruined some berths. Agatha joins me after a while and snorts at what we overhear.

'They think that the Lows' incursions will end,' she says.

'You think that they won't?'

'They're marking their territory,' she tells me. 'It's expansion. It's animal instinct.' I don't understand her, and I don't like to ask. 'But you're okay?' she asks.

'I'm fine,' I say. I don't tell her what happened. If she cared, she would already know.

'You don't look fine.' She glances at my chin and I look down, hiding the mark from her. 'You've been in a fight.'

'I'm fine,' I repeat.

'Your mother would be worried about you,' she replies, and that's it: she walks off, leaving me there, no comeback, no way to argue my case.

I take a break and leave the arboretum to stand on the gantry that runs back towards my berth. I watch the free people work to protect themselves against the Lows. The spaces between sections I and VI, and between III and IV – the stairwells, the only physical gaps that keep them from our half of the ship – are being stockpiled with whatever people can find. They're erecting jagged metal barriers, and tearing up the few remaining stairs and ladders to make it as hard as possible for the Lows to get across to us. It's happening on every floor that I can see.

People are scared.

This is the time of day when most Lows are asleep – most, but not all. Some are on watch, guarding, and I look at them in the distance, standing there, watching just as I am. They don't seem even slightly concerned.

Later, I'm working the vegetables – pulling turnips from the ground and cleaning them off, checking for mite-rot, and that they're safe to eat. I stay at ground level because I'm hoping that I might see the girl from last night and she only works the jobs that don't require her to use her useless arm. Even though Agatha's not with me I picture myself arguing with her, and I get angry with her – and with myself – because of everything that's not being said. I'm not saying what I did last night, because I'm scared of Agatha, and of how she'll react; and I'm not telling her that I'm angry with her, because she's breaking her promise to my mother that she would watch over me; and I'm not telling her that I miss her, because she won't let me.

Everything we harvest goes into the communal baskets, to be shared with all the free people. We all know that everyone who works in the arboretum steals some; that's our reward for working so hard. Today I steal more vegetables than I should, when nobody is watching me. I need to get myself a new weapon, and that's going to cost me.

*   *   *

The weapon seller is blind and makes no attempt to hide it, which is almost refreshing. I've met blind people before, and they lie until they're found out. They don't want to be seen as weak, but this one doesn't care even a little bit. He stands in his berth, knowing where everything is, avoiding eye contact. That's not rare on Australia. You probably wouldn't notice a thing until you actively tried to look at his eyes and saw that they were both missing. Instead, there are sunken black pockets with thick red scars on their outskirts. That's a Bell trick: a thumb in both sockets, pushing down until they're crushed.

'You want a knife?' he asks, 'Or a sword?'

'Maybe something in between,' I say. I can't have another blade as small as the last. It feels like I need something a bit more substantial. But a sword? I remember stories Mother used to tell me when I was a kid, about knights and dragons; and how the knights fought the dragons with swords. 'Long daggers,' she described them as, but clumsy. People always seemed to be taking these long, drawn-out swings: nothing nimble to them.

He laughs. 'What are you going to use it for?'

'The usual,' I reply. Here, that could be pretty much anything. 'How much is a cheap one?'

'Depends on who's buying. So who are you?'

'Chan Aitch,' I say.

'Chan Aitch. Daughter of Riadne?' He smiles. It used to surprise me when people knew her name – knew my name – but not any more.

'Yes,' I say.

'Your mother was a good woman: very good woman.

75

Kind, and fair.' He goes to a crate and lifts the cloth from the top, and he rifles through it, feeling the hilts of various blades until he finds the one that he wants. He doesn't touch a single sharp edge as he's doing it; his hands are a mess of old rough-skinned scars, where I guess he made that mistake too many times before. He finds whatever he's looking for and pulls it out: a black iron handle, grooved and indented for grip, made from one of the railings here. It's decorated around the hilt, some curlicued carving, and it's quite beautiful. The blade is the same colour: thick black metal that looks as if it's barely been used. He holds it out and I gauge the size of it in his hands: not quite a knife, but not quite a sword. It's just in the middle. 'Go on, try it,' he says, 'I trust you, Riadne's daughter.'

I take it from his hands. It's heavy, far heavier than any weapon I've ever carried before. The metal is cold to the touch, which is strange. For some reason, I always expect these things to be warm – usually, you touch a blade somebody else has given up, and there's blood on it. Blood is hardly ever cold.

'It's a single piece,' he says, 'which is good; it won't break at the hilt. There's more heft. Sturdy. You don't want your blade snapping off when you're . . . What did you say you were going to use it for?'

I didn't. 'I work in the arboretum,' I say.

'Okay.' His smile is so wide I swear it's about to tear his face apart. 'So, when you're cutting down fruit, or whatever it is you do there . . . Don't want it snapping, like I say.'

'No.' I swing it in the air, and I can hear the noise it makes, cutting through the space in front of me.

'It's good, eh?'

'How much is it?' I ask, instantly wary. I catch myself looking at my shoes, thinking about what they cost; or what they could have.

'What have you got?' I upend my day's haul to the table in front of him and he touches the vegetables, rolls them around, squeezes them, and he smiles. 'So, Riadne's daughter,' he says, 'this seems like it's more than enough.'

My new blade is different, and it's going to take some time to become accustomed to it. No more hiding it in my palm when I don't want it to be seen; and I'll need to keep it in my satchel, or else make a holder for it, something like that. I put it underneath my pillow and lie down, and I can feel the shape of it against my head: the blade itself right there, like a constant reminder. I wonder if I'll get used to it, but that thought quickly fades.

Of course I will: you can get used to pretty much anything, given enough time.

It's the middle of the night, although that doesn't mean anything. We only really have two times on the ship: day and night. The rest of the time slips by, hour by hour, and we only really notice it based on how tired we are. There are some clocks – some of the older people here still keep them, either running them off batteries made from apples, or they have the wind-up kind (though I can't believe that they're accurate) – and none of them show the exact same time. They're all just guesses. Still, night-time is night-time, that's a constant. Night is when the lights dim. Night is when those parts of the ship with broken light bulbs don't get the overspill from the brightness of the rest of the time, of the arboretum, of the floors that actually care. Night is when the stories happen: the kidnappings; the Nightman; and now, more than ever before, the Lows.

The Lows only come out at night. They sleep during the day – we watch their sections, I, II and III, falling quiet and still whilst the rest of us work to keep Australia running. But the night is theirs. I stand on the edge of the stairwell and watch them carrying on, like they have the past few nights: gathering up their torches, congregating, small packs of them travelling out into the rest of the ship to do whatever they're planning.

Expansion, that's what Agatha said. They aren't growing in number – God knows, the population on the ship is shrinking over time, with people less willing to have children than they were before, simply because of how hard it is to lose a child. But still, they want space. They want every single inch of Australia.

I want to find the girl I saved. I don't know why, exactly. I want to make sure that she's okay; and I realise that I want to help her, give her some lessons in self-defence, in case I can't be there next time. I take my new blade – the guy who sold it to me was right, it's certainly not just a knife – and I climb down to the forty-eighth floor, quiet as anything. She won't be in her berth, I know, but it's as good a place to start looking for her as any.

I'm outside the girl's berth when I see a Low coming towards me from their half of the ship. I look to the edge, to the stairwell between the sections, and there's a make-shift gangplank lowered across, and the stockpiled barricade has been tossed over the edge, leaving only fragments. Of course it didn't stop them.

There's a mace in one of the Low's hands, and my bruises ache, remembering the last time I met one of them. In the light of his torch, the glass shards on the mace head look even more brutal. I was lucky to only get hit by the side of the last one. Take that in the gut and you might as well throw yourself into the Pit. Some wounds there's no coming back from.

I step back, into a berth. There's a family inside – some people I know, who work in the arboretum. They're good people: a husband and wife, and their daughter. She's so young she's barely walking yet. I raise my finger to my mouth, telling them to be quiet.

'Sorry,' I whisper. They nod at me. We all stay quiet as the Low approaches, and as he walks past this berth, and to the now-vacant berth of the girl that they tried to kill. There's no noise. She won't be there.

I listen. There's the sound of his footsteps on the metal; then they stop, and there's a creak. His weight as he lies down on the bunk. I pull open the curtains at the front of this berth and peer down: the torch is propped against the wall, the flame lighting up the doorway. I can't see him. What's he waiting for? She's not there.

What were the words that Agatha used? *Incursion. Expansion.*

He's taking the berth for his own.

I leave the family, smiling at them, poking their daughter's nose – and that makes her gurgle this laugh at me, which her mother instantly silences – and I go back to the stairwell. I climb up, only one floor. I need to see what he's doing in there.

I find the berth directly above the girl's. The curtains are open. There's nobody here, but it's not vacant. I can see the remains of a stewpot, the contents long since burned; and drawings tied to the walls with fragments of rope. The pictures have been done in chalk, or ash, straight onto fragments of fabric, and they're quite beautiful. They're of imagined places, worlds that are maybe like Earth was: hills and seas and cities, things that have been described to us, that we've never actually seen. You'd think it would be hard to tell, without the colour in them – the blue of the water, the green of the grass – but it's not. They're how I've imagined them myself.

The floor is like every other berth: thin sheets of dark metal over the grating, not fastened together but fitted with one another to form a solid floor. Some berths are missing the flooring, because it's another resource, but the grating beneath wears hard on your feet. You get used to that, but for some it's about more. It's what makes a berth a home. As quietly as I can manage, I lift one of the panels, sliding it over its neighbour. Once that's done, I can see right through.

The Low is on the bed, lying back. His eyes are shut, but he's not sleeping. The mace is resting on his chest; the mess of spiked glass rests by his shoulder. Dangerous, that: he could cut himself.

He's waiting for something. I just don't know what.

This berth feels familiar, and yet totally alien. They all take on unique identities depending on who lives in them, which is amazing, given how similar they actually are. I'm in a space exactly like my own, but so different.

I watch all night, peering out from this berth at the Lows' side of the ship. They amass in the middle, right in the centre of section II, about twenty floors up from the Pit, just as they did last night. There's a huge group of them, riling each other up. Someone's shouting – I strain to listen, because maybe there's the hint in those voices being carried across the Pit, behind the thrum of the engine and the noise of everybody else on the ship, something to tell me what they want and what they're doing – and they pump their fists in the air, and they howl and scream when whoever's speaking to them is done. I look at the other parts of the ship. There's movement everywhere. Everyone's awake. Everyone's listening.

This is bad. I can feel the tension – whatever is going to happen – hanging in the air, drifting through the space between the sections. It's not like you could ever argue that Australia is a good place to be, but it's our place. We're used to it.

Now, something's wrong.

In the berth below me, the Low gets up and walks outside and picks up the torch. He stands on the edge of the gantry and he waves his torch, left to right. Across the ship, I can see the same thing happening, other Lows answering the call. Sections IV, V and VI are free. They've been free as long as I've been alive. I run to the gantry myself, and I crane my neck to see. Above me, across from me, I count fifteen, maybe twenty torches, all being swung the same way by other Lows, who have expanded the way this one did. I look back at the massing of Lows in their section, but they're not there any more. They're moving.

We have a few other forms of life on the ship. We used to have pigs, for food, but they were killed and eaten. We were too impatient to let them breed. There were fish in the river once, but they're gone as well – and whether you believe the story about the Pale Women poisoning them or not, that's a shame. But we have insects: ticks and lice, bugs and gnats and ants that get sucked into the systems and turned into the protein jelly we're meant to eat. It's easier if you don't think about what you're eating while you're doing it.

But insects are exactly what the Lows remind me of now. Insects scurry when there's food dropped, something that they can scavenge. The Lows run with the same desperation, spreading out, heading for the lights of the torches, scavenging. I watch them reach their gangplanks and walkways, ladders and bolted-together sheets of metal that they swing down to attach the free sections to theirs. I watch as they pour across in small packs, heading to different parts of the ship.

I watch as the first group of Lows climb to reach one of their number (someone like the Low below me), waiting in a berth that they've taken. They greet each other, almost clubbing their fists together. The people in the berth next to where they're standing are terrified: two men who back away, starting to leave. One manages it; the other gets tangled in the thick red curtain that they've draped over the front of their home, almost tripping. The Lows turn from their greeting to pounce. They cut him, and they drag him to the edge, and they hold him over the Pit, two of them gripping him by his ankles, shaking him. His body smacks against the iron railing and he screams for a while until he suddenly stops, and he stops struggling. He's passed out, or already dead, and they let him go.

Better to die like that: not being able to see the Pit coming.

The Lows move on, scaring the family on the other side, watching them scatter before them. The family clutches at each other, the mother swinging her fists to keep the Lows back. They're seizing two berths for every one they've already taken, one on either side of the original.

It's happening all over the ship.

The noise of the engines is lost under the screams and yells of the scared free people on this – on *my* – side of Australia. Below me, the solitary Low in the girl's berth waits. This is my chance.

I grab the railing at the edge of the gantry and I climb over and prepare myself. I'm going to grab the railing and swing down and drop onto the next floor. I have to do it silently. I have to do it without slipping, without letting go. I have to do it without dying. And I have to do it one-handed. My new blade is in my satchel, but I might have to fight the Low the moment I land. I don't want to be fumbling with the weapon. So I take it out, and I clutch it in my left hand, and I breathe. I rock up and down on my toes. I've done this before.

When I was a kid, we used to have a game. There were some other children who lived near us, and my mother knew their parents, so we were allowed to play together. We came up with this thing that we did when our parents weren't looking, like a dare. We would climb over the railings and we would dangle ourselves out over the Pit, to see who could hang there the longest. It wasn't about strength; it was about nerve. One time, I slipped, because I knew that I was strong and brave, and that made me lazy. For a second, as I fell, I was sure that I was going to die. You fall faster than you can ever imagine. Somehow I caught the railing on the floor below, though, and I dangled there until my friends came and pulled me up and over. I told them that I did it on purpose. I have no idea if they believed me, but I tried to convince them. Maybe even tried to convince myself.

They're all dead, now, those friends. Dead or Lows; and from where I'm standing there's not really very much difference between the two.

I step backwards, off the gantry. I don't even stop to think how stupid what I'm about to do is. Instead, I drop.

With my right hand, I reach out and grab the railing of the floor below. My feet, somehow – don't ask me how, because I'll never know – land right on the lip of the gantry. The Low is right there, straight in front of me. He gasps in surprise as he sees me, his mouth open, his breath stalled. He doesn't understand where I've come from.

'You,' he says.

'Me,' I reply. I raise my blade up and bring it down on his arm, and it slices clean through his hand. The hand – and the mace he was holding – fall to the floor, and he clutches the wounded wrist to his body and screams. His screams don't sound very different to anybody else's. He falls backwards, and the torch he's holding slips from his grip. I kick it towards him, and the flame touches the strange hair-fur he's wearing around his waist, and it burns.

It's the second fastest fire I've ever seen.

He stands up and runs, in pain. I could help him, maybe, but I don't. I let him fumble, stagger, slam into the walls of the berth. The pictures in there catch on fire, the paper crumpling and charring. I watch as the flames rise around him, spreading to the other fragments of clothing that he's wearing, his skin seeming to catch alight, the fire tearing around his body as he spins and cries. He comes for me and I swing away from him. He hits the railing at the edge of the gantry and he tumbles. He's too heavy, in too much pain to stop himself. I watch him drop into the Pit. From the light of his burning body, I can trace exactly how long it takes him to fall. I watch him burn out, a solitary light down in the darkness.

'What are you doing?' a voice asks and I spin around, startled. It's Agatha. She grabs my arm, practically hauls me into the berth. I notice the pictures that were stuck to the wall, now almost entirely gone. Fragments cinder on the floor. 'What in the hell are you doing? And what is this?' She pulls my new blade towards her and examines it. 'Chan,' she says, and I can hear the disappointment in her voice.

'Have you seen them? They're in these sections, and they're—'

'You think you did anything? You'll just draw attention to yourself. We have to go.'

'There was a girl who lived here. They would have killed her if I hadn't come here.'

'And now they'll kill you. If they see you, they'll mark you and hunt you down.'

'I had to do something,' I say, and she sighs.

'And now you have to hide. You have to go back to your berth, and you have to stay there.' She lets go of my hand and I rub at my wrist. Where she was grabbing me is red and sore, that's how tight her grip was. 'You have to look out for yourself.'

Around us, there are more screams. The Lows are still staking out territory. No one even noticed my fight. Agatha marches me to the stairwell, and she watches as I climb up. She follows me to my berth, and she stands outside as I go in, and neither of us says anything.

I can't sleep. I think about the Low, and how I killed him. Maybe not directly, but it was my fault. He might not have died from his injury, I tell myself; people have survived far worse. And it wasn't my fault that the torch landed where it did, or that what he was wearing burned up as fast as it did.

But he's the first person I've ever killed by myself. My mother's hand was on mine when she died. The old leader of the Lows, who I stabbed in the neck, was finished by somebody else. But this Low? His death is the first time I've truly felt the guilt of having somebody else's blood on my hands.

I ask my mother to not be disappointed in me. I ask her forgiveness, because I know that she wouldn't be happy. I shut my eyes, and I try to not picture him burning: the smell of him, the screams as he fell; and then I try to not see my mother's body burning as well, but I can't.

I hear a noise outside my berth. My hand creeps to my

new blade, lying on the floor next to my bed, still covered in the blood from the Low's hand. Not one set of feet, but two, maybe even three.

'Go away,' I say, loud enough that they'll hear. Agatha must have gone, but I don't know when. I should have been more alert. It makes me complacent, thinking that she's watching out for me. She can't be. She isn't, not any more.

The feet don't retreat. They're waiting; stalling.

I stand up and stride to my curtain. 'I told you,' I say, and I swing them wide. It's the family that I visited earlier, that I told to be quiet: the husband and wife and their little girl. She's terrified, looking me up and down, her eyes wide. I hide my blade behind my back and she holds something out. Her hands shake as she presents it to me. It's shiny and blue, a fragment of something that I'm sure was once much more impressive: a gemstone. It looks far larger in her hands than it does in mine. 'This is beautiful,' I tell her. 'What is this?'

'It's for you,' her father says. 'They left us alone, and . . .' He shrugs. *We survived another night*, the gesture says. 'Sophia picked it. We've got a few of them, and she chose the one that she thought you would like. So, yeah, that's yours. Thanks.'

'I didn't do anything,' I say. Something like this stone, that's worth money here. Anything even remotely rare or precious like this, people will trade the world for. Or worse.

'The Lows would have come and done what they did in the rest of the sections,' Sophia's mother says. 'They would have chased us out.' And that's that. She closes my hand on the precious stone and we stand together and watch the

Lows making their way back across to their sections, their expansion complete for the time being. They've scared us, and they've hurt us.

And they'll do it again.

FOUR

My mother's rule about staying away from the gangs is nearly impossible to maintain. While the Lows might stick to their part of the ship, the Pale Women and the Bells are a different matter. They wander among us, doing whatever it is that they do: the Bells picking fights, to prove something; the Pale Women preaching their gospels, trying to convert us. They have their own pockets, like the Lows, and like us, the free people. They've broken all the lights up there on the top floors, and live in total darkness. We never go into their territories unless we have to, and we don't talk to them unless they talk to us first.

'Somebody's looking for you,' the blind knife-seller says, as I pass his berth on my way to work. I didn't say a word, so I have no idea how he knows it's me.

'Me?'

'Chan Aitch, daughter of Riadne,' he says. 'He's asking about you, where you live.'

'Who?' I ask.

'Smelled like Pale Women to me,' he says. 'Hope you haven't pissed them off.' That sticks with me as I head to the arboretum, as I walk out across from the forth floor towards the giant suspended plate it sits on. The walls are misted up, fogged with the heat coming from inside. As hot as it is out here, it's worse in there. I hope I haven't pissed them off as well. There are stories – I mean, of course there are stories, there are always stories – about what they used to be like. So, once upon a time, they went around the ship, saving those who needed saving and judging everyone they didn't save. They were vicious, punishing whoever they thought needed punishing. Those they saved, they took up to the top floor. And those people they took, they were never seen again. That's the story.

I'm surprised that there might be Pale Women down here on 40. They don't come into the light, that's pretty much the only thing we all know to be true. They stay in the darkness. Something about penitence.

But I'm not going looking for them. They want to speak with me for whatever reason, they can come find me. I open the doors to the arboretum, and there he is: their envoy. I can see his neck, underneath his hood, sweat running down his pale skin. He mops at it with the sleeve of his gown, and I notice that collar again: tight against his skin. Can't be comfortable, especially in this heat. Leather makes you sweat. He looks wrong here, in this green and growing place. He's meant to be in the shadows. There are no lights on the top floor, and there never have been. Who chooses to live there, where you can't see anything? Here, in the brightest part of the ship, he's totally conspicuous. People are staring.

'I was told that I would find you here,' he says. 'Sister has told me to find you, to extend an offer to you that you come and join us, live with us. She thinks that you would be an asset.' He stands back, his arms hanging by his side, as if he doesn't need to sell me on it any more than that. The Pale Women want me, and I'll obviously sign up. What possible reason would I have to say no?

'Thanks, but you can tell her that I'm fine,' I say. I walk past him, down towards the plum trees. There's nobody working them right now, which is perfect. They're easy to climb, which means their fruit is easy to pick. I look for Agatha, but she's nowhere to be seen. That's unlike her, to miss work, but not unheard of. Sometimes she just doesn't feel up to it. The envoy follows me as I walk.

'Did you read the *Testaments*?' he asks. He has long strides, nearly as big as two of mine, but he keeps staring at the ground, not looking at the trees. I don't know for sure, but if I were him, living up in the darkness, I think I'd be drinking in the sights and sounds of the arboretum: the rustle of leaves, the hum of insects, the scent of water, of grass, of fresh growing things.

I stop and I turn, and I see that he's fixated on the ground. I wonder suddenly if he's ever seen grass up close.

'You like it?' I ask.

'A garden,' he says. 'Like it is in the book. A garden, where life begins.'

'Yeah,' I say. He's a bit unsettling. Slightly too on the side of crazy. 'I read the book,' I tell him, 'but I don't know that I understood it. Thank you, though.'

'Sister was insistent,' he says, his voice raised slightly, almost angry. 'You should come.'

I don't like that tone, and my reply makes that pretty clear. 'I'm fine where I am,' I snap.

'She says that the end days – that war – is coming.' He looks up at me, and I see his eyes clearly for the first time: a green-grey that barely exists outside of paintings and tattoos, not even slightly natural. 'There is a protection offered, from the Father. We're ascending.'

'If the ship goes to war,' I say, 'then nothing will protect you.' I plant my hands on a branch and pull myself up, into the heart of the tree. 'Besides, if you've got a way to save a few of us, why not save everybody?'

I stop climbing in time to watch him turn and walk back to the entrance. He pulls at the collar around his neck and rubs at his head underneath his hood. They're not used to rejection, I suspect. Most people here are so scared when they're alone that they'll take anything resembling security, no matter how strange it might seem to the rest of us.

As he leaves, out onto the gantry, the hood falls from his head. The light here is better, and I see a shock of bright red hair, cut close to his scalp. And it's his, totally natural. I've never seen red hair that's not been dyed, before. And I can't remember having ever seen a colour like it.

My walk home after work is strange. It feels later than it is by the way that everybody is acting, rushing home, drawing the curtains tight across the front of their berths, being as quiet as they can. They are crossing their fingers that events of the past few nights were an aberration, but as I put the bruised and damaged fruit that I kept today away underneath my bed, I see the Lows massing again in their section.

Somehow – I have no idea how – there seem to be more of them tonight. With their torches lit and, clustered together as they are, it looks as if that part of the ship is on fire.

Bess and Peter come to me again and we huddle in my home. We watch as they leave their territory, as they branch out into the rest of the ship. Again, flames spring up, showing them where to head.

'Why is this happening?' Bess asks me.

'I don't know,' I say. I wish that I did. I wish that Agatha was here, because she might have more of an idea. In her stories, she talks about how they rose and fell over the years: not just the Lows, but other gangs and cults and groups. 'Stay here,' I say to them, and I go to the edge and look up to Agatha's part of the ship. She lives on the sixtieth floor, in section VI. Her floor is dark, under the ever-present lights, and there are no candles, no flames, no torches coming from any berths. Except hers. There's a light coming from her berth: a single flame, beckoning the Lows towards it. She wasn't at work today; the flame is burning tonight.

There's something wrong. There has to be. I tell Bess and Peter to stay where they are, and I take my new blade. I'm going to need a holder for it, I tell myself. I'll try and make myself one tomorrow. There's always tomorrow.

Agatha's floor is swarming with Lows by the time that I get there. They've come over from below and climbed up, and they're fast. Everyone on Australia is taut and lean, but there's something about living in their part of the ship, something about their lifestyle, that makes the Lows even more so. Some have let themselves go, true, and their muscles aren't as hard; and there are stories about those who live on the very bottom floors of the ship, and the state that they're in, but I've never seen those Lows myself. The only ones we free people ever see are the fighters.

I stay in the shadows where I can. On each floor, only about half the lights work any more. I wonder what this place was like when it was bright. Now, there are sections where I can crouch, empty berths – their inhabitants either panicked away, or long since gone – and I sneak through as I count Lows. Five of them already on this floor, with more on the way. I get closer to Agatha's berth. They must have her. They might have killed her: I can't hear her, and she would be fighting, I know that much.

I get out onto the gantry, and I pull my blade out and clasp it with both hands, ready for them. They aren't looking in my direction, so I sneak forward. I'm not going to kill them; at least, not intentionally. Accidents happen, sure, but I'm going to injure them where I can. No killing, not after that last one. I don't know that I can handle the guilt. But I have to stop them, that's for sure. If I can get there before they see me, I might be able to take out one or two of them without—

A hand across my face, across my mouth; and another, on my shoulder, pulling me backwards. I kick back, trying to free myself, and I turn, grabbing a handful of cloak; my attacker is hooded. I drop the knife and reach up to the head of my attacker, grabbing it at the back. The hood falls back, and it's Agatha. She lets go of me and in the darkness I see the rope-like scar of her lip twisting at me in a smile. She nods, and I do the same, and she takes me by the hand and pulls me with her, in the dark. In the stairwell between V and VI we climb, using the fragments of railings and stairs to pull ourselves up, again and again and again. She doesn't stop. Her knees must be killing her, I think; I ache enough myself, and she's much, much older than I am. Compared to most people still alive here, she's pretty ancient.

We pass the rusted remnants of the sign for the sixty-eighth floor and she finally stops. She stands on the gantry and puts her hands on her legs and bends forward, and I can hear her breathing. She sounds almost like a Low, it's so strained.

'What are you doing here?' she asks.

'Looking for you,' I say. 'I wanted to know where you were.'

'I've been watching them,' she replies. 'And watching you.'

'Me?'

'I promised your mother that I would,' she says, 'and I'd never break my word.' She stands up and stretches, and I hear everything in her back, muscles and bone, as they grind and click into place. 'Come with me. I've got something to show you.'

I follow her down the gantry. The berths here are like everywhere else: free people cowering, taking cover. They watch us as we go, suspicious and worried. The higher up the ship you get, the further from the arboretum and the markets, the more frail the people who live there, it seems. These floors house the elderly, the sick and the tortured. There's no help for any of these people, and no way out. Nothing will get better for them.

Agatha stops in the middle of the gantry, halfway between stairwells, and leans over the edge. 'Look down,' she says, so I do.

I can see them. They're at my berth. Bess is being dragged out, and I watch as the Lows raise their hands and slam them down on her body. She crumples to the gantry. I can't see details, because it's all so fast, but I can make out the Lows, Bess cowering in the middle of them. Peter is nowhere to be seen.

'I have to help her,' I say, but Agatha grabs my arm.

'You can't do anything,' she says. 'And you shouldn't try.'

'Let go of me,' I tell her. I taste blood in my mouth, and I don't know where from. It's just there, welling up: sharp and metallic.

'You aren't special, Chan. You can't change anything. The best you can do is survive. You survive, and you do whatever you can to keep surviving.' She sighs. 'We'll move up here together, move all of our things. They aren't coming this high up in the ship, not yet. We can buy some time.'

'No,' I tell her, and I slap her hand away and I run.

What happened to Bess is my fault, I tell myself, over and over as I climb down the stairwell. I invited Bess into my berth. She thought that she would be safe, and she wasn't. This is my fault.

I'm climbing down so fast that I'm almost slipping, losing my grip again and again because I'm pushing myself, trying to do things that I've never done before: dropping whole floors and landing on rubble, and attempting to not fall or hurt myself. The only thing worse would be if I died on my way to save her.

The sixtieth floor, the fifty-eighth, the fifty-fifth. I keep going.

The fifty-second, and I'm exhausted. I can't think when I've ever pushed myself so hard. Even when trying to save my own life I'm not sure I've moved this quickly.

Then I drop from 51 to 50, and I land awkwardly. When I stand my ankle hurts and my hands burn, the calluses on them rubbed sore. The ship never gets kinder, and we never treat it any better. But I don't stop. Last time I hesitated, people died. This time I charge at them, pulling my blade from my pack as I run, and I scream, to let them know that I'm coming. The pain almost helps.

One of them, a female, is kneeling down next to Bess, crouched by her head, whispering something to her. I throw a smoke pellet, clouding the area, and I rush in. The Low is who I aim for and I tear into her with my blade, pushing her backwards, kicking her in the neck. She crumples to the ground beside Bess, and the others all inhale at what seems like the same time, their thick wheezing suddenly all that I can hear. In this moment, the engine noise slips away, and the cries coming from the rest of the ship: there's just me and these Lows.

I fight.

And I win.

Bess thinks that I'm dead, but I'm not. I can still wriggle my toes, and my fingers, and I twitch them just to check that they're all there. The first few Lows were easy to deal with because they were surprised, but the rest of them had time to attack. Still, they all ran, or fell. They're not here any more. And I'm cut, I know that much: all across my side there are slashes, because one of them had blades stuck to their fingers in some sort of glove, and I remember the way it felt when he grabbed me with it. Bess gasps when she sees me moving, and she cradles my head.

'Peter,' she says, 'my son. They've got him.' That kicks me awake. My pain will go. My injuries aren't so bad that I won't heal. I can still breathe, and I can still move.

I push myself. 'They took him?'

'He's not here!' she yells, and she beats the ground. No, not the ground: one of the Lows, unconscious, barely breathing. As my eyes start to clear and everything stops blurring together, I focus on him. I should end this; stop him waking up, exacting revenge. Something from the Pale Women's *Testaments* leaps out at me: *kill or be killed*, one of the commandments that their god passed down.

In the *Testaments*, all of the stories have morals. Thinking about it, every story does.

'Where did they take him?' I ask, but she only shakes her head. 'Bess, you have to tell me,' I say, and I try to get to my feet, but the movement makes my head swim, and all I want is my bunk, but there's no time for that. Later. Now, I have to help. I have to make up to Bess what she lost because of me. I promised to *be selfish*, so I will be. If I don't help Bess, the guilt will likely be the end of me. 'I'll get him back, but you have to tell me what happened.'

She explains through heaved sputters of tears. They appeared, and they burst into my berth, and they dragged her out. She told Peter to hide, but she didn't see where he went, and now he's gone.

'You didn't see them take him?'

'No,' she says, shaking her head. 'But they must have. They must have.'

'He'll be hiding,' I say, and I want to tell her to help me look for him but she's in no shape to do anything. She'd be a danger to me, like this. The Lows are still roaming the ship, and there's no way I could protect her if we were jumped again. I couldn't even protect myself in the shape I'm in, my ankle hurting and my side bleeding.

'I'll find him.' She helps me stand, and she pulls me closer to her and cries into my shoulder, putting her weight on me. I don't tell her that I can barely hold myself up, because she needs me to be strong. And she hasn't said it, but I'm sure it's on the tip of her tongue: this is my fault. And it's true. I told them to wait there. I told them that they would be safe. 'I'll get him back now, okay? You go home and stay quiet.'

As I'm walking away, she speaks again. 'They were looking for you,' she says. I stare at her. 'They said your name, Chan. They wanted to know where you were.'

'Okay,' I say; and I watch as Bess rolls the Low to the edge of the gantry and then heaves him over.

This is all my fault. The words ring in my ears as I climb through the ship, calling his name when I know I can get away with it, hiding when I know that I can't. I'm good at apportioning blame.

I start by heading down, and keep going all night, avoiding trouble as much as I can. Everyone's scared and quiet, so there's not much trouble to be had. I don't know what might happen to Peter if he's not found. He has to be somewhere.

He can't have climbed far. Down is easier than up, that's a firm rule here, so this must have been the way that he went. As I search, I watch the Lows skulk away, their damage done; and then I can see what they've wrought. More bodies, more chaos and more terror. More expansion.

I check everywhere. I have never explored Australia so much as in this one night. Peter wouldn't have gone to the Lows' side of the ship, so at least there's that. If he did, then I'll never get him back.

Nobody will.

On my way back up, I drop by Bess's berth to make sure he hasn't returned on his own, and hear her sobbing; and I think about a story that Agatha once told me, about how my grandparents asked to find my mother when she went missing. She didn't give up. She said that she couldn't go back to them empty-handed.

That it would have killed them.

So I have to go up, and up again. On the sixty-fourth floor, I think I see him, but it's another kid: same tone of skin, same slightly outgrown hair. On the seventieth, somebody tells me that there was a little boy here, running around, no parents. They tried to stop them, but the kid bit them, and the man telling me the story shows me the tooth marks on the webbed bit between his thumb and finger; and all I can think is that his hand must have been over the mouth of whichever boy did this, and that I'm glad that that boy got away from him. On the seventy-sixth – and there's no way that Peter could have gotten up here, not without some help, because every stairwell this high up is gutted to the point of being barely existent, one of the hardest bits to negotiate in the whole of the ship – there's a woman who looks suspicious when I ask her, refusing to talk to me, running off.

Then I hear the cry. It's sad and small, high-pitched – definitely a child – and coming from only a few floors above me. I wait for a second, to hear if it stops. I don't want to go much higher – that's too close to Pale Women territory – but the noise doesn't stop. The cry is almost like a mimic, almost fake.

So I go to find it. I've got to.

When I get to the eighty-second floor – where the noise is coming from – I see that it's nearly abandoned. We're directly above the top of the oxygen purifiers, and they cough out this smell that's almost unbearable. It's rotten, dirty as anything, the smell of the rest of the ship pushed as far as it can go before you start to gag. Instead of living here, people have stripped the floor of everything, ripping out the metal walls, the bunks, the floor tiles, the light fittings, the plumbing. It's not fit for use any more. With everything gone, you can see the ship totally laid bare: just one empty box in a series, all linked together, on and on, almost as far as you can see.

The emptiness does mean that I can see where the crying is coming from, though. I see a shape: small and nearly curled into a ball, crouched at the edge of the gantry, over-looking the Pit. I get closer and see that it's a girl, not Peter. They're about the same size, same age, I reckon. An easy mistake to make. I crouch next to her. Nobody rushes over, no parent. She's up here alone. She stares up at me with these big dark eyes. Her skin is gritty with some sort of condition, eczema or something, bright red from where she's been scratching at it.

'Hello,' she says.

'Hello,' I say. She looks at my hair, which has maybe grown out too much. It's longer than hers, certainly. She reaches up and touches it, and I can feel my hair under her fingers: unclean, wiry against her skin. She doesn't care, doesn't ask permission or anything. She is younger than I ever remember being. 'I'm looking for a boy,' I say. 'He's called Peter. Have you seen him?'

'No boys up here,' she says. She has a pile of dolls between her feet. They make them in the markets: fabric and bone, bundled together to create this thing that only looks slightly human even if you're being generous. 'These are my brother's toys,' she says.

'Did he give them to you?' I ask.

'No,' she says. 'He died, so I took them.' She holds one up and dangles it over the edge.

'You should be careful,' I say, 'you might drop that.' She ignores me, the doll swinging between her fingers as she holds it by the hair. 'You sure you haven't seen a boy?' I ask.

'I haven't,' she says.

'Okay. Do you have parents near here? Your mother?' I ask, and she shakes her head. I can't worry about her now. I can't. Whoever's responsible for taking care of her must be somewhere close, I'm sure.

I call Peter's name one more time and then go back, towards the stairwell. When I reach it I hear the noise again: the scream that we thought was Peter. The little girl drops the doll she's been holding, and she leans forward and watches it fall down the stairwell, eighty-two floors to the Pit below, and she makes the noise again. She's mimicking the scream of a person as they plummet.

She's probably heard it enough. We all have.

Limbo, the Pale Women's floors: the last place to check before I'm forced to give up, and have to go back and tell Bess that I couldn't find her son. I don't want to be up here, I know that much. The eighty-eighth floor is where the ship becomes almost oppressively dark, no light trickling in from those floors with better lighting. The darkness settles like mist up here. I don't know. The darkness is not exactly tangible or anything, it's just *here*. Things get darker and darker, and then here it is: pitch blackness. It's a strange sensation, heading up and into the black.

It's also harder to hear the engines here. I can still feel them, perhaps even more than anywhere else – the vibrations of them that run through every inch of the ship, shaking against my feet when I stand still – but the sound sort of falls away. I can hear the gaps in it more, and the echoes of the noises of the rest of the ship. And then, as I get closer to Limbo, there's something else: like a humming. I can't pinpoint where it's coming from or what it is. It's not from this floor. There are people living here, but they're all broken: sick or old, too tired and sad to protect and defend themselves. They're here because there's nowhere else for them.

My mother used to bring food to these people. I've not done that since she died. I've not even considered doing it. It's easy to forget that they're even here: that people still live in this part. *Look after yourself*, she told me. *Be selfish*.

I walk the gantry and look into their berths, straining my eyes to see into them through the darkness. Bodies in bunks, coughing up Australia's air almost as fast as they can breathe it in; groups of people huddled around makeshift stoves; amputees cradling their bodies, knowing how much more dangerous this place is for them. People who some on the ship have denigrated for not being as normal as the rest of us – whatever that means.

I've not been here for years. I've had no reason to come here. I didn't remember that it was like this; maybe because I didn't want to. It's easier to forget the things that you just don't want to know exist. I stand outside one berth, lit by a single candle, and watch a mother cradling her son. The boy's body is twisted and his head is too heavy for his neck, and he looks as though he's suffering a pain that will never go away. His mother notices me looking at them, but I don't expect her to talk to me. Seems like there's not much she could say. She looks away from me and back to him, and I know then that this is the worst part of the ship. There are terrifying parts, parts where you shouldn't go; parts where the people will try to hurt you for their own pleasure. But none of them compares to the pain of being here. This is *misery*.

From the darkness at the back of the berth I can see somebody else. They're dressed entirely in black, only the pop of something white at their neck – the spiked collar of the Pale Women's envoys. This one steps towards the sick boy and puts something on his head: a cloth, soaking wet. The water runs down the boy's face. It's the same red-headed envoy who spoke to me in the arboretum.

'You,' I say. The envoy nods. He isn't wearing his hood, and as he steps forward I can just see the colour of his hair in the light of the candles. 'What are you doing?'

'They need help,' he says, and it feels hard to argue with that. Looking at this boy and his mother, at the other people relegated to these floors, it's obvious that he's right. We're all alone here, but some are more alone than others.

'I'm looking for a little boy,' I tell him. 'He ran away, I think.'

'From where?'

'The fiftieth floor.'

He shakes his head. 'He's not likely to be up here.' He stands up, pulling the rag away from the boy's head. His whole body has to move; he doesn't bend his neck at all. The skin of his neck – the scar lines – seems to almost shimmer in the reflections of the flame.

'What about up with the Women?' I ask.

'I don't think so,' he replies. 'You could check, but he wouldn't have been able to climb. The top floor is . . . separated.'

'If you see him, can you tell me?'

'I won't see him,' he says. 'He's already lost.' He soaks the cloth again in a bucket of water and puts it back on the boy's head, and he turns away from me. The conversation is over, and I've failed.

As I sit on the edge of the stairwell and start to lower myself down to the floor below, I look up. The stairwell leading to Limbo is spiky with the iron rearranged into patterns of railing, spikes that jut out to prevent anybody climbing up there. It's so dark up there that I can't see past the spikes; and then I hear the humming clearer and louder, coming down from that place. It's the Pale Women, their voices knotted and tripping over each other. The humming is them saying their prayers, over and over and over, until the words lose any meaning that they maybe once had.

It takes me forever to get back to my floor. Nothing to do with the ship, or the Lows; I'm just terrified of what I've got to say to Bess. I practise the words as I walk, mumbling them under my breath. 'I'm sorry,' I say to myself, 'but I couldn't find him. Peter's gone. I don't know where Peter is. I can't find your son.' I don't know what sounds best. I've never had to tell anybody news like this before.

I think back to when my mother told me that she was dying; how she decided that it was better to tell me quickly, short and sharp, get it over with. There would be tears, she knew that, and it was better to get them to come quickly. Nobody wants their pain to be drawn out any longer than it needs to be.

So I breathe in, and I try to fix the words in my mind, and I hope that she just knows, somehow, and that I won't even have to say anything. I stand outside her berth, and I say her name to get her attention. There's no sound coming from it. I say it again, louder.

'Bess, can I come in?' As I say the words, I think about how embedded what I'm going to say to her is; how she can't help but know. Peter would have just run right in. He would have been in her arms before I could even tell her that I'd found him.

I pause before going in. I always expect the worst of every

situation – we all do. That's how you survive. So I don't know what I'm going to find inside, but I brace myself, because I'm not sure I'll be able to take it.

Her berth is empty. She's not here. Everything is gone: the pictures that Peter drew, that had been fastened to the walls; all her clothes, her trinkets, anything that she cared enough about to cling to. It's totally empty. You'd never know that anybody had ever even lived here.

I step onto the gangway and call her name a few times, but she's gone. It's nearly morning now. The Lows have retreated back to their half of the ship. There's something like calm in the air, but it doesn't feel real. It's so delicate that it could just tear apart.

I don't know what else to do, so I go back to the eighty-eighth floor. It takes me a long time. I have to rest every few floors, and there's a point where I sit down and I feel like I could just shut my eyes and maybe let sleep take me, but I would regret that. I don't want to sleep. I want to do something. When I get to him, the envoy doesn't even seem surprised to see me. He hands me a cloth and a small flask of a sour-smelling ointment.

'There's a woman who needs help in the next berth,' he says. I go to her, and she's lying on her back, looking as though she's asleep, but she isn't. She doesn't respond until I touch her and then she recoils from me, arching her spine, her limbs locking into position.

'Shh,' I say, trying to calm her. I dip the cloth in water then lay it on her head, and I pull back her sheets – she tries to stop me, but she's too weak – and I see where she's wounded. Her skin is a mottled patchwork of what it once was, ripped apart by some sort of rust-brown rot. It smells rancid and I have to stop myself gagging. I take the ointment, and I drizzle it over the wound. Almost immediately she's calmer, the pain subsiding. The ointment seems to fizz on her wounds, and I imagine it should sting, but it evidently doesn't. She manages to look at me and she can't speak, but I know what she's thinking.

When I leave her, I see the envoy standing at the edge of the gantry, looking out over the ship. He doesn't turn as I approach, but he tenses. He knows that I'm there.

'She's going to die,' I tell him.

'I know,' he replies. 'Most of these people are dying, and faster than the rest of us.'

'So why do this? Why spend so much time here?'

'Because they're sick. Because they're in pain.' He bites his lip, thinking about what he's going to say next. 'When I was a baby, I didn't have parents. The Pale Women took me in. They found me, and they saved me, and they didn't care who I was, where I came from. I was sick, coughing up blood. They didn't believe that I had long to live. Some didn't want to accept a male into their faith, no matter how long I was likely to live. Better to put me out of my misery. But one Sister fought for me. She wanted to make sure that my life – what was left of it – was as good as it could be.' He still doesn't look at me. He stares out over the nothingness, over the drop down to the Pit, looking at the other sections of the ship – a ship that somehow abandoned him. He's telling his story to the ship, it seems, not just to me.

'The way she tells it, that's what saved my life. She says

that the Father gave me the strength to fight for myself, just as she fought for me.'

'And now you're here,' I say.

'Yes,' he says. And he smiles. 'I help them, because I can. Because I think I should. Because I owe the women my life, and it's right.'

'I never helped anybody,' I say. 'Until two days ago, I didn't help anybody at all.' I hate myself for saying that as soon as the words leave my mouth. Stupid. 'I promised my mother that I would be selfish,' I tell him, trying to make it better. 'Then she died. But I promised her.'

'And she'd be proud, I'm sure,' he replies, and then he turns, still not looking at me, but back to the berths behind us. 'I should get back to them.' He doesn't wait for me to reply; he just starts walking to the next berth.

'What can I do now?' I ask. Then he looks at me, and he smiles, the corner of his mouth rising just a little.

'There's a man two berths down who has forgotten who he is, where he is. You could talk to him,' he tells me.

'I can do that,' I reply.

I stay on the eighty-eighth floor until the envoy leaves. I don't ask him his name, and I tell myself that I have to, next time I see him. Then I go down, back to my berth, bone-tired, and I fall onto my bunk. I don't remember falling asleep.

When I wake I can hear voices. Somebody new is moving into Bess's berth. I have new neighbours. I listen as they shift their belongings: a woman and her children – a boy and a girl – lugging everything they own in slow, arduous trips. There's a gap in my curtains and I watch them dragging mattresses, taken from their old bunks. I think about telling them that the berth is occupied, that Bess will come back, but I can't. I'm pretty sure that's not true.

It takes me what feels like forever to get up. I've never hurt so much. Every muscle in my body feels like it's been pulled, yanked into some new position. Every step makes me ache, and I have to bite my lip to stop myself from hissing when I bend down to tie my shoelaces.

I pull back the curtains and see the woman who's moving in better. She's lithe, her body a rippling display of muscles. She may be the most muscular woman I've ever seen. Where Agatha hides everything underneath her cloak, this woman wears her body like a badge. The scars on her skin that run around her entire body; the missing toes on her feet, a mark of some torture or other; the burn marks on her face, across her left eye, running up to her scalp, that mean she can't grow hair over half of her head, that mean her eye is a cloudy grey-white colour. I try not to stare. People don't like it when you stare. It's only when I see her back that I know more about her, and how she got like this. The scars on her back give her away, their patterns and designs, carved and almost delicately arranged.

She used to be a Low.

I watch her as she tells her children – both younger than me, but only by a few years, and maybe they're twins, that's how alike they look – to unpack their belongings, as they try to make Bess's old berth a home. It is obviously smaller than where they've come from, from the kids' moaning about it – but the woman has a power about her that you rarely see here. A control. She's completely even-tempered, never losing her patience. Her children are dreadful. They're already lost. They will join a gang, if they're not already in one, or form one of their own, and soon they'll be somebody's nightmare. I can see that their mother knows this and despairs, but for now she's still got some control over them.

I don't know how old she is. Maybe she's the same age as my mother was, but it's difficult to tell, she has lived harder, a fighter rather than somebody who tried to stay away from trouble. But she cares for her children. She tells them off, but she watches over them while they work. She's protective. I recognise it, and miss it.

The Lows don't believe in family, not in the way that the free people do. They treat everybody as part of the whole, every child a Low rather than a son or a daughter. If they don't have enough of their own, they take ours. Children are swallowed by them, raised to be monsters. You have a kid when you're a Low, they're basically screwed, no chance for anything else. Probably a reasonably good chance they won't even see adulthood. Maybe they were able to be good, once. Maybe they would have been able to do something other than be a Low, but they aren't given the chance. I can't be sure, but I'm betting that my new neighbour wanted her children to have that opportunity: the opportunity not to be monsters.

I go and stand at the entrance to my berth as I pull my shoes on, thinking that I might introduce myself. It can't hurt. While I'm waiting for the woman to notice me, I spot Agatha at the far end of the gantry. She's sitting on a crate, head down, trying to go unnoticed. I would say that she's not very good at it, but I know that's a lie. She just wanted me to see her. I ignore her and finish getting myself ready.

By the time Agatha gets up and comes over, I've got my blade already tucked into my pack. I don't want to be without it, not anymore.

'Living here is getting more dangerous,' she says. 'You should move upstairs, with me.' There are no stairs, not any more, and yet we still say that. We really need new words. 'It's what your mother—'

'She's dead,' I say, and that's the end of the conversation. She can't go anywhere else with it.

'The Lows are starting a war. They're trying to take this section, this part of the ship. They want it, so they'll take it.'

'Let them try,' I say.

'You don't understand. They've done this before, and they have always succeeded. They've pushed people out, and they've killed anyone who has tried to resist them. This is just them warming up. This is preparation, and it will get so much worse.'

She suddenly looks old and scared, and I think back to yesterday – the quiet and the darkness of the eighty-eighth floor, of laying that wet cloth across the forehead of a sick woman, of talking to that old man whose mind was gone. Even looking for Peter – just doing *something* – was better than nothing.

I am tired of doing nothing. I like doing something. I've spent my whole life doing nothing. I don't care about the danger. Agatha does. She's scared, and I don't know why, but I'm almost ashamed of her. She shouldn't be. She's given up. 'If we fight them, they will kill us.'

'Then you won't be in any danger, will you?' I say. That stings her, I know, and it's nasty of me. But she's standing back. The Agatha that my mother used to talk about would never have stood back and let this chaos – this violence – happen around her. That Agatha wouldn't have hidden in the dark. She would have done something, helped people.

That Agatha would have helped me.

'I can't protect you if you stay here,' she says.

'I know,' I say. And I want to say so much more to her, but the words don't form in my mouth, and then Agatha turns and leaves, and it's too late.

It seems as though everybody starts screaming at once. The noise of it clangs around the ship, waking me up. I don't know how long I was asleep for, but it wasn't long enough. I'm amazed that I managed to sleep at all. I remember lying in my bed and trying to pretend that I was somewhere else. I've done it before: taken myself away, in that space between sleeping and waking. I've found a haven where we're not here, not on Australia. The fantasy of it is always so strong, because my mother is always alive in these dreams, and I can talk to her about everything. I have so much I wish to say to her. And we're always safe. We're never running or hiding. That's the last thing that I remember.

But the noise of the screaming – which is monotonous and repetitive, like an alarm – is too loud. I open my eyes, and everything is black. I think it's me at first, but it's not: shapes start to make themselves known in the darkness, the layout of my room emerges in dim outlines. I stand up and stumble to my curtains, and pull them apart. It's not just my room: something's happened to the lights all over the ship. In every other berth, there are the sounds of panic, of people telling their loved ones to not be afraid.

I can't see anything.

'What's happened?' I ask, into the darkness. Next door, the ex-Low lights a candle and the light floods out. Such a small flame, and yet the difference it makes is amazing. It's so bright.

'They've cut them,' she says. 'They've found a way to turn out the lights.' She points, somewhere over to section IV. 'There are wires, behind the walls. Cables. They must have found the right one.'

'It's so dark,' I say.

'You're scared?' She moves away from the candle, and I can't see her face any more. Her boys stir in their makeshift beds on the floor. 'I wouldn't have thought you'd be scared of anything. I know about your mother. I know who she was.' She comes towards me, through the darkness. I can see her silhouetted against the flicker of a flame behind her. 'And I know about you,' she says, and I can see that she doubts the stories that have spread about me.

I'm about to say something back to her – to defend myself – when there's a sound from section IV. It's colossal: a crash, the sound of metal collapsing onto metal, of screaming and terror, worse than before. I can't see what it is, but I have to. I pull on my clothes, my shoes, get my blade, and I run. Despite every ache in my body, every painful muscle screaming at me to rest, I run.

On the forty-third floor, at the edge of section IV, the gantry has collapsed in on itself. Too much has been taken away over the years, too many of the support beams that hold it in place chipped away for weapons or whatever. Apparently, whatever the free people had done to stop the Lows from crossing was the last straw: a few too many things taken from the edge, to widen the gap; or maybe whatever they piled up to use as a barricade was just too heavy. Either way, the contents of three berths have spilled out, the gantry bent down to the floor below. There are people trapped down there, a mixture of Lows and others, and the only way that we can see what's going on is in the flickering light of candles and torches reflecting off the dark metal.

I climb down and start helping as the free people from this section of the ship pull off the metal, yanking it away from where it's fallen, trying to free those who are trapped underneath. Nobody notices who I am, and nobody asks about the blade that I have with me, and nobody says anything about my mother's ghost or what I might want. We don't even talk, unless it's to coordinate lifting up the metal and pulling out the people trapped beneath it. Time passes. I don't know how much.

On the other side, at the edge of section III, I suddenly notice the Lows. They have torches: thick rods of metal soaked in something that burns so brightly that the flames are almost white. They stand and they breathe their sick huffs, and they scream.

And then I see her: Rex, their leader; the woman who was there the night that my mother died. She's more scarred now, that's for certain, with fresh welts running across her chest and face, and I'm sure that her hair is singed in places – short to the scalp on one half of her head. She looks at me, and then at the fallen gantry around us all. She has no expression on her face as she looks at the chaos.

And then she says, 'Take them.' I can see her lips move; I know that's what she says, even through the noise all around us. And at this, the Lows hoot and howl and they drop ladders and planks across the stairwell, onto the creaking mess of metal around us. I watch, frozen, and she stares back at me, and she smiles. I'm sure of it.

There are too many of them. We back off, those of us who were trying to help the trapped and fallen, because they outnumber us. Ten, fifteen, twenty I count, piling over the gap. We can't save the others and ourselves. We retreat, because there's nothing else that we can do.

Agatha was right. The incursions of the nights before weren't war.

This is.

AGATHA

Your mother was a pain in the backside. I think that's fair to say. She was a nightmare, and your grandparents couldn't control her, so they asked me to help. I was treated as a part of the family after I rescued her – maybe a distant relative, coming every so often for food and company – and they needed help. She was inquisitive. Here, people change, but she was different. There used to be a saying: a leopard never changes its spots. You've seen drawings of tigers? A leopard was like them, but spots, not stripes. That was your mother. She was twelve or thirteen, and she wanted more than Australia could offer her. She wanted some degree of freedom, which . . . She managed to forget what she was like, I think, when she was dealing with you. You were your own person, and yet so like her.

She was going out a lot in the mornings and then not coming home. Your grandmother wanted to teach her – they had bargained for books, and they wanted to give her something like an education, as much as they could manage – and she refused. She had better things to be doing, she told them. So they asked me to watch over her, to make sure

117

she was alright. What they meant was: find out what she is doing. They were worried. People should worry; it's a sign that they care.

So I followed her, and she had no idea. I'm good at it. I know the ship like the back of my hand, and I know where to hide. I knew what paths to take to be able to watch her as she went without being seen, and I got to watch everything that she did. Meeting with her friends, talking, sitting. The games that they played, daring each other to go to places in the ship that they weren't supposed to go to. Climb high, visit the Pale Women; walk into Bell territory and tell them a joke; go into the Lows' section and steal something. The dares got worse and worse, the children pushing themselves as far as they could go. One of them was caught by a Low one time, and killed. I didn't intervene. I stood back and watched their horror, and I thought, this will be the lesson. This will be what stops them.

Of course, it didn't. You know what your mother was like: you told her not to do something, and she proved as stubborn and defiant as anybody's ever been. They didn't stop the games. Quite the opposite. I had to watch as they put more pressure on each other to perform, to outclass one another. Her friends . . . eventually they grew up, got scared, learned to be afraid. But not Riadne.

Anyway: one day, I stopped her. I grabbed her, because they were throwing knives that they had stolen from somebody, tiny little things, sharp spikes with fins on the side. They stole them, and they made a game of it: trying to hit targets below by dropping them through the grating of the floor, to watch them plummet and stick somebody who didn't see it coming. I grabbed her and pulled her to one side, and I told her to stop.

She refused. Of course she refused, because I was just like her parents. Couldn't have been more similar, in her eyes. I made things worse, then, because I slapped her. I'm not proud of that, but there it was, and she was shocked, and she slapped me right back. So she took my criticism of her and then went further. She pushed harder.

This would have been the first time that she went down to the Pit. Everybody goes down there eventually – and I don't mean in some hazy, mystical way, I mean, to see what it's like down there. There are bodies, and everybody has to see it. I know about the first time you went down, even. It's a secret; a dare. We make it into a rite of passage. But it's a test.

Your mother dared her friends – four of them, I remember: three girls and one boy – to go down there, as they had done before. But this time, they were going into it. Not sitting on the side, not looking away as whatever grisly mess floated towards them; actually setting foot in it. She told them that she would go first. I tried to stop her, once I caught wind of what they were planning, but she wouldn't listen to me. They went, climbed down, and down, and they ended up on the bottom floor. I don't need to tell you what it's like down there. It's dark, and the ship seems to shake more than anywhere else, and the smell makes you retch. There's a kind of mist above it, from the bodies. That's why the stories about the ghosts came about: because down there, people swear that they hear voices. Your mother? She wanted to meet a ghost. That's what she said

119

the dare was about. Go down there, into the Pit, and meet one of the ghosts.

I waited two floors above and watched them. I didn't want to make her do anything that might actually result in her harming herself. And defying me? That could have been what pushed her over the edge. Her friends were nervous. I don't want to say that they were more sensible than she was, but they knew to be cautious. Your mother, though? She went in. She sat on the edge and she put her feet in, and then she went for it. She waded out, waist-deep in that mess, and she grinned as if she had achieved something truly great. She was the first person she knew who had done what she just did, and she was proud.

She was also foolish. She didn't see the Lows at the lip of their section, stepping in. They forage from the Pit, and they always have done, trawling it for anything that they can use. Weapons and clothes end up down there, and . . . There have always been stories. They don't eat from the arboretum, at least not that we know. Some people must trade with them, and they steal things, but there are enough of them that most of their food must come from somewhere else. The bug protein can't be enough to sustain them, we all know that. They take what they can get; that's always been their way. Your mother didn't see them, but I did. I was willing to bet that they wouldn't care what they found in there, living or dead. They don't tend to make the distinction at the best of times. She waded out backwards, facing her friends, and then they saw the Lows coming, and they pointed, and your mother turned and saw them too, and tried to run, but the Lows ran faster.

She should have been able to make it out, but she tripped and fell, and that was enough. Down and under she went, under the blood and the bodies. You've seen it; you know what it's like down there. It's never been any different. She tripped, and then she screamed. Her foot was caught on something.

Her friends abandoned her. They didn't wait even a moment, didn't offer her any help. They ran, because they didn't want the Lows to turn on them when they were done with her. She was alone – or, she would have been, if I hadn't been watching her.

I went in after her, and I dealt with them. They didn't make it out, but she did. And I dragged her home, coughing and spluttering, and I cleaned her off before her parents saw her, and I told her what we would say to them: that she was done with going off alone, and wanted to help them out more. She was going to be the ideal daughter, I told her, and she agreed. No more going off on her own. No more lying. No more secrets.

But she lied. She lied to them, and to me. She would always have her secrets, even from me.

FIVE

First, they destroy the Bells.

The Bells are . . . There's a story. There's always a story. This one goes that the Bells came from experiments, before we left Earth. They were soldiers, modified by doctors back then, bits of their brains limited to focus them. That's how wars were fought, with people turned into single-minded killing machines. On Australia, though, that kind of focus isn't useful, not without anybody to tell them what they should be doing. Here, they're nothing but muscle, driven by impulses rather than anything like logic. They're violent and they're angry, but they're also malleable. Get into a fight with them and you're dead; but it's pretty easy to talk your way out, if you're able to think on your feet. They're harmless.

Or, they *were*.

The Bells live below the collapsed part of section IV, those floors way beneath. Once we're all scared away – by their numbers, more than anything – the Lows move down, flooding into the twenty or so floors that the Bells call home, using the darkness to their advantage. And they tear them apart. The Lows bring their torches with them, and I can see the fighting. I watch as Bells are thrown into the Pit, as the Lows cut them with weapons; as they throw fire-bombs to burn them up, to drive them out. Before? That wasn't expanding. That was just the Lows flexing their muscles. This is the Lows expanding.

I stand at the gantry railing to watch, and the woman who now lives in Bess's berth joins me. She rolls her shoulders as she approaches, and she snorts rather than saying anything, nodding to acknowledge me.

'Are you scared of them?' she asks. Her voice is throaty and hoarse, like they all are. She can't lose that, I suppose.

'Yes,' I say. Better to be honest.

'There's no end to this,' she says. She pauses, seeming to weigh up the words before she says them. I try not to stare at the burn marks on her face. 'They won't stop, and what happens then? When they've taken the ship for their own? Then we're all Lows.'

'You've been one before,' I say, the words out of my mouth before I can even think about how they might sound. 'I'm sorry,' I say, backtracking.

But she smiles, almost, the corners of her lips tilting slightly. 'I was,' she says, 'when I was much younger. My parents were.' So that was how she grew up. But she left . . . I wonder why. But I don't ask any other questions. She seems nice, I think. I haven't seen her before, but that's often the way here. If you want to hide, you can. This ship is good for keeping secrets.

'The Bells will fight back,' she says, 'but they'll lose. The Lows will take as much of the ship as they want, and nobody will stop them.'

'But that's—'

'They'll hunt down anybody who threatens them, and when the only people left are the weak and sick and scared, they'll take the ship. Don't fight. Stand back and watch, and pray that you don't get in their way.'

As we watch, the Bells are decimated. Some of them run for their lives, scattering to other parts of the ship to nurse their wounds and mourn their dead friends. The Lows have separated them. But they're done. One night and they're all but destroyed, and nothing anybody can do now can help them.

And suddenly, as if we blinked and it happened, fast as anything, half of section IV belongs to the Lows: every floor, from the Pit up to 50. It's over, just like that, and we've lost more of the ship. And now we're unbalanced; the rest of section IV starts dragging their wounded and dead and sick and young over to section V, crowding in. We lost the lower half to war; we'll lose the upper half to abandonment. The Lows will take the entire section.

They now have more than half of Australia.

In our section, we make room, and we let others in. I find a man and his daughter, scared and wandering, turned away from other places, and I take them to the berth on 85 that Agatha had suggested that I move into, and I tell them that it is theirs now. They're grateful.

I go looking for Agatha. I check her new home but she's not there. I want to stay and wait for her, but I can't. Because there are more people who need help. If I can't help them, I ask myself, what can I do?

*　　*　　*

The morning means nothing here, in the new darkness. Some people with clocks might try to read them, but there's no sense. It's strange: when the lights were on all the time, and we made it night, you could feel the difference. Now? For some reason, the distinction is no longer there.

I sit in my berth and I talk to myself, or to my mother, I'm not really sure which. I tell the darkness in front of me about what's happening, talking it through as if that will change anything. Maybe it will, I don't know. Maybe hearing it out loud will make it all make sense.

I'm so tired. My body is so drained, and I feel like I've barely slept the past few days. What's it like, to not be here? What would it be like?

'Mother,' I say, but she's not there; and in the darkness, it makes me wonder if she ever was, or if all those years with her looking after me were only some dream I had.

I wake up. I can't remember having ever slept so heavily. There is a noise coming from outside my berth: breathing, the sounds of violence. The curtains are drawn closed. I don't remember doing that, but they are. I don't know what time it is, how long I've been asleep for; and I can't see how many Lows are out there, waiting for me, or about to burst in. I sit up as quietly as I can manage, and the bed stays as quiet as I need it to. This feels like routine now: shoes on, blade into my hand, ready. I don't think about anything else.

Don't die, my mother's voice says, again and again. It rattles around my head and I can't get rid of it. If only she knew that it wasn't as easy as it might once have been.

But they're not for me, not straight away. It's the woman next door. I've been woken up by the tail end of them destroying her and her family. I don't know how I slept through it, but I did. Who she is – who she was – doesn't mean anything. She defected, and now she's here, and she's a threat. They call her a traitor, and she tries to defend herself. She tells them that she was granted pardon. She begs. They don't care. She throws around names of Lows that she knows, that she was friends with; and she shows them her scars, says that she got them in fights with the same Lows who are there now, torturing her. She begs again, saying that their leader spared her life, that she's free now. They laugh. The leader who spared her is long dead, they tell her.

Don't die. I peek through gaps in the fabric. There are so many of them out there, spilling out onto the gantry, lit only by the torches that they're carrying. A pack of them: ten or so, maybe more inside the berth. They would kill me. I'd never make it through them alive. They haven't killed her yet, and I don't know why. They're keeping her alive. I can see an arm on the floor, and I assume it belongs to one of her sons. The other, I have no idea. Hopefully he wasn't with them when the Lows arrived.

Then the Lows fall silent. All I can hear is their breathing, and the gasps for air coming from my neighbour. There's the sound of feet on the gantry, in the distance. Metal soles on the shoes, the solid thud that they make as she walks. It's Rex, and she's here.

'Kill the rest of them,' she shouts. I remember her voice: so strangely monotonous, like there's nothing there behind it. It's terrifying, worse than any other Low.

I have to leave. I have to get out of here. I look down at my hands, and I see that my new blade is shaking; and it takes me a second to realise that both of my hands are shaking, that my whole body is. I should be stronger. I should be trying to help my new neighbour. She might have done wrong once, but not any more. She wanted away from them. I have to believe that she's a good person, and that what's being done to her isn't fair.

But I don't want to help as much as I want to live. I'm scared, and right now, there's nothing that I can do.

The Low who was my neighbour screams. The more noise she makes, the better chance I'll have to escape. I peek through the curtains and I can't see Rex. Maybe she's in the next berth; maybe she's left, gone somewhere else. I can't tell.

When my neighbour howls again – louder this time, and it makes me feel sick to my stomach to hear, because it's so loud and so pained – I open the curtain slightly, and I step out, ready to break into a run.

I don't get the chance.

Rex's hand clamps onto my throat, her nails digging in, tight and sharp. I don't want to scream, and I don't want to shut my eyes. She's so close to me. We're the same height, but she's stronger than I am. The muscles in her arm jut and swell as she grips me tighter. I wonder, in that second, if she might be able to lift me clean off my feet.

I can't breathe, and everything starts to go red. Lit by their torches, everything goes the same colour as the fire, and then there's blackness, deeper than the lack of light. I kick out. I somehow put my hands on her arm, and I try to prise her fingers open.

She digs her fingers deeper into my neck.

'Don't cry,' she says to me. 'Don't cry.' I didn't realise that I was crying. I somehow manage to take a breath, and I see her clearly for a second: her eyes huge and empty, her title carved into her chest still, now healed over into thick creamy welts that run over the thin skin. In her other hand, I see a knife: my mother's. It's the one that I used to kill her, that Rex in turn used to take her place as head of the Lows. She's kept it, and now she lifts it up to show it to me. She knows that I recognise it. She brings it close to my throat, resting it on the top of her hand, pressing it against my skin. She says something else, but I don't hear it. Her voice sounds like it's coming from another place, as the darkness swarms my vision again.

Everything goes black and then—

I drop. I'm suddenly on the floor, on my back, and I'm gasping in air, coughing it straight back up. The light – as little of it as there is – comes back, and I can see feet, a struggle of fighting in front of me; and blood, pouring from somewhere, is hitting the floor in front of my eyes, spattering onto my face. There's screaming again, but this is different. It's angry.

I'm wrenched to my feet, and I barely have time to see what's happened before Agatha is looking into my face. She pulls me close to her.

'You have to run!' she whispers. Behind her, the Lows cluster around their leader, who clutches at her arm. Her head is rocked back, mouth open, teeth bared. Some of them, I see, have been filed down into points. She never bares them, doesn't use them to scare. She's just done it because she liked it.

And then I see her hand, on the floor. It's still clutching my mother's knife.

'Where?' I ask Agatha, as Rex starts looking around, as the Lows gather their weapons, as they start towards us. I see Rex snatch a lit torch from one of her followers, and she drives her hand into it, screaming as she cauterises the wound. 'There's nowhere safe!'

'The Pale Women—' Agatha says, and she's cut off, like she's going to say more but can't, and that's all I've got.

I reach out and grab my blade from the floor and then I run, like she told me to. I don't know if Agatha is behind me. I'm more scared than I've ever been my whole life.

I climb up a floor when I reach the first gantry, and again, and then I see Lows, terrorising the fifty-third floor, so I go along, to try and reach the next stairwell, between sections V and VI, past the berths here as the Lows are in them; and I see them, and I think, *Don't die,* and I keep moving, because that's the only way I know to avoid the fighting; and I climb up another floor, and another, and another, and I'm exhausted and aching and shaking but I can't stop, so I don't; and then I climb again, and again, five floors in one go, and the coast is clear, so I leave the stairwell and run along the gantry, and suddenly there are more Lows; and it's so hard to see anything, because I'm relying on my gut instincts, on the occasional torch that's been left somewhere, on the reflections of fire in the metal walls that make up the berths. But I know that the Lows have light, they have fire, so that's what I stay away from, I decide; and then, on the sixty-sixth or sixty-seventh, or maybe even the seventieth floor – I can't tell because I've been moving and not worrying where I am, just trying to stay alive – there's so many of them that I have to find another way, so I look for one, but I can't get past them; and they look down at me, and they see me, not knowing who I am, but knowing that I'm running, and maybe also catching the glint of my blade. So they start to come for me, and I turn and I run again, back in the direction I came from. But I can't go back down, because there's nothing for me there but Rex; and I hear her, screaming my name, somehow still on her feet, somehow coming for me, which means that she's done with Agatha, however that particular fight ended. So there's only one path left, and that's across the ladder-bridge that they used to get to this section, over into section I, so I rush across it, into Low territory, right into where they have come from, where I have never ever been before.

There's a torch lying on an abandoned bunk, and matches. It's dangerous: the rest of this side of the ship is empty, and lighting it will make me a beacon. But I have to. I've got no idea what I'll find here. At least it's empty. Or, it looks like it's empty. I hold my breath and I strike the match, hold it to the fabric that is knotted around one end. The torch takes.

I've spent time staring at the Low sections before. You can see them from anywhere on the ship, but not close enough to pick out details. You don't know what it's like until you're in it, until it's lit up close by the yellow bright-ness of a flame. There are bones on the gantries, and ripped rags of fabric on the walls, all manner of colours and sizes. Pieces – remnants – of the people that they've killed. They have weapons here: blunt and broken, but probably useable. And there's so much blood. It stains the metal of the floor, and it stains the walls, and the ripped mattresses inside the berths that they sleep on.

It's not until I've made it up a few more floors in their half of the ship that I look back at where I came from. I pause, breathe for a second. Strange to think that it's quieter here, that I'm safer where I should be more terrified. But this part of the ship is empty. They're all in the free sections, waging their war.

I don't know how they became so lost, so willing to act like this. Something, once upon a time, triggered this. I have to believe that it's got a reason, or else . . . Or else it's just in them. It's in them, and maybe it could be in the rest of us.

Not far to go until the Pale Women. I can't rest now.

So I climb.

There's a noise, ten floors from the top of the ship. I mean, of course there are noises. There's nothing but noise. Up here, the echoes of the rest of the ship – the howling, the engines, the crying – drowns everything else out; and these sections, which seem abandoned, creak and moan as I travel through them, as I run along the rusting metal of their gantries. But there haven't been any Lows for a few floors, not until right this second.

He's above me: just a large, dark shape in the darkness. He doesn't have a torch, and the light of mine will only alert him that I'm here. He stands right near the edge of the stairwell, swaying, like there's something wrong with him:

I can see the shape of his body rocking back and forth. *Don't die*, my mother says.

'Alright,' I say, under my breath, 'I get it.' I snuff the torch out and start to climb, as quietly as I can. One Low: that's all, and he's in my way. I can do this. I'm level with the gantry, close enough that I can touch him. I can take his ankle and pull him, hopefully over the edge. At the very least he'll end up face down, giving me an advantage. It's only as I reach out that I see the bodies, lit by some flame far away. My eyes have adjusted to the darkness, now that I don't have the torch, and I can see their shapes: their heads tilted towards me, their eyes dead and staring. My fingers touch the Low's ankle, and his body tenses. He spins, and looks down at me, and there's a blade – no, *two* blades – slashing out at my hand, and I flinch away. I hang on, barely, as the Low's body flies past me, off into the Pit. Then I see another face, peering down at me: it's the Pale Women's envoy.

He kneels at the edge and reaches down, and he clamps his fingers around my wrist. I see his knuckles go white as he holds me, as he starts to heave me back up to the floor.

'What are you doing here?' I ask him. He looks down at the bodies around him: all Lows, all with their throats cut. There's a lot of blood, and I'm grateful I don't have more light to see by. I wouldn't want to be able to see how much.

The envoy doesn't answer. He's cut, I see: across the side of his face, a tear that's swollen and thick with redness, glistening in the dim light. I reach out to touch it, and he flinches. 'Don't,' I say. 'This needs cleaning.' He might be dangerous, I think; but he killed them. What it that they say? The enemy of my enemy is my friend? And he's killed Lows.

'It hurts,' he says. I'm not surprised, but I don't say that. He puts a hand to it and brings it away, and looks at his palm, covered in blood. The wound is pretty bad, anybody could tell that.

'You need help,' I say. 'I can clean it for you.' He nods and hands me his satchel, the rags and ointments he was using to help the sickly on the eighty-sixth floor; and he pushes his hood back to his shoulders. His collar is still on, the spikes nudging against the scars on his skin. I take out a strip of fabric and soak it with the ointment, and I press it up to his face, washing off the blood that's there. Some is from the cut, but some definitely isn't.

'Hold still,' I say, and he does. I press the cloth to his skin, and the water soaks through it. It runs down his cheek, taking the blood with it. I press again, and harder, and then drag the cloth along the cut itself, trying to make sure it's clean, that there isn't a shard of anything stuck in it. He flinches.

'What's your name?' I ask.

'My name?' He sucks in air, a hiss of pain through his teeth. 'Jonah,' he says.

'Jonah,' I repeat, trying it out. 'That's from your *Testaments*.'

'It's an important name,' he says, as if that explains everything; and, in some ways, it does. Makes sense they'd use those books for naming. They use them for everything else.

'Why were you here?' I ask him.

'This is what I do,' he says. He opens his hands at his side – the knives he had, they're missing now, secreted somewhere in his cloak – and he indicates the bodies. 'They were a threat, and they . . .' Again, he stumbles over the words, and he breathes in deeply. This time, I'm not hurting him. This time, it's something else. 'They were judged, and I carried out their judgement.'

'Judged,' I say, and he nods. He's carrying himself differently than before: where his head is usually bowed, now he's tall, his shoulders back and tense. He takes my hand and pulls it away from his face.

'I have to go,' he says.

'I was trying to get up to find you,' I say. I correct myself. 'To find the Women. I'm being chased.'

'You won't be welcome,' he tells me. 'You shunned them when they gave you the books, when they made their offer for you to join them. Sister says—'

'Then I take it back. I take back what I said, and I'll listen to their stories.'

'It's not as easy as that.' He pulls his hood back up. 'We're nearing ascension, Sister says. It's too late for you.'

'They'll kill me.' And he looks sad; I swear that he looks sad. He knows I don't deserve whatever's coming. 'Their leader's been hurt, and she'll want me. She won't stop.'

'Come and talk to Sister,' he says then, and he moves without pause, running down to the stairwell and leaping up from the edge, to clutch the lip of the floor above. He doesn't look back. I climb up after him, and we go up there together.

* * *

He doesn't talk, which really annoys me, even more than when Agatha is silent. I try; I ask him about what he was doing down there, why those Lows were dead at his feet, why he wears the collar. Everything is met with grunts or, if I'm lucky, a justification that *it's in the book*. I've read the book, and it doesn't say anything about collars or knives. It's nothing but old language and mystery and inconsistent characters.

So as we climb, and as the Lows' part of the ship becomes something more like what I'm used to, as we get higher, I stop asking him questions. No sense. Sometimes he breaks into a run, and he tries to move fast enough that it's almost as if he wants to lose me, but there's no chance of that. My hands hurt, and my body aches, but I keep following. I can't stop now.

When we're a couple of floors below Limbo, he stops climbing up and instead takes off towards our half of the ship. You almost wouldn't know what was going on below from here. Things seem to have quietened down; the echoes of sound from down there have faded away. The sick, the injured: the Lows haven't made their way up here yet. Maybe they know that this is the part of Australia that will offer them the least resistance. Might as well leave it until after the harder work is done.

'Sister will ask you what you believe,' he says as he walks. I almost miss it, as he moves faster than I can comfortably keep up with.

'And I'll tell her,' I say.

'That's how she'll give you sanctuary,' he says. 'That's what they work on. You'll abandon who you were, and take

135

up our cause.' Their cause? As far as I can see, they stay in the darkness of the top floors and pray over their old books. The only one of them I've ever seen actually doing something is Jonah. 'That's the only way that she will offer you protection, you know.'

'Okay, sure,' I tell him. He's preachy. It's annoying. I don't understand why they wouldn't just help me because it's the right thing to do. Even in their book, that's the suggestion: you do what's right and just and fair. You shouldn't have to swear allegiance to them to get that. 'Agatha should be here as well,' I tell him. 'She said she would meet me.'

'The old woman?'

'Yes,' I say, and that makes me smile. I'm not sure she'd like being talked of in that way. Something burns me, then: the thought that she might not be here. I don't know what happened between her and Rex, after I ran. But she must be okay. She's always okay.

I suppose that's the one truth of life that always holds, though: you're always okay until suddenly you're not. What if this time is the *suddenly*?

'Here,' he says, pointing up to the ninetieth floor. The ninetieth floor is a lie: it's actually the ninety-first, but there's a floor missing in between. One day, over a hundred years ago, it collapsed, down onto the eighty-ninth. The floor itself was salvaged for metal, the people who lived on or below it dead, crushed or fallen down to the Pit. So the climb up to Limbo is harder: not a case of looking for the next floor, of finding some way to reach it and then hauling yourself up; more like finding handholds in the side, actually having to scale something that's dangerous. And the Pale Women stripped the stairwells of stairs, ladders, everything. There's no immediate sign of how you climb this. No one knows how the Pale Women get in and out. So I copy Jonah, putting my hands where his have been as we climb. He knows the way, but I can see he's still cautious. He keeps pausing, listening to the ship, trying to tell what's happening.

There's something wrong, and we both know it. We climb onto the gantry of the eighty-ninth floor, and we hear the noise from above, and see the flames, and the flashes of weapons through the floor above us. We climb again, faster, Jonah almost furious in his movement. I can feel the shake of the feet on the ninetieth floor as I put my hands onto the edge of the gantry; as the fighting explodes around us.

I've never seen the Women fight before, but they're vicious. I only catch glimpses of them in the darkness, in the brief moments that they're directly lit by the flames of torches, but they're brutal and relentless, tearing throats and throwing knives. The stories about them said as much, but I never really believed it, not until now.

This whole area is a mess of Lows and blood and weapons, and Jonah and I stand on the lip of the gantry and watch them. He clenches his hands, I notice, opening and closing his fists.

Limbo isn't safe either. I don't know why I thought it would be. And then, without a word, Jonah disappears into the fray, and he's just another black-robed body in a swarm of them. I don't know what to do. I could get involved, but I'm exhausted, not prepared. Still, I've got a weapon, and I can breathe, and I can move. Limbo isn't a safe place, but it could be, it could—

Then she's there. Again, Rex. She's here, with the rest of them, nursing the stump of her arm, which is wrapped in cloth. There's no blood. She's at the other end of the gantry, but I can see her in the light of their torches, now that this part of the ship is lit up for the first time in who knows how long. I can also see that there's writing all over the walls: scratched in, clawed in, layers and layers. I recognise phrases from the Women's book.

Rex. Rex, focus on Rex. I look for Jonah, but he's invisible. The Women fall, because there aren't enough of them.

Rex. She lowers her head and looks down the gantry, and she sees me. I'm here, and I'm alone; and, as she notices me, as she starts to walk towards me, as she pulls my mother's knife out of her sheath and holds it in front of her, as she smiles, I take my own blade out and I stand firm, because I don't know what else I can do.

So, we fight. We fight, and it's over as soon as it's begun, because I'm no match for her. Even one-handed, as full of anger as she is, she wants victory more than I do. I'm not fighting to beat her; I'm fighting to survive.

I swing my blade, and she ducks underneath it and stabs me. The knife slides into my side, my mother's knife, all the way up to the hilt. And then she twists it, and she tugs it out, doing as much damage as she can. I feel it at first, and then it all fades away. All the pain, it's just gone, replaced with a kind of numbness.

She kicks me off the lip of the gantry, down into the stairwell. I drop a few floors, and then I collide with something – a barricade across gantries – slamming my back into the metal, and the last few things that I see (her peering at me, cradling the space where her hand was, her scars, and then Jonah slashing at her, taking the fight back, doing *something*), those last images slide away into nothingness, and blackness, blacker even than the darkness of the ship itself. I turn my head and I can see down, off the edge, all the way to the bottom of the ship; but I don't know if it's the darkness of the Pit itself or just the darkness of everything else. Still, I think, if that's where I'm headed, at least I know it's only as dark down there as it's always been.

Don't die, my mother's voice says. I wish I could tell her how hard I'm trying not to.

PART
TWO

PART

TWO

SIX

I open my eyes for fragments of time and nothing more, and I see the fires around me, all around, and—

I'm awake when they drag me down, floor by floor, two of them, four hands, pressing against me, carrying me, but I can't hear what they're saying, their words—

and the sound of fighting, as they put me down somewhere and they—

and it's so wet, all over me, and I cough, and that makes one of their hands come up to my face, and I see—

'Agatha!' I yell, the only word I can actually manage to get out, but—

over and over, falling back into the darkness, and nothing has ever scared me so much as it has, nothing ever, not my whole life, not even the day when my mother told me that she was dying and that I would be—

'Breathe,' she says, Agatha's voice, Agatha's words, which means I'm safe, I know that I'm safe, because I have to be safe if she's got me, and there's the light of a torch, the flames of one, and I look around—

we're in the Pit, oh god, we're in the Pit, how did we get down here

and there's a hand on my face, over my mouth, and she whispers into my ears, 'hold your breath,' and then I'm submerged, and it's like being in the river in the arboretum, like washing, but it is warm and dense and slimy and awful, and I struggle and fight but she keeps her hand steady—

I open my eyes again, and it's light. Bright, burning light, brighter than I've ever seen before in my entire life, and I can't keep my eyes open because it actually hurts.

'You're safe now,' she says, and I so want to believe her.

My mother and I found moments of peace on Australia that only we shared. We would pull the cloth across the doorway of our berth and we would sit on the bed, and she would tell me stories. She remembered books from when she was little, books that her mother had read to her when they were still available on the ship, before they had completely deteriorated, and she told the stories to me. Every story had a girl about my age in it; every story was about that girl becoming who she should be. I am sure that my mother changed them, because they were never exactly the same from one telling to the next. Every story had an ending, and it always ended with the girl – who was always called Chan, because that made me so happy – winning. It was every night, as soon as the lights dimmed: just me and her on the bed; just her hands on mine, clasped together, her voice whispered and hushed to hide the story from the rest of the world, and keep it for me alone.

She said, 'One day, you can tell these stories to your children.'

'You can tell them as well,' I said. She smiled. She knew then, maybe. Or maybe she just knew how cruel Australia was to the people who live inside her.

When I wake up, I'm alone. I start with my hands: touching – squeezing – the mattress underneath me, which is thicker than I've felt before. I can't even feel the bed frame itself. And it's wider, because I can move my arms out and they don't find the edge or the wall, not until I stretch. That hurts, a pain that runs all up my spine and into my neck, and then down through the rest of me.

'Hello?' I say, and it feels like testing my voice. It echoes, and then it hits me: I can't hear anything else. There's no screaming, no sounds of violence and no throb of engines.

I open my eyes.

The room is a blur of colour and shapes, and it takes my eyes a second to focus on what these things are that are all around me, apparently painted onto the walls. They're animals. I recognise some from books, like elephants and tigers and giraffes. Then there are others, brown-furred things like little half-men, and things that look like tigers but bigger and solid yellow, and almost-dwarven elephants with giant white stumps of teeth jutting from their mouths. Others, more and more. Birds! There are birds in groups, flying across the heads of every other creature, and pools of water, and grass, as green as I imagined it would be. There's very little light in the berth: only a single bar above my head that is soft, muted, tinged with amber.

I move as much as I can, as slowly as possible. My legs onto the floor, and then my body to sitting, and I crick my neck. The pain doesn't dull, not even slightly. It's worse, and I try to reach behind me to feel for cuts and bruises, but my shoulder screams. Then I realise that, underneath my feet, there's something that isn't metal. It's soft and yellow, and it looks like the grass in the arboretum, almost, when it's been cut right back to nearly nothing.

Standing. I need to try standing. I support myself on the wall, and I get up to my feet, and that alone feels like a miracle. Taking a step is harder, because it hurts. I stop, and the pain dulls away slightly. Behind me, the sheet is stained, yellow and red and brown in the outline of my body. I wonder how long I have been lying there for.

There's a door in front of me, closed. A handle. None of the berths I've seen before have doors. Where am I?

I open it, and the light hits me hard. My eyes sting, and it takes a few seconds for them to adjust. My head is full, it feels like, and it feels so heavy on my neck. When I pull myself together I'm left staring down a passageway that I don't recognise.

It is like a picture from a book. The walls on either side of the path are solid bright colours, lighter than the grey of the Australia's metal. The lights don't flicker. And there's a noise, coming quietly from far away: tinny and vague. I tread softly towards it, and it clears up: it's music. I've never heard music like it, but it's music.

Everything else I've ever known on Australia feels like a lie, suddenly.

Where everything I've known is open, here things are closed: there are closed doors leading off this main passage, and everything is quiet. I run my fingers along the walls; hanging from them are pictures of various things that I do not recognise, shapes and faces and places. Some are so clear, so realistic that I can't even believe them; but they're in front of me, as real as anything else I've ever seen.

There's another door on my left, and I push it open. Right in front of me, there's a mirror. They have them in some of the shops, metal that's been polished so bright that it shines and reflects yourself right back as you stare at it, but none of them are as clean as this. None of them have ever let me see myself as I do now. My face and hair are covered in blood; my skin has marks all over it, scratches and bruises, some imperceptible, most dark enough to look as sore as they feel; and my clothes are just as torn, hanging seams and loose threads. But beneath it all I can see my skin: my mother's skin, and her mother's, and her mother's. I spit on my hand and wipe some of the dirt and blood away from around my mouth and eyes. It barely makes a dent, but it's something.

I go back out to the passage, and the music is louder, and I'm no longer alone; because there's Agatha and Jonah, and in their hands there's a body, and behind them an open door, and more bodies, piles and piles of them.

'You're awake,' is all that Agatha says, and that does me, exhausted and overwhelmed, and I drop to my knees, and I cry.

She turns the music off and sits with me; and then she explains a little, but not enough. I want to press her, and I keep interrupting, even though I know how much she hates that. I keep asking where we are, but she persists in explaining what happened after I fell, doing things in the right order. I can fill in those gaps, I try and say, but she's so stubborn she barely pauses.

'You fell, and she,' meaning Rex, 'was climbing down to check you were dead. You weren't moving when I got there.'

'I don't remember anything,' I say.

'He saved you,' she tells me, looking over at Jonah. 'I watched – I wasn't close enough – as he dragged you away. I thought that you were dead.' I notice that Jonah isn't quite with us in the conversation. He's got his hood down, and he's playing with something around his neck, something on a chain that runs underneath his collar and down into his cloak. 'But he took you down, and away from her.'

'The Women?'

'Dead, most of them.' Jonah flinches as she says it. 'Some will have escaped, more than likely. But the ship—'

'Where are we?' I ask again.

'We're safe,' she says, 'and that's all that matters.'

'I've never seen this place,' I tell her.

'No,' she says. 'We carried you away from there, the two of us. It took too long, and I was worried. You were breathing, but we didn't know how injured you were, Chan.

We just couldn't tell. When we got you here, we thought it was best to let you sleep. We were worried about how bad your injuries were going to be when you woke up.' She smiles. 'But you're okay.'

'Yes,' I say. I don't tell her how much I hurt, because there's no point. She knows. We all hurt, no sense in making a big deal out of it. 'Where are we? And who were those bodies?'

'Tell her,' Jonah says. It's the most passionate I've heard him, the most emphatic. And then, to look at him, he's lost the calm that he held so constant before, and there's anger there behind his eyes. Green eyes, tinged with red, and his skin – now that I can see it, in the light – freckled softly, so pale that it's like it's been drawn in chalk. Agatha takes my hands.

'Take a shower, and I'll cook something to eat. And then I'll tell you everything.'

I'm nearly too distracted to enjoy the shower, but not quite. This is a room dedicated to showering, white-tiled and clean and bright. There's a toilet here. I'm used to toilets that are metal bowls plugged into the walls, the ship taking the waste and recycling it. This one is white, in a material that's like the cups some of the artisan sellers make. There's a seat on it, and a lid and, next to it, a door, made of frosted glass. Beyond the door, on the wall above my head, there is a spigot shaped like a flower, and there are a hundred tiny holes in the head. I'm used to taking showers in big communal rooms, standing under rusted pipes that drip out cold water. They're always unpleasant, and I've never spent longer than I had to taking one. Now I run the tap, and the water coughs out at first in spurts; and then flows, each hole in the flower spigot a tiny stream, as clear as any water that I have ever seen. I taste it, holding my mouth open and sticking my tongue out underneath the stream, and it's warm and beautiful. I strip off my clothes and step into it. The water is too hot, but I don't mind. There's a bar of soap, and it's soft, and it froths up when I rub it between my hands, smelling of something almost indescribably sweet. I've only ever used soap that comes from lye, and it burns the skin until it's washed completely away. The soap I'm used to can scar.

I don't know how long I stay under the water. But I'm there until long after my fingers have wrinkled. When I'm done, I wash my clothes as well. I hold them underneath the water and rub them with the soap, and I watch the filth run out of them. It's disgusting to see dirt like this, in this clean white room. Strange, I think, to only find it revolting now. When I'm done, I hang my clothes on a rail – a polished metal rod that's so hot to the touch it actually stings when I touch it – and I realise that I've got nothing to wear. It's not that Agatha would balk at my nakedness, but Jonah? I don't know. It seems like the sort of thing that would upset him, and I don't want that. I don't want him to see me so . . . exposed. So I open the cupboards, which are empty; and then go back to the berth that I slept in, and explore the cupboards there. There are piles of blue clothes: each garment has a torso and arms and legs all sewn together into one outfit. It takes me a while to find one that fits, but when I do, it's amazing. The fabric is so much softer than anything I've felt before. There's a hood at the back, and I pull it over my head, and then I sit on the floor – the soft floor – and I feel almost dizzy for a second, because this is all so different.

But then I remember that this place must have been here the entire time, and Agatha has just never told me. There are questions I have to ask, and she's got the answers.

Agatha is cooking something, and whatever it is it smells amazing. The room that they're in is strange. There's a counter, and pots and pans heating on something without a flame; and then humming machines, all with doors; and a pair of giant metal doors on one side, that I see Agatha opening to a hiss of freezing cold air, which bundles out and envelops her. There are tables and chairs made from metal that are neater and cleaner than any I've ever seen before. I'm used to cracked cooking pots: thick black things built up with char from years and years of use, burnt food on improvised flames. Jonah's already sitting down, and Agatha tells me to sit next to him.

'This is nearly done,' she says, tasting whatever's in the pot that she's got boiling. 'Real meat, Chan. You've never tasted anything like it.'

There's meat here?

She puts a bowl down in front of me, and I nudge the broth around with the spoon she gives me. It's rich and creamy, and there are chunks of vegetables that I recognise from the arboretum – leeks and cauliflower and potato – and something else, white and soft. I take a spoonful, and it burns my mouth, but it tastes ridiculous. Just ridiculous, sweet and spicy in equal measure, and so flavourful; and the taste seems to change as I eat it, starting as one thing, becoming another as it travels across my tongue. Another spoon, and another, one after the other.

'How did you make this?' I manage to ask, the broth dripping out of my mouth and down the front of my blue jumpsuit.

'There are books,' she says, and she passes me one. Every page has a different guide on it, a different thing that can be cooked. All the ingredients, and how you prepare it. This is a stew of some sort, and it's so different to what we have above. The recipe includes herbs and spices, and preparations that we'd never dream of doing when cooking in our berths. 'And there are more books. Lots of them.'

We eat the rest of the meal in silence. I need answers, yes; but for this moment, I need this more. Myself, Jonah and Agatha, all three of us eat the scalding hot food, and we love every single mouthful.

'Whose are the bodies?' I ask. 'Who are they?'

'They are people,' Agatha says, 'normal people. They died here, and we were . . . ' She trails off, waving her hand in the air, as if it's all self-explanatory.

'We were what? Where are we?' I ask again. Jonah is piling the plates up on the counter, and he stops when I ask, and he rests his hands on the counter and bows his head. I look to Agatha.

'Tell her,' Jonah says.

'Okay,' she says, nodding at Jonah. 'We're below the Pit. All of this? It's below the Pit.'

AGATHA

The worst things on Australia *aren't the Lows, Chan. The Lows are chaos and violence, but some people are even worse. You know that. Some people are liars, hiding the dangers that they pose behind stories. Like your father.*

Your mother met a man. She met this man, and she was smitten, but she was young and foolish. He was awful – artless and crass – an oaf. I could tell he was a bully the first time I met him, and he didn't like me, not one bit. He rolled his eyes when I was there, and spoke quietly to your mother, so that only she could hear. Your grandparents were dead by then, but I still watched over her. When they died, your mother went even more wild. She went to the furthest parts of the ship, and she picked up where she had left off a few years before: pushing herself, taking too many risks. That's when she met Ellis.

We didn't recognise him, even though we knew pretty much everybody on the ship, but this one day he appeared, these foods in his hands that we had never tasted before. He was wearing a blue suit, head to toe – just the same as the one that you are wearing – and he carried vegetables or chocolates with him. Nothing like the chocolates that we have, that you can buy here, but something so much better. She gave me one, once, and it was so rich that it hurt my teeth and my belly to eat, but I loved it. And that was how he won her: he gave her what nobody else could. And he promised her even more. He promised her the world. He promised her warmth, and food. He said – this came from her to me, and I always wondered the truth of it, but now I know – he said that he could take her somewhere else, and that he could offer her a new life. A different place to the Australia that she knew. And what alternative did she have? She thought that she had lost everything. How could she refuse?

He never stayed long, and she never knew when he would be back. He would come to her, and they would hide from everybody in the shadows, and then he'd be gone, and she didn't know where. She was so in love, she didn't care about his secrets. I did, though. I watched him, and followed him, to see where he came from. I never trusted him. I learned that he had a deal with the Lows, to pass through their section unscathed. He gave them supplies, clothing and materials, and they left him alone. He – and his friends, because there were more of them, I discovered – they built the Lows up. They fed them and made them stronger. I assumed that they lived with the Lows.

In the end, your mother became pregnant. He didn't take her with him, though. Even as she grew, week by week, he told her to wait, letting her grow larger, more tired, and then bringing her food, as if that was all she needed to get by. But she'd never listen to me about him. His promises were stronger than any truth she already knew, somehow.

Being pregnant is hard. It makes you slow, and being slow makes you a target. So I protected her, because I couldn't do anything else for her. I cooked for her – this is when I began working in the arboretum, so we had more fruits and vegetables than we had ever had before – and I watched over her. I found her the berth you grew up in, and helped her move in there. Before that, she'd lived higher up. This new one was easier. I never even told her what I paid for it, and she never asked. She was just grateful that I was there when he wasn't.

But he was gone so much, and he wouldn't have excuses. Maybe she started to see him for what he was. I knew what he was already, of course. I followed him, and he did things that, when I told her, your mother refused to believe. There were other women, Chan, and he got them pregnant as well. He treated them the same, and gave them the same promises. It was like a secret that they all shared. He told them the same thing he told your mother: that, when they gave birth, he would take them somewhere better. He would take them somewhere safe.

I watched one of those other girls give birth a few days before your mother was due. She was living two sections over. The man was there for the birth, and he helped her. He gave her drugs that I had never seen, to help with the pain. The birth was hard, and the child was stillborn and, when he saw that, he left, left the mother lying on the floor of her berth, bleeding. I had suspected but then I knew: the mother was nothing to him. I tried to help but it was too late, and she died, crying for her child.

I woke your mother up, and I dragged her to that poor

girl's berth, and I told her to look at the body. It felt cruel, but it was all I had. After that, she made me promise that I would not leave her during the birth, and that I would not allow him to do the same to her. I swore it. Maybe I gave her too much, but she meant everything to me. She was a daughter to me.

I told her that we had to move, just as her waters broke. We went to my berth, closed it off with as many rags as we could find, and we stayed there, hoping that he would never find her. But he did, and too quickly. We assumed that somebody gave her up, told him where we were. He asked her if it was time. She said, Not yet, and she smiled through the pain as best she could manage. I hope it comes soon, she said, I just want it out of me. Soon, he promised, and he said that he would be back. As soon as he was gone, we tried to move forward with your birth, and she bit down on rags to muffle the screams. Birth screams are different from any other that I have heard. They come from somewhere else in the body. When she was done, it was your turn; you came out and you howled. Of course you did: imagine your first taste of air being the air of up there. At first, you held your breath, so I slapped you; and then you gulped it in. You screamed, and so I took you and I hid you. That was what I had promised: to hide you from him.

But he'd found us once. So, to protect your mother, we needed a lie. We needed a baby, to hand to your father, to appease him.

I went to the bottom of the ship, to the Pit, and I waded out into that mess. There had been other children, other babies. I would need to find one, and we would have to pass *it off as your mother's. There was little other choice, and sometimes you have to do the worst thing you can imagine to stop something even more terrible from happening.*

I still have had nightmares about that search. What it took to find the baby's body . . . As I was leaving the Pit, I saw him: your father. He was climbing down into the Pit from the Lows' section. Nobody was watching him – apart from me. I sank down low and I held my breath as long as I could. He looked all around but didn't see me; and then he put something over his face – covering his eyes and mouth, a mask of some sort – and he disappeared underneath the mess. I saw him moving into the middle of the Pit, and then he was gone. He didn't resurface, and I didn't have the time to investigate him there and then. I had to take the body back to your mother, and I didn't know when he would next appear.

I held that cold, dead body and handed it to your mother while you were up with the Pale Women, being kept quiet. They owed me a favour, and I called them on it. Your mother's face, Chan . . . You cannot imagine it, because she wanted to be holding you, and she had the corpse instead. He came up that night, to check, and she presented it to him: his dead heir. It was days old, blue and reeking from the Pit, but we swaddled it and hoped that he wouldn't look too closely. And he left. He said nothing, just abandoned her.

Of course, your mother wanted you back, but I told her to wait. I told her that it wouldn't be safe. I had to make sure that it was, that he wasn't watching or suspicious. She didn't know what I planned; only that I told her that everything would be alright, in the end.

I followed him again that night, to check what I had seen the first time around. He was angry. He went down to the bottom again, through the Lows' section, and he put that mask onto his face, and he pulled a blue suit identical to the one he was wearing from a berth and put it on over his clothes, and he went into the Pit. After a minute, I followed him. I went out to the middle where it was so dark I could barely see what was around me. I dove down and felt the floor for something – anything – that might indicate where he had gone. I found a lever, and I gripped it and pulled it, and something whirred: a stir of machinery, that would be lost in the noise of the rest of the ship. By feeling around I discovered that the lever had opened a door to a vestibule. I climbed in and the door shut. I was in a pod, just barely big enough to stand up in, surrounded by the mess that had followed me in. I wiped my eyes and saw a vent in the wall, a fan, and it spun so quickly, and most of the mess was sucked out, pulled into it, leaving only the objects too big in the pod. Bones, rags of clothes. And I saw another lever, which I pulled without even hesitating.

Looking back on it, I was so reckless. I didn't know what would happen when I pulled that lever, or what I might find. I was so cautious in those days, even more so than now. Below me, another door slid open. There was a ladder, and I climbed down it. Suddenly I was in a place that I had never seen before, a chamber with pictures on the walls and a soft rug that ran from wall to wall on the floor. I was down here. I was scared and I was still dripping from the Pit, and I was angry: with Ellis, with his promises and stories and lies, and with what he was hiding from the women he made promises to. I started forward. I had a weapon and I drew it, and I went to find your father.

I found him first. He was in one of the berths, removing the suit he wore over his cleaner clothes, bundling the bloody ones he'd worn to climb through the Pit into a pile. I caught him unawares, and he only noticed me in the doorway when he turned to leave.

'Oh,' he said, and his face was terrified, as if he knew what I meant. I had a knife with me, and I dealt with him, and I left his body on the floor of that room. There was no ceremony to it. I wiped my knife clean on his clothes.

When I left the berth, there were other men in the hall waiting. Six of them, all ages: some younger than him, two of them very old. They all had weapons in their hands, and they attacked me. I was better than them, and I killed them all. They nearly overwhelmed me, but . . . They didn't know how to fight. They were reliant on their weapons, and they hadn't lived the life that I had. They'd never had to fight, not really.

But one of them I didn't kill.

I had questions.

SEVEN

'What did he say?' I look at Agatha, and then Jonah. He's angry now, and growing angrier, his teeth gritted, his brow creased up.

'Chan—' Agatha starts to say, reaching across and taking my hand, but Jonah doesn't let her finish her sentence.

'He was a guard. They were all guards,' he says. 'This ship – Australia – is a prison.'

I know the stories, because we all do. We all know about the floods, and about the fires, and about the Earth tearing itself apart. My whole life, full of stories about what was before. But we've never had any pictures, and we've never had details. The Pale Women have their story about the loading of the ark, and how the animals went into it in twos: two of every creature. That's something. Our story: we loaded ourselves, two by two, into our own ark, and that ark was the Australia, and we went into space to find somewhere else. Somewhere better. And someday we will. That's our story. We've never questioned the story, because there has never been any reason to. Because, why would anyone choose to live like this? Why, for any other reason, would anybody live like this? Being here has to be for the distant hope of a better life.

'The last guard bargained. It's human nature to try to live, to do whatever we can. It was what he could offer me. He told me everything, and I didn't even have to ask him. I didn't have to press my knife to his throat: he was simply too terrified of dying. He told me about this place. Our ancestors were sent up here before, on this ship. They weren't fleeing: they were criminals, the worst of the worst. This was a way of keeping them out of sight.'

'But Earth was destroyed,' I say. My voice is quiet. Everything is wrenched away from me, everything that I ever believed. The closest thing I can equate it to is the feeling of sitting there with my mother's knife in my hands, her body bleeding out. Agatha shakes her head.

'It wasn't,' she says. 'Only for us. The guards were prisoners themselves, but fraudsters, not murderers. This was a way of giving them their life back. They were free to do as they chose. They lived here, as best I can tell, and they did as we did. They just had more control.' She smiles as she says that. I wonder what control that was, that meant that they felt it acceptable to treat people – my mother – as they did. 'They did what they wanted, and so did we. We fell apart.'

'It wasn't always like this,' Jonah says.

'No,' Agatha agrees. 'It used to be locked down. At some point, we overthrew the guards. At some point . . . ' She shrugs. 'At some point, we changed the story. We started lying to ourselves.'

She stands up and leads us into another room, just off the kitchen. 'This is where they watched us,' she says. There's a chair here – one solitary chair – in front of a series of black boxes, shined and glossy, stacked on top of each other. On a table at the side of the room, there are books of hand-written names and details. *Ledger #1, #2, #3* printed on the front of them in delicate writing. I open them and flick through entries for men and women, and then hastily scrawled details about their children, about their families, and crimes, and where they're living. These books are old. I don't recognise any names. I look for myself and I'm not there. I look for my mother and she's not there. I look for Agatha, and she's not there.

I close the book I'm holding. I don't understand yet.

'What do these do?' I ask her, pointing at the screens

'They show the rest of the ship,' she says. And she presses one of them, strokes it with her fingers, and they burst into light, each one suddenly showing a picture. It takes me a second to work out what the pictures are, because they're grainy and not in colour, and they're small, each picture split into four sections showing different things. But I know them all, what they show. Each of them has a small part of the ship on display, all of the sections. Some of the pictures are a wash of grey, but most of them are showing some-thing. This is the ship, the rest of the ship, and what I'm seeing is what's happening up there right this second.

'How?'

'I don't know,' Agatha says. 'I've looked, but I can't find out.'

'What happened after?' I ask. 'When the guard told you all this?' I can't stop looking at the pictures. They're showing exactly what the ship is like: the chaos, the madness. From down here, clean and – suddenly, somehow – safe, it almost looks unbelievable.

'He died. He died, and I left.'

'We could have come here,' I say. I think that I should speak up; that maybe, I should be angry about this. I spent my life up there, and this was here the entire time.

'This place is a lie,' she replies. 'Up there is the truth. It's where we come from, who we are. We weren't meant to be down here.'

'But this place is safe,' I say. It's empty, and it's warm, and it's clean. I imagine having grown up here instead of up there. What my life might have been like, with showers to take and food to eat and no worrying about the threat of somebody trying to kill me, all day, every single day of my life. I wonder what that might have been like.

I wonder if it somehow might have stopped my mother from dying.

'It wasn't safe, not then. There were things that I didn't understand here, Chan. I didn't know what this place was, and I didn't feel—'

'You should have told us!' I scream at her. The anger has swollen up in me, and it bursts. 'You should have brought us down here, and we could have . . . We could have lived here.' I'm in tears. This hurts so much, to know that this was here the entire time.

'I couldn't,' she says. 'I couldn't.'

'But why?' I ask. She doesn't have an answer for that. She just looks away from me.

* * *

163

I'm sitting alone in my room when there's a noise outside, in the corridor. I stand up and open the door, and Jonah is there, waiting. He seems almost surprised to see me, as if he hadn't planned to come in.

'Can I sit?' he asks, and I nod. I can't hear Agatha now, and I don't know what she's doing. I don't care. I'm so angry at her. I don't really want to talk, that's for certain, but he does. He was there for me, and I owe him that.

'It's cruel,' he says, out of nowhere. 'There's something almost cruel about finding this place.' I nod, because that's all I can manage. He slides his finger underneath his collar and pulls it away slightly, to give his neck room. 'Being on Australia was never something good, not like the Women said. Everything we live through – the hell of it all, the chaos and the nightmares, and there was never a reward owed to us.'

'A reward for what?' I ask. Keep him talking, and maybe I won't have to think about my own problems.

'For living. Life here was purgatory, and we were on our way to be rewarded with a better world. After the revelations on Earth, we ascended. We were going to find heaven.' There are tears in his eyes as well, and that stings me too, for some reason. At least I haven't been living my life expecting a payoff in the end. I've lived day by day, not hoping for the future. But he hasn't. His whole life has been about that: about the promise of what comes after. In some ways, he's lost more than I have by learning about this place. 'We were meant to be finding somewhere better.'

'Maybe we still are,' I tell him. If we land – if we're alive when we find a place to land – there will at least be a planet. A new home. We can start again.

'Doesn't matter,' he replies, 'look what we come from. *Who* we come from. What sort of person is so dreadful that they're sent away, imprisoned and exiled? In *The Book*, only the worst . . . ' His voice fades off. The *Testaments* of the Pale Women: they mean nothing now. His finger runs around underneath his collar, stretching it. He's sweating, and it hurts him.

'Wait there,' I say, and I leave the berth and head to the kitchen. Agatha is sitting at the table, her hands clasped around a cup of something steaming and sweet-smelling.

'You can't know what it was like to make the choices I had to make,' she says, looking up, her face ravaged with grief.

'No,' I tell her, 'I don't. I was never given the chance.' I take a knife from a drawer and head back to Jonah, slamming the door to the kitchen behind me. This knife is small, but almost impossibly sharp. Looking down the blade, I daren't run my finger along it to test. I know that it will just give me another scar I can't get rid of.

He looks up as I show it to him, tensing his body, suddenly on his guard.

'Don't worry,' I say, 'I'm good with one of these. Just don't flinch.' I take the back of his head in my hand, holding onto his scalp with the tips of my fingers, holding his head steady, moving it to one side. The band that runs around his neck is stitched together, the threads thick and hard, with metal staples pushed through. It's tight and, underneath the leather, I can see where it's rubbed, scarring his skin. I slide the blade of the knife beneath it, holding it angled against the inside of the strap, where the threads are joined.

'I'll try not to choke you,' I say, and I start pulling the knife towards me. The threads fray and then snap, and the collar falls to his lap. 'There,' I say, and then I notice that I've cut him slightly, where the tip of the blade has dug into his skin. I rub it, and the blood spreads. I lick my finger and wipe it off. The nick on his skin is barely noticeable.

'Thank you,' he says. He turns the leather strap over in his hands, feeling the metal studs with his fingers.

'How long were you wearing that for?' I ask.

'As long as I can remember.' He looks up at me. 'It was a reminder, they told me: that man is born in sin. I could look forward to my eternal judgement, when it would finally be removed. They told me how favourably I would be looked upon for wearing it; how it would make up for my being a man.'

'And did it work?'

'Yes,' he says, and he smiles. 'I suppose that it did. It made me never forget my potential to sin. Because of it, I've always tried to help people.' It's only the second time that I've seen him smile; it softens his face, makes his eyes light up.

'You're a good person,' I say. I don't know what makes me say it, but I think that he needs to hear it.

'Maybe,' he says. 'But I don't . . . I couldn't help the Pale Women.'

'You helped me.'

'They raised me. They loved me.' I don't know what to say to that. Nothing I can say will help. 'So what happens now?' he asks.

'I don't know,' I tell him. He rubs at his neck, so hard that it's even redder now than it was before; but at least, I suppose, he's in control of that.

We stay together in silence for a long time, and only emerge much later. Agatha cooks something for us. Bread and meats and cheese on top of it, a recipe that she's found amongst the pages of the cooking book, the one that's dog-eared from being thumbed too much. She puts it down on the table and she doesn't say a word, so neither do Jonah or I.

But it's almost nice, almost comforting; eating in this silence.

I struggle to fall asleep. The bed's too soft, and it's far too quiet. I miss the noise of the engines; of the people being happy and sad and just alive and around me; of the chaos; the heat of the engines, their rumble through the metal, up into the mattresses and through every other part of your berth, to the point where you wonder if your teeth are rattling in your head; the smell that's so distinct, that I only notice now that it's gone; and the taste of metal in the air, that you're never sure if it's iron or blood.

This stillness is wrong in so many ways.

But it's not just that. I sit up, on the edge of the bed, in the darkness. There's a light that I found, down in the wall, plugged in. It's in the shape of an animal's head, I don't know which one. But you flick a switch and it glows orange, a soothing shade that gives just enough light to the berth to let you see that you're alone. The door is shut, and I feel safe. Nobody knows we're here, and yet I've still put my blade underneath my pillow, and I was still clutching it as I tossed and turned and tried to sleep. So I get up. I get dressed and I creep to my door and gently push it open. Agatha and Jonah are in their own beds, and I can hear them both from here: the gentle sounds of their breathing in the night. That's good. I need some time to myself, and now I have it.

I walk to the kitchen, and I open up one of the giant metal doors that the food is hidden behind. There are shelves and shelves of food, all sealed up and labelled, and I barely recognise any of the names. *Ice Cream*, one says. There's a picture on the tub, of a boy and girl grinning, spooning stuff into their mouths. I peel back the lid, and there it is: a cold substance of pink and brown swirls. I touch it. My finger sinks in, and I draw it out and put it to my lips, and I can smell it, and then I taste it, and oh my.

Oh my.

I take the container and find a spoon in one of the drawers and go into the control room, where there's the one chair, and I sit in it, and for a few minutes I eat and eat – until my teeth hurt and my belly aches. When I'm done I put what's left in the tub down, and I look at the empty black pictures.

I need to see this. I need to see what it's like up there. I touch the pictures, just as Agatha did. They flick into life in exactly the same way, and they show me what's happening in the rest of Australia

And what's happening is war. It's still going on. The Lows are still attacking, still fighting, still expanding, still taking. Rex is still leading. The free people are losing. Everyone I've ever known, ever so much as spoken to: they're running, or begging, or dying.

Or dead.

I sit back and I watch the war that's happening above, and I feel totally and utterly powerless, more than I ever have before the whole of my life.

I watch the pictures for hours. I don't even know how long. Finally, I hear someone else awake, coming towards me. I know it's Agatha without even having to look at her. I don't say anything. She walks close to the screens and peers into them. I'm reminded that her eyesight isn't what it once was. She fixates on one screen in particular, and I move over to see what she's looking at. I know it. It's the berth that I lived in with my mother. It's been destroyed, torn apart. Amongst all the war and carnage, I hadn't noticed it until now. I can see that it's full of Lows, and there's a body with them, somebody that they've killed. Even from here I can see that they've torn their neck open. They're dipping their hands into the blood and writing on the wall, and we watch them until they're finished, until they stand back and admire their handiwork as if this is art to them, as if this is something to be proud of.

There is no ghost, the writing says.

'Can you see the Pale Women?' Jonah asks then. I didn't realise he'd come in. We look for the Pale Women, but there's no sign of them: not of their floors, or even any of their outfits.

'They might be in one of the darker sections,' I say, 'and some parts we can't see.'

'They won't have survived,' he says. 'I should have stayed and fought for them.' I don't say it, but I'm glad that he didn't. If he had, I might be dead now, and we wouldn't be here. This is a second chance, maybe. It's a chance to do something, certainly.

I just don't know what.

I start to feel sick. I try to tell myself that it's the ice cream, that I've eaten too much, but I know that it's not that. What I feel is a different kind of ache, a gnawing deep inside me that feels like it's trying to force its way out. I watch people being murdered, killed for territory or – it seems – for fun. All of this seems so *wrong*. All anybody here did was be born in the wrong time, the wrong place, punished for crimes that somebody in the past committed. That's so deeply unfair. These are innocent people, and children, and—

I spot her, in one of the darkest corners of the ship. The little girl that I met before, way up high, throwing her brother's dolls into the Pit. She's covered in bruises, right across her eyes. I don't know what she escaped from, but something – someone – tried to hurt her. She's got one doll left, and she's hugging it to her chest as she cowers next to an abandoned berth. I look at the screens around hers, and there are Lows everywhere. They haven't found her yet, but they will.

I get up and go into the kitchen. 'How do I get back up there?' I ask.

'What?' Agatha stands up and looks at me. 'No,' she says.

'I'm going,' I tell her, and I'm sure that I say it in a way that suggests I'm not messing around. But she slams her hand onto the table, and she shuts her eyes. She looks so old, and so tired.

'You can't, Chan. I made promises to your mother—'

'So did I,' I say. 'So did I, and I'm not going to break them. I told her that I wouldn't die, and I won't. Not yet. Now,' I say, walking down the corridor, away from the kitchen, 'tell me how I get up there.'

'Why?' she asks. 'Give me one good reason.'

'I'll show you,' I say, and I drag her into the control room. The girl is still on the screen, still terrified. The Lows are closer. They'll find her soon, and this will end just like every story here does: in blood.

'I'm going to find her,' I say.

'And what will you do when you get to her?' Agatha asks, gently, like she's trying to talk down a hysterical child.

'I'm going to save her,' I say. 'I'll bring her down here.' I haven't thought it through, but that's what comes out of my mouth, and so that's what I'll do. That's the answer. We have somewhere here that's safe and protected, where she won't be threatened. I can give her what I never had.

'No,' Agatha says.

'I never knew you were so selfish,' I reply. It hurts to say that, and it hurts her more to hear it, even if she doesn't show it.

'It won't end with her,' Agatha says, and she's right. Even as she says it, I know that's the truth. We can't be alone, I know that. I've been so selfish. I look at Jonah, trying to be good, even succeeding, and I feel guilty. I've wasted so much time trying to protect myself. But I'm stronger than that. I'm stronger than sitting back and watching. I can make a difference, and I will. I know that, now.

'Does that matter? If I bring others down here, what difference does that make?'

'You can't save everybody. You have to look after yourself. You promised your mother. You promised her that you would look after yourself.'

'My mother's dead,' I shout.

'You don't get to make this decision. You're only a child,' she says.

'I'm older than my mother was when she had me.'

'And she was just as stupid.' She spits the word out at me, and it hurts. 'Being rash – being naive – was how your mother got into her mess' she says. I stand up and walk away, but she follows me and grabs my arm.

'Get away from me,' I say. I want to scream it, but I can't. It hurts, and I don't want her to know how much.

'All of this would have happened with or without you,' she says. 'The Lows were ready to boil over. They have always been violent. Nothing you can do will change that. You're not special; none of us is.' She sighs and leans against the wall. Our argument is taking all her strength. 'You're safe here. Maybe you don't understand the value of that yet, but you will. I was stupid, maybe, to not bring you here before. But now you're finally safe.'

'I might be, but she isn't.' We both look back at the screen. The little girl is terrified. 'I have to do something.'

'Why do you?'

'Because my mother was selfish, and it didn't save her. It's not an answer.' That feels defiant; an end to the argument.

'You're a fool,' Agatha says. She is disappointed, her voice tinged with anger.

'I am what you made me,' I reply, and she knows that I mean all of them: my mother; the guard who was my father; Agatha; and Australia itself. She lets go of me.

'Go, then,' she says. I do. I walk out into the kitchen, then the corridor, where Jonah is waiting, acting as though he didn't hear the argument.

'Where is it?' I ask him.

'It's down here,' he says, and he rushes ahead of me, down to the far end of the corridor. There's a panel on the wall, and he presses it. A hatch opens in the ceiling and a ladder drops down, the machinery that powers it sounding rickety and tired. There's rust on the insides of it, all the way down the mechanism. Here, in the shining cleanliness of this down-below, it stands out: an intrusion from the real Australia.

'I'll be back soon,' I say, and then I see Agatha behind him, running towards me.

'Wait.' She takes my hand, and she holds it between both of hers. I'm expecting her to plead with me to stay, to give me some reason that I shouldn't go up. 'Come with me,' she says instead, and she pulls me back down the passageway, into the berth where she has been sleeping. It looks the same as all the others, but more drab, the walls a pale grey instead of the cream that's everywhere else. There's no bed: just her blanket and a pillow on the floor. And the cupboard doors are metal, not the strange material that's everywhere else. She opens one and stands back. 'You might want to use these,' she says, and I see what's inside: black and shiny rods with handles, the word *Striker* decorating their sides in small white print.

Agatha reaches in and takes one of the rods. She hands it to me, and I curl my fingers around it. 'This is what they tried to use on me when I came down here before,' she says, and I inadvertently squeeze the handle. The black rod fizzes and a streak of blue electricity runs up and over it. It shakes, struggling against my arm; but I tense, and control it. It's dangerous, I can tell. She reaches to the bottom of the cupboard and brings out a mask: two eyeholes and a piece that goes into my mouth. 'They wore this when they went into the Pit,' she says. 'It let them see where they were going, somehow; even in the darkness.' I press the mask to my face and it suctions onto my skin, the mouthpiece going between my teeth. There are grooves for me to bite onto, and I do, and my lungs fill with air. It's incredible, and it rushes to my head. I stumble and she grabs me, steadies me. The view through the mask is different, flashing bright before stabilising into greys, showing me the darkness and light better than it was before. It's disorientating, and I need Agatha's support.

'Thank you,' I mumble, spitting the mouthpiece out.

'Come back,' she says, and I nod.

'I will.' I walk out, striker in my hand. I stop in my berth and grab my blade as well, and then I climb the ladder into the vestibule embedded in the ceiling, and I find the lever that Agatha spoke of, and I tug it. There's no time to waste.

The roof of the pod comes out in the middle of the Pit and, as soon as it's open, the mulch starts to pour in, over my face and shoulders. Even with the mask on, I close my eyes and hold my breath, because I'm so worried about what it will be like if the breathing apparatus fails – and because I don't much like the idea of seeing exactly what's underneath the surface of this, what's sunk to the bottom of the Pit after so many years – decades or centuries, I don't know – of bodies. It's hard to push against it, so much thicker than the water of the arboretum's river. The Pit itself is like a bowl, deeper in the middle than at the sides, so the wading is even harder. I am afraid to take a breath and don't until my lungs are screaming, but the device works perfectly. That helps me calm down, and I push through the Pit until I can stand. I keep my eyes shut. I don't want to see this.

When I reach the side, I heave myself up. I don't know what section this is, and that worries me, but I'm ready for whatever. It's quiet, for a second; and then my ears clear, and the rush of the rest of Australia comes flooding back to me: the noise of it all, and the smell, and the darkness. It takes a second for my eyes to adjust, and then I hear a whizz, a noise in my face, and suddenly I can see. The mask shows me what's around me. It looks just like the pictures in the down-below: grainy and slightly vague, tinged with greenish grey. But I can see.

I'm in section IV, the numbers marked in pale, faded, worn-away print on the wall. I'm relieved that I didn't wind up on the Lows' side of the ship. I get up, walk to the nearest stairwell and start to climb. There's a long way to go, and I have no idea how much time I've got before the Lows find the girl.

Getting to her means hiding, skulking, creeping my way through the chaos. I am focused; but I can't ignore what I see. I can help people. I can fight. And, when I've fought, maybe there's something I can do to stop the Lows ever getting to the people who I've helped again. There's a whole part of the ship that they don't know about.

On the thirtieth floor, the market floor, I meet my first bunch of Lows. There are crates and boxes, and fragments of fabric hanging from rafters. They are moving in, bringing their possessions over from their territory to here. I don't know what happened to the free people who used to live here.

The Lows are jittery. I get close enough to hear them wheezing, talking.

'Rex wants this done,' one says to the other. His voice trembles: he's terrified. They never call her by whatever her name was before: now she is just Rex, some ancient king come to wreak havoc and destroy everything we have. *Rex wrecks*, like some bad joke.

I get closer and see that the berth they're moving into isn't empty. There's a family inside; I recognise the father from the arboretum. He's crying, begging for his life. Not his family's life; just his own. The children are crying as well, but his wife isn't; she holds firm, because she has to. He is gutless. *Selfish*. She can see that now. He doesn't resist when the Lows step towards them.

'Spare me,' he begs, asking only for his life. Doesn't matter what happens to the rest of them. His wife doesn't plead. She screams at the Lows, defending her children, and she lashes out, but they sidestep her. One of the Lows kills the father, gouging out his throat with some hacked-up half-broken knife. The man's blood washes out of his body. The children stare, noiseless and terrified. I check my weapons in my hands, that my grip is good. As I'm moving in to do something, they kill the mother. I thought that they would leave her until last, but I was wrong. I can't – and don't – hesitate.

The first Low goes down with the striker to the back of his neck. It fizzes and he falls, his eyes rolling back in his head. The other takes a second to register what's happened. He starts to say something to me, but I don't wait to hear it. I kick the first to one side and drive the striker into the face of the second, letting the blue electricity roar into his skull. He screams, and the children scream. The Low drops to his knees, smoke pouring from the socket where his eye used to be. He's breathing, but only just. Whatever happens, he's not a problem any more. He's not dangerous.

I kneel by the two boys and I snap my fingers. 'Listen to me,' I say. 'Do you have any other relatives? Is there anybody else you can go to?' They don't reply. They don't even seem to register what I'm saying. 'Okay,' I say, 'I have to take you somewhere else. You need to come with me, and I'll make you safe, okay? We have to go now, and you need to be quiet.' I guess at their ages: under five, certainly. The younger one is sucking his thumb now, and I worry that he has blood on it from what I did. His older brother has no shoes on. I can save these kids as well.

This is a delay to finding the little girl: taking these two down to the bottom. Agatha will be furious, that the first people I've saved aren't even who I came up here for. I look down the gantry, seeing everything in my shades of green and black: more Lows heading here, to find out what the commotion is. They don't know what's happened yet, but they will, and they'll be angry.

'Come with me,' I say, and I take their hands, and I start towards the stairwell. I have to be quick.

'I'll take them,' Jonah says. I whirl around in surprise. He's on the floor below, looking up through the grated flooring, dressed in one of the blue suits, mask on his face. His hood is down over his face, coated in a slick layer of blood from the Pit. But through my own mask, it looks almost pure white, like fire. 'Pass them down,' he says. I nod, and look at the boys' faces again. I hold a finger to my lips to tell them to be quiet. They mimic me. This is a gesture that they recognise. Jonah takes them as I lift them down, setting them gently on the floor by his side. Then, holding their hands, he turns to go. 'Be safe,' he whispers up at me, so quietly that I barely hear it; and then he's gone, stepping off the edge, taking the children with him. I pause for breath; but only for a second.

When I finally reach the floor where I once found her, where I saw her on the videos, there is no sign of the little girl. The Lows have been through here, and they've done what they do. It's empty, almost terrifyingly quiet. When I softly ask if there's anybody here, my voice echoes around in whispers. It makes me think of the ship's ghosts, the stories people tell to scare children. Here, it feels as though they're everywhere, and yet I know they've never been real. My mother's ghost, the ghosts in the Pit – which, now, I realise must have been based on the truth of the guards, of my father and whoever else lived there with him. I never believed in them.

This emptiness is the closest I've come to believing in them myself.

Then I see the little girl's rag-and-bone doll lying on the floor; or, at least, its torso. The head is missing, and one of the legs. I tell myself to move on; that I cannot become fixated on finding her. She's gone, and I have to abandon any hope of rescuing her. I can't dwell on this. The longer I stay out here, the more dangerous it is for me.

As I turn to go back to the stairwell I notice a shape, tucked in a corner behind a ripped-up mattress. It's her, as close to the wall as she can manage. I kneel down and pull off my mask, so that she can see my face. No sense in terrifying her any more than she already is.

'Don't panic,' I say, 'but I'm here to help you.' She looks towards me, and through my mask I can see her face, terror giving way to relief.

'It's you,' she says. I push the hood back from my face and hand her the remnants of her doll. She clutches it to her chest, both hands, tight as I've ever seen anybody grip anything.

'Where are your parents now?'

'I don't know,' she says. They're long dead, is most likely. Probably they've been dead for a while.

'Okay. I want to take you someplace safe. Would you like that?'

Her lip twitches. 'Not here?'

'Somewhere else. You won't have to hide, okay?' She nods, and then she starts crying. Real, huge, racking sobs. She crawls towards me, bawling her eyes out, and she puts her arms around me. I shush her, holding her to me. She buries her face in my chest and I beg her to be quiet, because her tears will bring the Lows if she's not careful. 'I don't know your name yet, anyway,' I say, trying to distract her from the tears. 'I'm Chan. Can you spell? See-aitch-eh-enn.' I trace the letters out in the air. 'What's yours?'

'Mae,' she says, her voice so quiet I can barely hear; but it works, and the tears start to dry up, and she sniffs.

'Mae. That's a beautiful name,' I say. I take her hands and squeeze them. 'It'll be okay,' I tell her.

She doesn't say a word after that. She clings to me, wrapping her arms around my neck, clutching me so tightly I couldn't shake her if I tried. The climb down is hard, and it's tough to hide with her attached to me, but she's good: quiet when she needs to be, not panicking when I scratch my hand on the metal of a stairwell and we slip, nearly falling. By the time we reach the bottom I've almost forgotten that I'm carrying her. I've gotten used to her weight.

I stop and put her down, and I kneel in front of her.

'When I tell you to, you have to shut your eyes, okay?'

'Why?'

'Because I said so.' Because, I think, there are some things you shouldn't have to see. And maybe now she can go her whole life without ever seeing them. 'And you have to hold your breath. You know how to do that? You breathe in—' I do it, and then I don't let it out, pulling an exaggerated face, then finally puffing out, and we both laugh. 'You breathe in, and you hold it. Don't breathe until I tell you. Okay?'

'Okay,' she says, still smiling.

'So you're ready?' She nods. I pick her up, and I push her head into my shoulder, her eyes into the cloth of my outfit, and I hold her head there with one hand and climb down with the other.

And then we're in the Pit, and I'm wading, and the mess is up around my waist, then my shoulders, and she wriggles but I hold her tight; and I tell her to take that one big deep breath, and she does, and we're suddenly under. With my free hand I feel for the lever, and then we're in hatch, in the space between the Pit and safety; and then we're on the ladder, and down below.

'You can open your eyes now,' I say to her, and she does.

EIGHT

Agatha talks quietly to me as we cook. In the other room, there's noise: Jonah sitting and talking with the children, then the quick transition into that becoming some game. I can't remember ever having heard anything like this: the voices of children – and happy voices, at that – without the backdrop of everything else.

'How does it feel?' Agatha asks, pulling pots from the stove.

'Like we can do more,' I reply. She sighs. I know what she's thinking, and that she's right: we can't help everybody. It's impossible. And if we did, what would we do? Bring them down here? There's not enough room. We would lose this place, as it is now; it would be swallowed by the rest of the ship. There's only so much food, and only so many beds.

But then dinner is ready, and Agatha takes it to the table, and I forget about the rest of the ship for the moment. The children swarm over to us. It's strings of something, in a sauce. According to the cooking book, this is spaghetti with tomato sauce. We eat it with our hands, spooning it up in our palms and sucking it down, sauce everywhere. It looks like a massacre. The kids don't stop, even when they should be full. They're overeating, and they'll all have bellyaches tonight, but that's probably okay. They're all so skinny, and I imagine them as they might be in the future, always full and content. When no one can eat any more, the three of them slope off, hardly able to move from the feeding. Mae is the most hesitant; she doesn't want to be away from me, it seems. It'll take a lot to teach her that she's safe now.

Agatha, Jonah and I do the dishes. We stand in a line at the sink, and Agatha empties the remnants into a trash chute, Jonah dunks them into hot water, and I wipe them dry. It feels nice, comfortable. I'm content, for a second, with all of this.

'I have to know if the Pale Women survived,' Jonah says, out of nowhere. 'If they're alive, then I would like to save them. To bring them here.' He breaks the work line, leaving his current dish soaking in the water, his hands dunked in up to their wrists. 'They were good to me, and I—'

'It's okay,' I say. Agatha waits for me to tell him that we can't go looking for them, but I won't, so I just leave his last words hanging in the air; and I reach over and pull the dish out of the sink for him, and I dry it, and leave it on the side.

While everybody else sleeps, I make myself a suit.

I've got materials taken from three different uniforms, and tools and weapons. I tear apart the different materials, and I size them against my body. The suit I've been wearing barely fits, and it's clumsy. It'll snag, or I could trip over the too-long trouser legs. I cut the fabric apart and sew the new bits together.

There's a knock on my door. 'Come in,' I say, and it pushes open. It's Agatha. I don't know why, but I sort of expected Jonah. I maybe hoped for Jonah. She looks down at what I'm doing, at me sitting cross-legged on the floor, surrounded by all of this stuff.

'You look like you could use my help,' she says. She's better with a needle than I am, and she sits next to me, and she goes over every seam that I've already sewn, and she makes them all stronger. I watch her; and sometimes I notice that her fingers are shaking, and she breathes and tries to steady them before carrying on again. She doesn't want me to see that, and she pauses, stops sewing when she notices me looking, then resumes when I go back to my own work.

'Your hands,' I say, the third time I notice it and she tries to hide it from me. 'Are you okay?'

'I'm not what I was,' she says. I don't know if she's ill, or if it's just tiredness. But after that, she stops hiding it.

When we're done I stand up and she helps me into the suit; and we check the measurements, and that I can still move in it. I need to be able to run and climb and duck without having it fall apart on me. When we're satisfied, I take the outfit off and we start decorating. And this bit? It's pretty fun. It feels like something from before, when Agatha and Mother and I would sit together and make our clothes beautiful with beads and whatever else we had that could brighten up the fabrics. Now, Agatha also adds straps, sheaths for my blade, for the striker; and she adds pockets, getting me to hold the fabric as tight as I can while she sews them. They're big enough for me to carry anything I might need. Then she adds protection (armour, she calls it): thick plates of what feels like metal under taut, coarse material. We cut it apart and attach the pieces to the chest and to the thighs. We tweak the hood, adding a drawstring so that it holds down over my face rather than being in any danger of falling off.

And when it's all done, I stand in the mirror and look at myself, as I pull the outfit on again. I look ready, and I'm pleased by that. I'm not sure for what, yet; I don't know how far I'm going to go down this path. I can save more people: innocent people. Maybe I should focus on the children. There are a lot of them, many orphaned and lost. They'll be taken by the Lows and, if they are, their futures are all but decided for them. But I can save them.

I pull the hood down, over the stubble of my hair. The hood is peaked at the front to set it rigid over my forehead. I can barely see my face in the mirror now: only the bottom of my chin, my lips. When I speak, trying out words, I can hardly make out my mouth moving. Agatha stands back and watches me, as I breathe in and out. The outfit's dark, which will help me stay hidden; but if somebody should see me – one of the Lows, even Rex – I want them to stay away from me.

I look like I should be feared.

I look like something out of the stories we tell on this ship: the Nightman, the ghosts. The stories get told because we fear them. And the Lows are going to fear me.

I'm lying on my bed in my room, the suit hanging up in front of me, and I'm watching it, staring at its shape. It looks almost full, even when there's nobody inside it. I hear my door creak just as I shut my eyes, and my hand darts to my pillow to grab my blade, reflex kicking in before I can even think.

'Chan?' Mae asks.

'Hey,' I say. I relax. 'Hey, come here.' She pads across the carpet and clambers onto the bed, and immediately lies down next to me, draping her arms around my neck. I'm so tired and achey that it hurts, but I don't let on.

'I can't sleep,' she says. I checked on her earlier and she was flat out. Still, she's woken up now, and I know all too well what sort of dreams she might have been having. 'Can I sleep here?'

'Of course you can,' I say, and I lie there with her, stroking her hair. It only takes a few minutes before I feel her body settle as she goes under, and I shut my own eyes and breathe.

Just as I'm drifting off, I think that I can hear footsteps outside my berth, outside my door; but they fade, just like everything else does.

Agatha wakes me, gently shaking me. I don't know how long I've been asleep for, but Mae is gone and I'm alone. I hear Agatha's knees crick as she kneels down

'Jonah's gone,' she says. 'When I woke up, I couldn't find him. I've checked the screens, and he's out there. He's looking for the Women.' I sit up, rubbing my face. I'm groggy, and my body feels like it's weighted down by something that I can't see, my muscles rebelling against my trying to make them move. It's been a long, long time since I've slept like that. I'm not sure that I ever have before.

'Where have you seen him?' I ask.

'All over, searching, first on the top floors, then working his way down.' She hands me something, a cup of something hot. 'This is called coffee,' she says, 'and it will help.' I take a sip, and it's scalding and foul and bitter, but I persist. She knows best about these things. 'He won't find them, Chan. They're dead, or they're hiding. He'll get himself caught.'

'I know,' I say, and I stand up and stumble to the cupboard, where I get the outfit down and lay it on the bed. I'm slow to pull it on, but I can't tell if that's tiredness or something else. Fear. I don't want to have to go up there again, not when I'm not completely ready. I'd been planning to hide, to slip around in the shadows, only fight if I was discovered and attacked. But Jonah isn't cowering in a corner; he won't be hiding. He'll be looking for the most dangerous bits of the ship that he can find, hoping that they'll lead him to the women who brought him up.

I walk through with Agatha to the control room, past the kids in the kitchen. They're eating again – they always seem to be eating – and they wave at me as I walk past. They're happy. They're not worried about the worst case of what could happen. Maybe I shouldn't be either.

'Are you going to be alright looking after them?' I ask Agatha, and she nods.

'You think I haven't done it before?' She never had children of her own. I'm so quick to forget how present she was during my own childhood, and all the things that she did for me. And my mother.

I bring up the screens, the views of Australia, and I search

187

for Jonah. I can't see him anywhere, but I do see Rex. She's sitting in a berth, nursing her destroyed arm, cradling it. It's wrapped up, and she's rubbing at the edges of what must be the wound. I've heard that it itches like crazy when you lose a part of yourself, when that flesh starts to heal. The end of her arm is covered in a rag, and I can't see what it looks like, but I'm guessing it's not pretty. She'll blame me for what she's lost, I'm sure; as soon as she knows that I'm still alive.

'You should go,' Agatha says.

'I thought you'd be trying to stop me.'

'Would you listen to me?'

'No,' I say.

'Well, then. I'll watch you. If you need help, signal to me. Like this,' and she makes a gesture, her fingers curled into an OK circle. 'Got it?'

'Got it,' I say, but we both know that I'm not going to ask her to come and save me, to leave the kids. I'm going to find Jonah by myself. She doesn't come with me as I walk to the hatch, or as I attach my mask, or as I go back up into the Pit.

On the fiftieth floor, where I once lived, I attack before they can. I hang over the edge of the railing, and I use the striker to take out two Lows who were in the middle of torturing a man I know. As much as possible, I want to save Jonah without there being any more deaths, not even of Lows. Killing makes me no better than the Lows. This striker weapon is far neater than a knife; less blood, less mess, less noise and not inevitably fatal. The man who they were hurting, one-legged and vulnerable, thanks me, his face full of tears. I ask him if he's seen Jonah. I describe his suit, and when that gets no reaction I focus on the details: his red hair, his green-grey eyes, his pale skin. The man doesn't know. He's seen a lot of people, and he starts to tell me a story, about how I should be careful; that there are rumours the Nightman is up to his old tricks. I don't have time for this. I leave him.

I work quickly. I rush and strike a group of Lows three floors up, right in my path for the easiest route to the top floors of the ship. To them, I'm a blur, that's all. Again, I try to leave them alive: injured enough that they can't heal within the next few days, but still breathing. I just don't want them coming after me if I can help it.

I fight Lows when I meet them, and as I'm catching my breath between encounters, I imagine how we might decorate the new berths, making them more personal, putting up pictures that the children have painted. I save a family on the sixty-second floor. The Lows are stringing them up, in front of their berth – likely as some sort of warning – and I cut the back of one Low's tendons and shock the other, and then slice through the rope that's tying the family together.

As I run, I imagine the cooking that we will do down below, the food that we will prepare. I imagine a school, teaching the children to read books, to write and learn all the stories, the real ones as well as the lies. And we will do that all by ourselves, telling the little ones what we have discovered. Imparting knowledge, so no one will ever forget where we came from.

On the sixty-fifth floor, I save a little boy who is alone, covered in blood. I do not know what happened to his parents, but there are so many Lows around him I have to act. They are discussing what to do with him, like it's a game. They are dividing up the pain that they'll cause him between them. I don't just save him: I ruin them. I kick one to the floor, jamming the stick into his mouth, smashing his teeth and frying his tongue until he howls in agony; I throw the other to the floor, my knife cutting his thigh deep, his blood a fountain.

I take the boy with me, just as I carried Mae, and I don't even think about the burden, because if I didn't do this, he would die. Simple as that. On 70, I save a family, but I don't fight the Lows that are advancing towards them. There are far too many of them. It would be suicide. I pull the family by their hands and I tell them to stay quiet. I lead them into the darkness, away from the Lows. As we run, the woman slips and falls, trapping her foot in a hole I didn't see in the grating, and she screams. Her ankle is broken and I can see the bone jutting through her torn skin. I don't have time to save her, because her screams tell the Lows where we are. I put my hand over the mouth of one of the boys to stop him calling out his mother's name, and the man does the same to the other, and we carry them into the darkness, leaving her. We wait, and we hear what happens: the sickening sounds of death. And then I signal to Agatha, into the nothingness, hoping that she's watching, knowing that she'll be angry with me – three more little mouths to feed, and the first adult let in; and I send the motherless children down to the bottom of the ship in the care of their father, along with the boy I saved before.

I keep going; I keep trying.

* * *

On the eighty-eighth floor, I look for Jonah. I remember meeting him, for the briefest of moments; working here with him, trying to help the people who can't help themselves.

But he's not on this floor. Nobody is. All of the people from before, the sick and injured, they're gone. The berths are burnt out, destroyed, and even in the green light of my goggles it doesn't look any less terrible. The people who lived here won't have been able to protect themselves, I know that much. I wonder what sort of pleasure the Lows took from killing the woman I put ointment on before. She was in so much pain, every single movement she took hurt her more than anything I can even imagine.

I wonder if they cared. I wonder if they even relished it.

I go back to the stairwell, and I climb up. The last time I was here, I nearly died. Last time, I could copy what Jonah did as we climbed. If I didn't have my mask, I'm not sure that I'd be able to do this. But now I can see the bits I should cling to, even in the darkness. I look down, and there's a clear drop for six or seven floors. I fell that once and survived it. Not sure the same would happen again. That's enough to focus me, and I take it slowly: hand by hand, foot by foot. It feels darker, suddenly. Colder, maybe. Doesn't hot air rise? Isn't that what's meant to happen? That's not how it is, though. Even with the lights gone everywhere else in the ship, somehow I think that the darkness here is darker. Like it has settled in. It's made the top of Australia its home.

I don't announce myself. I don't know what's waiting up here for me. The Lows: they could be here, still. Maybe they're catching up on their reading, staring at the writing on the walls. That makes me laugh, and I have to hold myself back, and that makes it worse. Don't laugh, don't laugh; but I can't help it, picturing them all lined up, reading the words on the walls as if they're in class. I snicker, and that turns into a full laugh, a single Ha! that echoes all around me. Get it together, Chan. Get. It. Together.

He's not here. There's nothing here. The ninetieth floor of the ship is the only part where you can see all the way along, with no berths to interrupt your line of sight. Nothing but gantry. There's nobody up here, not a single soul, and no possessions, no blankets, no beds. There's blood on the floor in places – remnants of the fight from before – and scraps of torn fabric, a few twisted, bent bits of weapons. But no sign of Jonah, or the woman that he called Sister.

I sit down. I'm tired, and I have to. I stare at the walls, at the writing that's there – even in the darkness, I can see it in green, on the black walls. Some of it is clearer than others; some of the scratches deeper. I read it: it tells the same story as the *Testaments*, about the making of man and animals and the Earth (the same Earth which, at the end of the story, would be torn apart). *The Father made a garden in the East*, I read.

A garden. The arboretum.

It's not meant to be dark in here. Trees, fruit, vegetables, crops; they thrive in the light of the artificial sun that hangs above all of us, and now that that's off, this place feels wrong. All of the trees seem to loom over me, the same green as everything else through my goggles. There's a fire burning on one side of this place: some of the crops have been set alight, their thin stalks now fizzing into ash. And then I see Jonah in the distance, by the apple trees. Somehow, having read their book, I should have known this is where he would be. He's not alone. I can see another shape with him, its colours less distinct, less bright through the mask's view: a body, cradled in his arms.

'Jonah. It's me,' I say, as I get close and see him tensing at the sound. 'I came to find you.'

'She's dying,' he says. She's propped up against the tree, her head lolling. It's the Sister. It's a miracle she's still alive. 'I don't know what to do for her.' He's got his ointment in one hand, and he's daubing it onto her skin. I take my mask off, to see as best I can. Lit in the flames of the burning crops, I can see how bloody her gown is, soaked through with darkness. Her neck is cut, but not badly enough to just end her. This is a slow death. 'Rex did this,' he says, 'she did this, and she . . . It isn't right.'

'I know,' I reply. I know that my words are meaningless. Doesn't mean that they won't be what he needs to hear: what I need to say.

'All of this. Sister wanted to help people. She wanted peace.'

'And she found it.' The stories about who they were faded over time: the Pale Women of old were a story more than a reality. We don't know if the stories were ever even true. Probably doesn't matter, not any more.

'Maybe she was wrong. Maybe death is . . . Maybe that's better. What Rex deserves.'

'Maybe.' I kneel next to him. 'You have to let her go,' I say. I brush the hair from the Sister's eyes. Brown eyes, almost the exact same colour as her skin. She doesn't focus her eyes on me, or on anything else. She's all but gone already.

'I can still try to help her.'

'No. I don't think you can,' I say. I put my hand on his back, and then around him; and I pull him close to me. He stops touching her, stops rubbing the ointment on her wounds. It won't help, anyway, that ointment. It's just another lie, I think. She's in terrible pain, and it's only going to get worse.

We're sitting, quiet, in the dark, when I hear the voice: Rex's voice, preceded by the hissed throats of the Lows that she brings with her.

'Keep quiet,' I tell Jonah, even though he's not said a word, and I move us behind the tree, behind the Sister's body. I put the mask back on and watch them, coming in from the opposite side of the arboretum, behind the burning crops. They won't see us, I know. It's too dark and we're hidden by the bright light of the fire that lies between us and them. That means I've got the upper hand. Now, it's just a matter of what I do with it. 'Wait here,' I tell Jonah, and I creep forward, close enough that I can hear what they're saying.

'We're nearly finished,' Rex says. Her voice is more broken than I remember, her speech slowed down, slurred. She rubs at the stump of her hand, itching and pulling at it, wincing as she does so. I really hope that it's infected. I hope that it turns, and rots, and that the fever sets in.

'The ship is nearly ours,' she says. 'The rest of them can try to fight back, but we'll kill them. This arboretum,' she stumbles over the word, 'is already ours now. They'll have no access to food. Let them hide, or wait. They'll have nothing. They'll starve, or join us.'

She's chaos, pure and simple. I watch as she takes an unlit torch and dips it into the dying flames at her feet. 'This is how we take our freedom,' she says, like they've been oppressed, like they haven't been terrifying the rest of us for as long as anybody can remember. The flame takes and she carries it to the trees. She stands under one and holds it to the trunk, and the bark starts to crackle. Her Lows throw things high into the trees: small vials that explode, the liquid that's inside them running down, catching fire as it goes. The tree is lost in seconds, the flames up to the very top of the branches. The colours, through my mask, are almost too vibrant, too bright. I pull it off. I've climbed that tree. I've spent hours in that tree. When I was younger, I would climb it and hide and read the fragments of whatever books my mother had managed to salvage for me. I watch now as the branches snap and fall; as the Lows light the next tree, and the next. They'll burn it all down. The trees give us oxygen and food, and I'm sure work harder than the almost-broken air generators that have kept us alive for so long. The Lows are going to damn everybody. They're going to kill us all, even themselves. I have to stop them, I know; but I don't know how.

Then, the water starts. From above us – right in the roof of the ship – it comes, spitting, gently at first; and then it flows faster and faster, water gushing from all around it, spraying everywhere, hitting everything. It's just like the shower down below, but on a much greater scale. It's rain.

I've never seen such a thing before. I have always known that the plants irrigate from below, from the river. This must be for emergencies, and it's amazing: water flows in great clattering sheets. The Lows are terrified, shouting, panicking, watching their flames sputter and die; watching their light disappear.

This is my chance. Mask down, I run. Blade in one hand, striker in the other, I plough into them. They don't even hear me coming, because the rain is so loud, and we're soaked, pounded by it, drenched. I slam through them, one by one, and they scream and howl, and I get two of them down before the others even realise it's not just the water that they're screaming about. A third one hits me, a lucky accident, but I can see him, and he can't see me; I duck, and I get behind him, and I discover what happens when you use a striker on somebody who's wet: the effect is amplified.

Through the grainy vision of my mask, everybody looks the same. I suddenly worry about Jonah, but then I see him, waving his arms around, hear him shouting my name so that I know where he is. He's helping. He's in the fray. There are ten of them, I think, maybe more; and only two of us. But I don't care about any of them apart from Rex. I search for her, trying to get a glimpse of her half-shaven head, her scars. I worry that she's gone, that I've lost my chance.

And then I spot her. There's only one person here missing a hand. That makes her easier to identify: a space in my vision where there's usually something. She sees me across the melee, strides to me, pushing other Lows out of the way, unstoppable. My legs shake. I plant them in the soil, which is turning to wet mud, and I try to brace them. I can't shake.

I can't balk, not now. She's got one good arm, but I've got two. That surely gives me an advantage.

I don't know what I'm expecting, but when she's close enough, she leaps. She takes off, and she comes at me, the stump at the end of her ruined arm extended towards me. I hold my ground, because the impact will hurt her more than it hurts me. I ready my blade, and she hits me but slips and falls to the ground, and I swipe as she goes, getting her on the back, and she lands on her knees in front of me. I once saw the Lows worship her the way she is now, in front of me.

She laughs, and that's when the pain hits me. I reach up and knock the goggles off my head, and I look down at where her stump is pressed against my side. She's still laughing. She pulls her hand back and I see what my goggles missed: that my mother's blade is fastened to her stump, embedded in the flesh, pushed in deep and firm. Tightly wrapped gauze runs round it, holding it in place. I'm sure that it must hurt her just to have it in there. But as she pulls the blade out of me, she only laughs harder.

Jonah slams into her from behind, tackling her, pushing her away, but she's on her feet straight away, slashing at him. Through the rain, I only catch glimpses of them as they fight. I put my hand to where she cut me, and I feel for blood, but feel only the wetness of the rain. The wound aches, but doesn't hurt as much as I imagined that it would. I step forward. The pain is manageable, for now. I pick my mask up from the mud and wipe it off, and I put it on. I can see them fighting, almost a dance between them, back and forth.

Rex doesn't see me behind her, and doesn't hear me. She only hears the sound of the striker warming up; the fizz of the rain as it hits the blue lightning wrapped round it; and then the sound of her own skin crackling where I slam it into her neck.

She crumples like a pile of ash to the floor, still breathing, eyes wide open.

'You're hurt,' Jonah says, his face drenched.

'It's fine.'

'You're bleeding.'

I look down at Rex and I see it now; my blood is mixing with the rain, running down me and pooling at my feet.

'You need—'

'I need to finish this fight,' I say. I draw my blade. I can do this, I tell myself. She's a bad person, a terrible person. I've tried to avoid killing where I can, tried to incapacitate. But she wouldn't give me the same consideration. She wouldn't hesitate to kill me, just as she hasn't hesitated to kill so many good people on this ship. If good people die, why shouldn't she? My mother, the Sister: they were good people. They were . . .

I drop to my knees and Jonah rushes to catch me, to support me. His arm under mine, his shoulder propping me up.

'You're not a killer,' he says. He helps me away from her, back down the gantry, back to the main body of the ship. I lead him to what was my home for so many years; and we sit on the shattered metal frame of what's left of my old bed, and he helps me with the zip of my outfit, pulling it down. He can see the wound better than I can. 'It's not as bad as it could have been,' he says. 'This' – tapping the armoured plates that Agatha sewed in for me – 'took most of it. It'll need stitches.'

'I can't see it properly,' I say, and he pushes my hand down, gets close to my skin. He takes his kit from his pocket and finds a needle, then takes some thread and loops it through. It's wet from the rain, but it's fine. It'll do. He doesn't look me in the eye as he cleans the wound with his ointment and wipes it dry; and then, as he pushes the wound together, sliding the needle into the skin, winding and looping it through, pulling my skin tight. It hurts, but not enough to make a fuss. Not enough to let him know. When he's done, he bites the thread to cut it, his face close enough now to my skin that I can feel his breath on it. 'There,' he says.

'Thank you,' I say. And then we're both on that bed frame, still, and it's uncomfortable, but better than standing. He's warm, and that's nice; as the coldness of the water that soaked us fades and we sit in the warmth of the darkness, unseen, unlit; and we start to dry. I feel his hand reaching for mine, and I take it.

We both shut our eyes, and I think how easy it would be to sleep, somehow, even here, even now.

It takes Jonah standing to break that moment. He helps me to my feet. I'm fine. It hurts, but I know that it'll heal. I look at the stitches, at how neat they are, and I smile at him as I fasten up my suit. 'We have to deal with her,' I say. I walk back towards the arboretum, picking up speed until I'm almost running.

'What will you do?' he asks as we go. The rest of the ship is strangely quiet. I picture everybody who's left, huddled together, terrified and quiet, praying for the war to be over, the darkness to end.

'I don't know,' I say, and I don't, not now. He was right when he said I shouldn't kill her. So what happens after that? Maybe we should take her down below; take her prisoner, lock her in a berth and stop her getting out.

But, maybe there's been too much imprisonment. I don't know where we go if we start down the path. What happens next?

I can see that she's gone before we're even in the arboretum. I stand where she fell, and I hold my head back, letting the rain patter down onto my face. It's refreshing, cooling. As I'm standing there, it stops, slowing to a dribble, and then just the drops of emptying pipes. I look around, and I see rustling in the bushes, over towards the river.

'What now?' Jonah asks. Quiet as I can, I track her down. She's trying to hide, but she won't. She can't. She's underneath the blackberries, trying to recover from the blow the striker gave her. The Lows abandoned her. I reach in, and I find her one hand.

'Get out of there,' I order, and I pull her out. She doesn't fight me. She's too weak.

'What are we doing with her?' Jonah asks. He pulls his blade out, as if he knows the answer. I won't kill her, he knows, but he could. There's already much more blood on his hands than there is on mine.

'We don't kill her,' I say, 'We're taking her with us.' And that surprises me, to hear my mother's words come out of my mouth, almost as much as it surprises him.

'We can't,' he says. 'She'll . . . She'll know.' He whispers that, trying to protect our secrets.

'It's the best way. She's not a threat, not any more.' She struggles, tries to stand. I know she'll fight us with whatever she has left, but right now that's barely anything.

I use the striker once more, on her skull. Knocking her out might save us some hassle.

By the time we get back below the Pit, we're tired and broken, weighed down and covered in grime. Seven more people came down with us – eight, with Rex: one family of three and four orphaned children. Three of the orphans are placid, maybe shocked by the things that they've seen; the other kicks and bites when I try to lift him down into the Pit – tearing at me, trying to get free. He's terrified, and he should be. It isn't until he sees the lights of the down-below that he calms down, breathing more deeply, relaxing.

The one little girl who has her parents with her seems to be adjusting faster than the others. But the one who fights me – he's more scared of what's happening than the rest of them. Agatha stands and watches them all, and then stares as Jonah drags Rex's body from the hatch, dropping her down from the ladder into our corridor. Her limp body lies on the floor, staining the carpet with the muck from the Pit that's clinging to her skin.

'What have you done?' Agatha asks, her voice low, shocked.

'Find me a berth we don't use,' I say, 'we're going to keep her in it.'

'She's a murderer,' Agatha says.

'Yes,' I reply, 'but I'm not.' I drag her down the corridor myself, as she starts to stir; and Jonah finds a closed door, an empty berth. We take out everything that we might want or need – even the sheets and pillow from the bed – and I lay her on the bare mattress, and I think that this is still a better place than any she's known before. Maybe what we're doing isn't fair. In one way, it is almost a reward for all the dreadful things she's done.

'Pull out her blade,' Agatha says. I look down at it, jammed so far into her arm. The flesh is starting to heal, the blade becoming a part of her. Some part of me thinks how apt that is; another wants it back. It was my mother's.

'No,' I say. 'She might bleed out.' I don't want her to die, I tell myself; but then I wonder if leaving her with the blade – alone, locked in a room by herself, no way out – is my way of taking that choice away from me; leaving matters in her own hands, in some sick way.

We shut the door; and I take another striker from the cupboard and I slide it through the handle so that it locks, so that she can't get the door open. Agatha grabs me when I'm finished, when I'm standing alone in the corridor.

'What you're doing won't change anything. They'll find a new leader, as they always do.'

'Right,' I say, 'but it will slow them down. It might even stop the war.'

'Enough. This is enough, now. You've done what you can, and you've pushed your luck. Soon enough it will run out.' She takes my face in her hands. 'You aren't special, Chan. None of us are.'

'I'm not special,' I say, 'that's right. I'm really not.

Anybody could have done what I'm doing, but they didn't. So I am going to. Maybe that's enough.'

I'm angry with Agatha, with her selfishness. I'm tired of selfishness. Survival should be more. I storm off, back to my room. I don't want to fight any more. Agatha doesn't get it, and I don't have the strength to persuade her. Mae is in my bed again, curled up in the corner, pressed to the wall. I shrug out of my dirty suit and sit on the bed beside her. She turns to me and puts her arms round me, warm against my cold skin.

'Tell me a story,' she says, shutting her eyes. So I tell her the stories that my mother told me: about ghosts, about Earth, about who we are. They're lies, but it's easier to tell them than the truth. How do you explain that we are damned because of a crime that we didn't commit?

I don't notice when Mae falls asleep. It doesn't take her long, that's for certain. I'm not tired though, not yet. There's still adrenalin running through me, telling me that there's more I can do. I don't need to stop yet. I think about Jonah: about how hard everything that's happened must be for him. He's gone through a lot, and lost just as much as I have. The Pale Women might not have been his blood, but they were everything to him, all the family that he had. At least I know where I come from. He doesn't even know his real name. I wonder about what might have been; if everything here had been different. If we weren't all so broken. I slip out from underneath Mae's clinging grip, and I go to the room where we have been keeping all the suits.

I start to make a new suit for him. I don't have him try it

as I go, guessing at the size instead. I'm sure it'll fit him, when I'm finished. Pretty sure.

As I'm sewing – and thinking about Jonah's own sewing, the stitches in my side – I hear noise coming from Rex's room. She's murmuring something, and I listen as she walks the room, beating the walls, looking for a way out, and then as she starts to scream for her freedom, as if she has any idea what the word even means.

In my room, I work all night, until I'm so tired I can barely keep my eyes open; until Jonah's new suit is finished.

The next day I waste no time. I wake Jonah as soon as I'm up, barging my way into his room. He's lying on his bed, no sheet, and it takes me a second to realise that he's naked. It takes me a second longer to look away. Not that he seems to care.

'Get dressed,' I say, from the darkness of the doorway to his room, and I throw his new suit onto the bed. 'We're going hunting.' He picks it up, and he looks surprised. When I see him next, he's wearing it. It's a little tight around the chest – that's the armour, I'm sure of it – but it fits. It's quiet in Rex's room. She kept the noise up for hours, then went totally silent. Maybe she's tired herself out.

Or maybe she's killed herself, lying on the floor, waiting to be saved. I don't have the time to check now; or maybe, I just don't have the inclination. I can't be sure.

Jonah and I don't talk as we climb up into the Pit and then, floor by floor, up through the ship. We're looking for trouble. On the thirty-second floor, section IV, we see a little boy being thrown by a group of Lows like he's a toy. One drops him, and he tumbles to the gantry and skids towards the edge. Jonah and I know what to do without having to say it. I ignore the Lows and go for the boy, and I grab his arm just as he goes over, gripping him tightly; but there's a click and a howl from him, and then he goes limp, passed out. Jonah goes for the Lows, hitting one, knocking the other back. That's the best way to fight them: divide them, then deal with them one by one.

I haul the boy up and push him to one side, getting him out of the way of the fight, and I join Jonah. We're back to back, dealing with them. This is fine, two on two; and then I see them coming for us, more of them. Tens of them. We don't balk, because we can't. We do as we should: cut through them, divide them up, knock them down where we can. The Lows seem confused. They must know Rex is gone by now. I wonder why none of them have risen up to take her place.

That confusion makes them sloppy. We fight enough of them to make a dent, and then grab the boy and run. Jonah and I pass the kid between us, taking turns at mowing through them while we carry him. It makes getting down through the ship easier; passing him off to Agatha, who waits at the bottom, even though we didn't tell her we were leaving; and then making our way back up again. We've got a system now, and it works. No sense in messing with that.

We save a family on the sixty-third floor. They're all injured in one way or another, the smallest – three or four months old, nothing more – infected with something, probably only a week from death. We incapacitate the Lows and then the family backs away from us. They ask me if I'm the Nightman, come to take them away. They're scared, but I reassure them. I'm not going to hurt them; I'm going to save them. Jonah escorts them to the path to the bottom of the ship. I write a message on one of the walls, aimed at the Lows: *Stay Away.*

We save a young couple, younger than us. Thirteen, fourteen years old, maybe, living on the seventieth floor. She's injured so badly she can't move, and we stop them as he's about to kill them both – something about living in paradise together – but I tell him that there is no paradise; there's only below the Pit. He carries her down. He's an idiot, but it's kind of sweet.

We save a tiny kid as his family cowers at the edge of the gantry into Low territory. We grab him as he's running right up to a sleeping group of murderers, still coated in the blood of the people they killed last. I use the striker on them as they sleep. It would have felt wrong to leave them there. I return him to his parents and then send the family down, telling them about the Pit. Telling them to be careful, but there's somewhere else.

'You don't need to be scared anymore,' I say to them.

In the kitchen, I see how many we've saved so far. We're busy, the tables full, the floor cramped. There's only room for thirty or so people here, and that's assuming we sleep crammed into the small rooms, sharing beds. I look at the food in the cold storage compartment, counting how much we've got. What's the plan? I haven't thought past today, not really. How long are we here for? What happens when we run out of food? What happens to the arboretum, now that it's burnt and dark?

And then, the bigger questions: if there's no food, do we just wait it out down here for the Lows to die? What about the people who I don't save? There are free people up there, innocents. There are, and we – I – can't do anything. I lean against the back wall inside the cold room. I push against it, feeling my muscles stretch against the freezing wall. I've never felt this cold before.

'It's hard,' Agatha says, from the doorway. 'You have to make choices, harder than you've ever had to make before.'

'How long will all our supplies last?' I ask her.

'A year if we're clever, if we don't bring any more people down here. If,' she says, 'we don't feed *her.*'

'I'm not letting her starve,' I say.

'Then we'll run out that much faster.'

'Please,' I tell her, and I turn to look at her.

'You can't save any more people, Chan. You're choosing who lives and who dies. You're choosing who's saved. That's—'

'It's not even a choice any more,' I say, and that feels like the end of the conversation. There's nothing more to be said.

NINE

I'm three floors up in the ship when I see Bess, who once lived in the berth beside mine. How long has it been? She looks so different: a total change in everything about her. She should be dead, but she isn't. She's alive, and she's dressed like a Low. Torn clothes, fresh tattoos on her skin, paint on her face, clutching a jagged metal spike with fabric wrapped around one end, a crude torch. She's facing the stairwell as I pull myself up. It takes me a second to recognise her. 'The Nightman,' she gasps as she sees me.

'No,' I say, as I pull my mask off so that she can see my face. That changes nothing; she doesn't look any less shocked.

'You're alive,' she says.

'Yes.' I notice a fresh scar on her skin, on her chest: the letter P, carved deep. 'I'm sorry about Peter,' I tell her. I'll never forget losing him, and not being able to find him. Maybe it was my fault, maybe it wasn't.

'It's fine,' she says. She coughs, her throat ragged. She isn't breathing like them yet. She hasn't had to live in their half of the ship long enough. Whatever happens to the air over there, it's not quite gotten to her yet.

'They're destroying the ship,' I say. 'They would have killed you. They probably killed Peter.' I see that sting her. I shouldn't have said it, I know. That was cruel of me. But I want her back. She doesn't belong there. 'How can you trust them?'

'I don't. But I don't trust anyone.'

'So don't stay with them.'

'Being with them will keep me safe,' she says, and she turns away from me and starts to run off.

'We have somewhere,' I shout, 'somewhere safe. If you change your mind.' But I don't know that she hears me, because she's gone, up into the darkness.

The arboretum is all but gone. Looking at the remains of the plants, of the crops and grains, of the trees – they're burnt out and dead. Some greenery struggles through, but through my goggles, it's all just the same shade of grey.

But I stay here. I sit on the ground, near the river – which still flows, just as it always did, as it always has, part of the ship's innards doing their job, their cycle of constancy – and I take my shoes off, and I remember where they came from; and I wash my feet in the water, because they're sore, and because here, alone, I can. I haven't had a shower today. I'm not taking proper advantage of it. My mother would want—

No.

This isn't about her, not any more. This is about me, and those kids. And Jonah, now. We have something, something that we can build; something that we can do to make this all better. That's worth concentrating on. That's what I need to focus on.

I hear a child crying. I don't know where, but I don't wait. I put my wet feet back into my shoes and I run towards it, because it won't stop until I reach it, or somebody else does.

When I get back down beneath the Pit, the child and another family with me, there's a crowd in the corridor: the few adults I've saved, Agatha and Jonah. Jonah is breathing heavily, his chest rising and falling, sweat on his brow.

'She broke the door,' Agatha says, and I see that they're outside the berth that we've been keeping Rex in. The door is barricaded, but cracks run down the length of it and the handle is halfway to snapped off

'What did she do?' I ask.

'She used her body,' Jonah says, 'slammed against it, over and over. We heard her.'

'Jonah stopped her,' Agatha says. He's bleeding, I notice: a bite mark on his arm, the blood a nearly perfect imprint of Rex's mouth full of sharpened teeth. 'We can't keep her here,' Agatha says, which means something different than moving her, I know.

'I'll talk to her,' I say.

'And say what?'

'I'll tell her that she's safe now.' She's scared, I think. We're all scared. 'Get back from here,' I tell them all, directing it at the kids, but aiming it at Agatha. I don't know what Rex will do, given half a chance; and I pull my striker from its sheath, and I start moving the barricade to one side. She doesn't make an attempt on the door, but she'll be ready, just as I am.

She's in the corner furthest from the door, pressed into it, her arms stretched out and almost clinging onto the walls. There are scratch marks down the walls around her, and through the dug-out colour I can see that the underneath is metal; cleaner metal than upstairs, shiny and polished rather than the dull black. The fingers of her good hand are bleeding, and the blade – my mother's blade, I remind myself, another thing that she left me, that came back to haunt me – is blunted, the metal bent. It's still dangerous, maybe now more than ever.

'Riadne's daughter,' she says. 'Chan.' I don't know that I've heard her say my name before. I don't say her name. I don't know it, not the one that she originally had. Nobody does any more, I wouldn't think. She's Rex. I wonder if she even remembers her name, or if this new one has taken all the space she had for it.

'You can't escape,' I tell her.

'I'll kill you. I'll kill you and all of these people.' But as she says it, I can see she's lying. I was right. She's terrified. Take her away from her people, from the ship that she knew better than anybody else, that she was on the verge of ruling, and she's just like me. She's only a bit older than me, I think: a year older, maybe. Hard to tell through the scars, but her eyes are young still. I can see her better here, in this light, and everything that was frightening about her is

211

clearer to me. Her scars aren't marks of power now. They're pain. She's had chunks taken out of her, over and over. The name on her chest is the same as all the rest. It's healed up in puckered slashes, uneven, and it still looks so sore; and there's a bit on the R, where she started her journey, where the line wavers, where the cut isn't as deep as the rest. She was unsure about it. She regretted it as soon as she did it, maybe. It hurt too much.

'You're not with your people any more,' I tell her. 'You're alone, with us. And you're safe here.'

'So you're going to keep me here?' Her wheezing is already better, I realise. A few days away from the air filters on the Lows' side of the ship, and already she's sounding closer to normal. 'Where are we?'

'We're somewhere safe.' I can't believe that I'm saying that. Weeks ago, safety – real safety – would have seemed an impossible dream.

'Nowhere is safe,' she says.

'Who are you?' I ask.

'I'm Rex.' She says it in a slightly different voice, the tone that she takes when she's their leader. Defensive and defiant all at the same time.

'Your real name?' She smirks. She won't tell. Not that it matters. She scratches at herself, at her scars. Or, no, at one particular scar, the one on her belly, that runs across the top of her pelvis. Only in this light can I see that it's actually neater than most, and not scratched or torn. It's a medical scar. 'You're a mother?' I ask, and she immediately stops touching it and moves from the wall, coming towards me. I step backwards with one foot, worried, stick my striker out in front of me, squeeze the handle. The blue flame tears up the stick and she balks.

'You don't know anything about me,' she says, 'and you can't, and you won't. I will kill you, and I will kill the old woman, and I will kill every single one of you who stands in my way. And I will take this place.'

'No, you won't,' I tell her. 'Because I won't let you.' I swing the striker, and it hits her on the arm. She collapses, and I shout for help.

'What are we doing with her?' Jonah asks, walking in and looking down at Rex's unconscious body.

'We're putting her in the cold rooms,' I say.

We move everything out of one of them, piling it into the other. The door is sturdier, and there's no handle on the inside, no way for her to get herself free. There's a dial on the wall to change how cold it is. I turn that up. It'll still be cold, but not too cold. I hope. We'll still need to give her clothes, to stop her from freezing to death.

If we ever land, I think, I'll set her free. I'll let her go, see what happens if she's given a chance. Here, you never have a chance. But then, we'll never land. We're prisoners; we're not looking for a home. We're out here waiting to die.

When it's empty, I drag her down the corridor. The children stand in the doorways and they watch, and their parents – or, the few adults that are here, looking after them, taking them on in immediate and chaotic adoptions – try and get them to turn away. They say that she's something to be scared of.

'Shut up,' I tell one man who hisses at her like she's a character from one of the plays that the Shopkeepers used to put on when I was young. I don't want people scared to be down here. That's not what holding her prisoner is about. I pull Rex through the kitchen and into the freezer, where Jonah is putting spare blankets inside. It's already thawing, the ice that had formed around the shelves dripping down, making the air damp. She might catch a cold from that, but she'll survive. I push her to the end, up against the wall. She's limp. Out of the corner of my eye, looking back at the door, I see Mae clutching the remains of her doll. It's a pretty good likeness, I think, looking down at Rex now. She's broken.

She's done.

Jonah and I sit in the control room and look at the screens, trying to find anybody else we can save. I'm focused, looking for children. They seem the easiest targets, both for the Lows and for us.

'What about him?' Jonah asks, pointing to a man in one screen, being beaten by two Lows. They're taking it in turns, punching him with weak fists, gently kicking him. It's attrition rather than anything more brutal: stretching out the torture, so that he lasts longer. The man is bruised and bloodied, but he's awake, and he's struggling. 'He'll heal better here, if they let him live.'

It's the Shopkeeper who tried to sell me my shoes. He's a bad man, I know that. What he wanted from me . . . I don't want him down here. The Lows are doling out something that's almost like accidental justice. Part of me hopes that they kill him. So I don't look at Jonah, but I shake my head.

'No,' I say, 'not him.'

'He needs help,' Jonah says.

'He's a bad person.' I look at the other screens, trying to find somebody, so that I can move this on.

'How do you know?'

'Because he is,' I say. I don't want to get drawn into an argument.

'He needs saving.'

'You don't know what he would have done to me. Just because he's—'

'People can change,' he says, his voice wavering.

'Not all people,' I say. Jonah keeps quiet. He doesn't want to fight, and neither do I. I change tack. 'We're getting full. There won't be enough food. We'll have to go back up there sooner, if we're not careful.' I'm not going back up there. I won't do it. 'We save people who can't save themselves, who need saving. That's it.'

'Chan—'

'No!' I say, and I slam my hand onto one of the screens, 'Look at them! None of them can save themselves. That's why we've had to step in; why you've had to take charge.' He's just as angry as I am. But I *am* in charge. This is on me. The kids; bringing them down here; fighting back against the Lows: it's all been at my urging, and I will defend my choice until the end.

Jonah cycles through the screens, showing the parts of the ship that we haven't gotten to yet; where the Lows are still waging their war, where the free people are still hiding, trying to fight back, trying to survive. 'There's still so much to do,' I say, and Jonah doesn't disagree.

* * *

215

Outside of the arguments, Jonah and I make a hell of a team. We've got a language between us that doesn't need to be spoken. He distracts the Lows and I swoop in, saving whoever needs to be saved, and then we deal with the Lows together; or, I pile in, taking one out, he takes another and we fight around the children, screaming at them to keep out of the way of our weapons; or, we pick the Lows off, one by one, without them noticing. I hang from the floors above and I strike the backs of their necks, knocking them out, while Jonah climbs up from below, and he pulls the incapacitated Lows out, sending them down to the Pit. Killing comes easier to him, but he still hates it. Taking a life hurts him. I catch him praying once or twice after he's done it, mumbling words with tightly pursed lips.

The Lows are easier to deal with now that Rex is gone. They're shaken, missing their leader. There's still no new Rex, so far as we can tell, nobody who's risen up to take that mantle. Maybe they don't know she's gone for good. Maybe they're waiting it out, hoping she'll be back.

'Shall I take it down?' Jonah asks, when we find a baby, terrified, mewling with fear. I wonder how it knows to be scared: if the fear is ingrained in a newborn.

I nod. 'I'll stay here. See if I find any more.' This is how it is: we watch for where to start, then we come up and we do what we can; and then repeat that, over and over. Until we're full, or until we're done, whichever comes first.

I watch him carry the baby, gently climbing down level by level. It doesn't cry while he's holding it. I watch until they're so swallowed by the darkness that my goggles can't pick them out any more.

I hear a scream. Section VI; probably five or six floors up. It's a young voice, a kid. I climb, quick as I can manage. Could be nothing: could be a child afraid of the dark. I'll get there and her parents will be holding her, telling her that it's alright; that there will be light again soon, somebody will fix it and then everything will be okay. She screams again, and again, and soon it's just one long burst, only stopping when it makes her voice croak and cough. She's struggling. Come on, Chan. Faster.

The screams have stopped. I don't know what that means.

I think I've got the right floor, but I can't see where the scream was coming from. I walk down the gantry, looking into the berths. Huddled free people, not seeing me, or not wanting to. One woman makes eye contact and then turns away, and I know the look in her eyes: fear. She's scared of me. They don't know what I'm trying to do for them. Then, a few berths down, frantic moving shapes. I can't make them out at first, just a mess of the flame-red and yellow and orange that the goggles show me. They've got a torch lit, so I take the mask off, just as I reach the berth.

The Lows have gone, and the little girl is dead. I try to save her – I've seen it done before, people beating their fists on chests, breathing air into lungs – but she stays dead. She can't come back, and I shouldn't even try. The berth is a mess. They've used her blood to leave me a message. A reply. Die, the message says, over and over. Die. A wish, an invocation. Almost a prayer.

I can't leave her body, I know. They'll . . . I don't know. I can't leave it. She's not going into the Pit, though. I can't do that to her. She deserves better than that. I pick her up, and

I hold her to me as I climb down the stairwells, and as I cross the gantry to the arboretum. I put her down next to the river, which is running black with ash and soot, and I kneel there, where the soil is wet. I dig at it with my hands and with my blade, carving a trough in the ground big enough to put her in, and when it's done I lay her down. I put the soil over her, back where it came from. This little shape in the ground, barely visible. Through the goggles, I watch the last of her heat die out. Whatever was left in her body is truly gone.

When I get back down below the Pit, I don't let anybody know that I'm here. I go to my berth and I don't even take my clothes off, I just stand underneath the hot water gushing from the shower faucet, and I try and keep myself together. Because if I don't, I don't see how I can do this any more. If I don't, I think that I might just fall apart.

I hear Agatha in the corridor, telling Mae that it's better to leave me alone tonight; that I need sleep. I need the rest, that's her excuse. My lights are off, and I'm trying to sleep. Trying, but failing.

'It's fine,' I shout, and that's enough for Mae, who bundles into my room, all grins and energy.

'I missed you,' she says. She clambers onto the bed and lies next to me. She sucks her thumb. I look at her, and all I can see now is the little dead girl. That can't happen to Mae. It just can't. Agatha follows her, trying to usher her out. It's impossible.

'I saw what happened,' Agatha says. 'You couldn't have done anything.'

'I know,' I reply. It's not about that.

'You've done good.'

'Maybe.' I'm glad that she can't see my face in the darkness.

'And now we have to stop,' she tells me. I don't reply. I don't know if she's right or not. I don't know how I can save everybody else. It's impossible. She leaves the berth, pulling the door closed. I clutch Mae, pulling her tight to me. She smells of soap. The scent of Australia – whatever was there before, ingrained in her skin – is gone.

'You're shaking,' she says.

'I'm sorry,' I say, and I try to stop, but I can't.

Mae shakes me awake, grabbing my shoulders and yanking them up and down.

'Wake up, wake up!' she says, 'there's somebody at the door.' There's knocking. I didn't hear it. I don't know what time I fell asleep, but I feel awful. Groggy. Aching. I don't want to get up.

'Come in,' I say, and it opens. It's Jonah. He stands awkwardly in the doorway, like he doesn't quite fit into it; he tilts his head, and his hair – which is clean, I notice, different from when we were living above; changed by the showers and the soap and maybe just the air down here – is soft, slightly fluffy, already showing signs of growing out. He notices me looking at it, and he runs a hand through it, suddenly self-conscious, and I look away.

'Agatha wants you. She says that it's important,' he says.

'He's strange,' Mae says, after he's gone.

'He is,' I tell her. 'But I like him.'

I get changed. I've found my old trousers, my top, clean and fresh. I'm not going up above today. Maybe not ever again. There's food cooking, but the smell makes my stomach churn. I can't face eating yet. I yawn. Some of the people we've saved are sitting at the table, eating food that I don't recognise. We're still trying everything, seeing if we can work out what's good and what's not. This meal smells like meat. I wonder if what they're eating was normal breakfast food, back on Earth, or if maybe we're breaking all the rules.

'Where are they?' I ask, and one of the people points to the control room. They don't go in there. We didn't make that a rule or anything. They just don't. Maybe it makes them feel guilty to see everyone else, still up above. Live down here; pretend that the rest of the ship doesn't exist any more. That's easiest.

I wonder if I can do that.

I open the door to the control room. Agatha is sitting in the chair, touching screens, moving them between views. She stops and looks at me.

'You've got a message,' she says, and she points to the screen right in the middle. I can see a Low there, and I get closer to see better. It's Bess. She's sitting, cross-legged, in a berth. I'd know that berth without any indicators: it's mine, my mother's. And behind her, scrawled on the wall, one word, begging me to come, to find her.

Chan, it says. I think that's the first time since my mother was alive that I've actually seen my name written down.

'Has she done anything else?'

'She's just sitting there,' Agatha says. 'Nothing else. And she's alone.'

'Okay.' I stretch, reaching down to touch my toes, bending back to crick my shoulder bones. 'I'd probably better go and see her, then.'

I go to the section over from mine, to get a vantage point. Through my goggles, I can see the distant scramble of the rest of the ship's inhabitants, all fighting, moving, scurrying. I don't care about them, not right now. I care about Bess. The entire floor is deserted now, everybody else moved on – one way or another. She's on the fragments of the bed, and she's waiting for me. It doesn't feel like a trap, I tell myself. But then, I suppose traps never really do; not until they're sprung.

I slip into the berth right on top of hers, and I check around us again. There's nobody around, not that I can see. The Lows don't know about the goggles, so they can't protect against them. This isn't a trap.

'Bess,' I say, standing at the edge of the gantry, and she looks up.

'You came,' she says.

'Are you okay?'

'Yes,' she says. 'Yes. I . . .' She fumbles her words, twists her hands against each other. She coughs, her voice with that slight wheeze behind it. 'You said that there was somewhere safe.'

'There is.'

'I want to be safe,' she says, and then, 'Please.' She steps forward, until our heads are pretty much even, and she looks right up into my eyes – past the goggles, past everything. 'I'm so scared,' she tells me. 'I've got nothing left.'

That's true. She's a good person, confused and lost, that's all. She went to the Lows because they were there; because they might have had her son. But she hasn't found him, and never will. We both know it.

'Come with me,' I say.

She stands at the edge of the Pit, and she recoils as I wade into it. She might be a Low, but she's not fallen so far as to be comfortable with this, not yet. We both know what's in here; and what's unspoken is that Peter might be here as well. Maybe she'll see him, as we trudge through it.

I pull off my mask and hand it to her.

'Wear this,' I say, 'it'll help. And you can breathe with it.' I can hold my breath, I know. I take her hand and I move forward, toward the centre, and she follows. I have to pull, to keep her moving. She doesn't make a sound, and I don't want to look at her. If I stop, if I let her think about what we're doing, she might panic.

When we have to go under the mulch, I just do it, and I don't let go of her hand. She doesn't struggle, and I pull her after me and yank the lever, and then we're in the hatch, and then we're out of there, down below.

'You can take the mask off,' I say, spitting the blood away from my mouth, going into the closest berth and grabbing one of the towels that I've put there for this very reason. I wipe my face. 'You're okay now.' I watch her pull the goggles from her head and try to take this all in. This first room, which is basically nothing, not in the grand scale of what we've got here, but still: it's clean and light and open and safe, and she's never seen that before.

'What is this place?' she asks. I pass her the towel.

'Better if I just show you,' I say. I lead her down the corridor, past the bedrooms, their doors open. The kids in them stop and look at her, balking when they see her. She's what they've been told to be afraid of. Another Low, and how do they know what makes her different to Rex? 'Wave at them,' I say, 'let them know that you're not a threat.' She does, a half-hearted shimmer of her hand. I can tell that it's painful for her, looking at these young faces. In another time, she would have been here with Peter. Maybe they could have lived here, and he would never have been taken. That must hurt her, imagining that. I see Mae and call her forward, and I kneel down and whisper to her. 'This is Bess,' I say, 'and you should be nice to her. She's scared.' Mae nods, knowing. We've all been there. Scared is something that we all share.

'Do you want to play?' Mae asks, holding out the broken doll that she just won't let go of.

'Maybe after I've cleaned myself up,' Bess says. Her voice trembles. We carry on, into the kitchens. Agatha and Jonah are there, and the other adults, and they stare. One stares in open-mouthed horror.

'It's fine,' I tell them. 'This is Bess, and she's a friend.' Agatha knows her. She comes over and looks Bess in the eyes, not smiling, ruthlessly sizing her up, and Bess starts to cry. I hold her, putting myself in between her and Agatha. 'It's fine,' I say. That doesn't stop the tears.

I help her with what happens next: showing her how the showers work, giving her new clothes from the quickly diminishing pile of blue uniforms. We all look the same down here now, apart from Agatha. She refuses to change, washing her old clothes instead, waiting naked in her berth until they're as close to dry as she can stand, and then putting them on again. Bess isn't as fussy. I take the remnants of her clothes and throw them into the trash, and I hand her a towel. She's not shy about her nudity, and I see her body as she gets dressed: the bruises and marks that cover almost every bit of her skin. They all look fresh. That's how quickly the Lows infect you.

'What's happening with the Lows now?' I ask, when she's sitting in a chair and I'm behind her, shaving her hair where's it's started to grow out. We don't have lice here, not yet, and it would be nice to never get them. Maybe I'd like to grow my hair long, one day. I've never tried it. I wonder what I would look like.

'They're the same as they ever were,' she tells me. She stares straight ahead, watching her own face as I cut away the hair. Now that she's clean, she can see what she looks like. This is part of the ritual we've created for new people: clean them, shave them in front of a mirror, let them see themselves clearly for the first time. 'Maybe worse. They're uncontrolled.'

'They lost their leader.'

'Yes,' she says. 'They think she's still out there. She was strong.' She looks at me, straight into my eyes. I stop cutting her hair. 'You killed her, though.'

'I didn't,' I say, 'I brought her down here.' I watch her face shift.

'She's here?'

'Not like you are. She's a . . .' Prisoner. She's a prisoner. We're all prisoners. I can't stand to tell the others, because of what it might do. For now, they're all still free. Our history – the lies that we've been fed for generations – is still a truth. Earth was destroyed. We escaped.

Good for us.

'She's dangerous,' Bess says.

'Not here she's not. She's in a room. It's locked.'

'I want to see,' she says, and she stands up. 'Please.'

In the kitchen, before the cold storage where Rex is, Bess touches the door. 'She can't get out?'

'Not a chance,' I tell her. Bess already looks so different. The change in her being clean . . . She looks just like the rest of us. Orphaned, kicked out of our homes, wearing what we can, finding somewhere new.

'Good,' she says. She stands in front of it, pushes it, testing to see that it's shut. She's scared of Rex, even here, even through thick metal and a lock that can't be broken. 'Can I see the children now?'

'Of course,' I say, and she goes down the corridor to the room where Mae and the others are playing. I hear her introduce herself, giving them a chance to take in the new version of her. When I turn back, Agatha's staring at me. 'She'll be fine,' I say. 'I'm sure of it.'

Bess handles the children at dinnertime. She asks Agatha if she can cook for them. Agatha doesn't mind, and stands aside, handing Bess the utensils. She's probably grateful for the night off. Bess looks at the books, picks one out and finds a picture of a delicious-looking stew, then pauses, touching the image with her fingertips.

'I can't read,' she quietly says, but that's okay. She shuts the book and cooks by instinct, taking food out of the cupboards, raiding the freezer next to the one where we're keeping Rex; and she chops and tastes and puts things into a boiling pot. She uses everything she can, and it smells amazing and then overpowering, but she's excited. When it's done, she dishes it up into bowls, and I taste mine. It's almost too much, too many flavours going on at one time. I grin at her.

'This is wonderful,' I say, and she's so happy to hear that. We're all served, all eating quickly, as if the food is going to disappear if we don't get to it quickly enough. I notice another bowl on the side, steam coming off the top.

'It's for Rex,' Bess says. 'Do we feed her?'

'Yes,' I say, and I reach for the bowl, to take it over. 'Open the door for me?' I ask, and she nods. She does it slowly, methodically, the heft of the door making her struggle a little. Inside, Rex sits at the back, cowering under her blanket. The cold has been turned off, but she's still feeling it. Her breath comes out in puffs of steam. She shivers.

'I'll hurt you,' she says, her mouth tense, her teeth snapping together between the words. 'You can't keep me here forever.' I hand her the bowl. If only she knew. She takes it, because she thinks that she needs her strength, and I back out.

'Shut it,' I say to Bess. 'She stays locked in there.' Bess doesn't hesitate.

Then it's like that moment never happened. Bess leads the children from the table, takes them to a berth, sits on the floor with them; and she plays just as they do, inventing stories, making up characters, joining in as if this is the easiest thing in the world for her.

'She's adapting well,' Agatha says to me as we stand watching them.

'We all are.' I want her to tell me that I was right. That it is possible to help people.

'You must be tired,' she says.

'Only as tired as you,' I tell her. 'You're doing so much down here.' That makes her laugh. She reaches over and puts her hand on my back, up by my neck. We move together without thinking, like she's hugging me, like when I was young. It's so comforting, and I let my head rest on her shoulder for a second, and I shut my eyes, and I listen to the laughter coming from the kids, and from Bess.

The darkness of the ship means that only glimmers come through on the screens. Only when there's fire somewhere nearby can you see anything, and then it's patchy, grainy and grey. Shapes and movement are pretty much all you get. I can't sleep, so I sit in front of them, and I watch. There's something almost hypnotic about the screens, watching the Lows rampaging, still. We've saved twenty-seven people, if I include Rex. Twenty-seven people – mostly children – who would have been punished, tortured, likely even killed, and now they're safe. I wish it could be more. I wish that I could save every single person here. But I can't, I know that. I'm more powerless than I would like.

On the screen I watch somebody struggling to get away from a lone Low, watch as they kick out, as the Low reaches for them, swipes a knife, misses, but doesn't give up. It's a constant pursuit that won't end until something more drastic happens. Maybe taking Rex out of the equation was a good first step, but that's all it was. There's still so much suffering.

'You've been doing something good,' Jonah says. He comes to my side and leans against the wall. I think it's the first time I've seen him looking truly comfortable and relaxed. It doesn't come easily to him. 'It's helped, you know that. You should be proud.'

'I don't know about that,' I reply, 'it's more that it's the right thing to do. My mother told me to do what was right.'

'Agatha says that she also told you to be selfish.'

'The two can't coexist. I had to pick one.' I smile at him. 'She also told me to not die. That one I'm planning on sticking to.'

'I wish that I'd known her.'

'She would have liked you,' I tell him. 'She liked faith. She always said that it was good to believe in something, whatever that was. That's the Lows' problem: they only believe in themselves, only believe in power. That's why—' I nearly tell him what I did; about the part I played in my mother's death; about my being complicit in it. I haven't thought about that in so long. Feels like a lifetime ago, that night in our berth, holding the knife . . . The guilt I feel about that act, which now has been somehow replaced by something else entirely.

He asks me something. I don't hear it. I'm picturing my mother, and her final few moments.

'What?'

'Do you have faith?' he asks again.

'I believe in this,' I say, looking around the room. 'I believe in us here, and now.' I watch him reach his hand to his neck, to rub at the skin there. It's rough but healed, no longer the sore red that it was before. 'I think it's the same as what you believe in, really. Something good.'

'I don't know what to believe,' he says. 'Everything was lies, wasn't it? Why we're here, who we are. We're not blessed. We're not ascending. We're drifting.' He smiles, but it's not coming from happiness; more like acceptance. 'There's nothing left.'

On the screens, I see another kid, just a fragment of a tiny shape, crawling around somewhere on the thirty-fourth floor, in the Low section. Maybe they're the child of a Low; maybe they've been kidnapped. I don't know either way, but they're scared, scrabbling around, trying to escape something that I can't see.

'I should go,' I say. I pull the zip up on my suit, adjust the hood onto my head.

'Do you want me to come?' he asks.

'It's fine,' I say. 'I'll be back soon enough.' And then, as I'm leaving the room, as the door to the kitchen is open, this small control room flooded with light, he grabs my arm, gently, holding me. I turn and look at him.

'I believe in you,' he says.

I've never felt like this before, like my skin is singing where he touched me as I go to the hatch, up into the Pit, climbing out; as I save the little girl and bring her back, telling her that it's okay, that she can stop crying now. And then seeing him there when I towel the blood from her face, waiting for me. Smiling.

When I go to my room, Mae isn't there. She's in the next room over, with a couple of the other kids. They're all curled up on the bed, holding each other. That's better for her, I think. I pull the door shut behind me as I leave them in the darkness. I want to be alone with this new thing that I'm feeling, anyway.

I hear screaming, and it makes its way into my dreams, so that I'm not sure if the noise is real or a part of whatever's happening to me as I sleep. Everything slips into everything else.

But it persists, and I'm pulled awake by it, so I throw myself out of bed and rush to the door. The screaming is from everybody – adults and children both – and full of panic and danger. Something is happening now. My door won't open. It's shut, somehow, locked tight. I struggle with the handle, but it doesn't move, so I beat on the door with my hands.

'Please!' I shout, hoping that somebody will hear me. There's the sound of struggling. They've found us, I think. I have to be out there. I hear the voice of a little girl – Mae, I know that it's Mae – and, out of nowhere, a scream, louder than anything I've ever heard. A scream so terrible that it's terrifying: it echoes everywhere.

After that, there's only the faint rumble of the hatch door opening and closing; and then silence. No more voices. Just a hush.

I hit the door harder, throwing my shoulder into it, but it doesn't give; so I take up my striker, and I beat the handle with it, over and over. Eventually the handle snaps, showing me the insides of the door, and I reach in, pulling the lock mechanism back. There's a click, and I pull it open.

I see Agatha. She's on the floor, blood pooled around her. Jonah is holding her, pressing his hands to her side. His hands are soaked red.

She looks at me, her eyes flitting closed, rolling back. 'Rex,' she says. Just that. Jonah presses her chest.

'Help me,' he says. But I can only stand there. On the carpet around them are the footsteps that Rex left on her retreat.

'I have to get her,' I say.

'You can't, not yet,' Jonah tells me. 'She's got Mae.'

Bess betrayed us. While we slept, she crept into the kitchen and she opened that door, and she let Rex free. I trusted her. I was an idiot. Bess helped Rex down the corridor – the wet footprints from the floor of the freezer attest to that – and then they took Mae. When Agatha tried to stop them, Rex stabbed her: the blade I decided to leave Rex with went right into her gut.

But they didn't kill me. They could have come into my room and slit my throat and left me there to bleed out, letting the Lows into this place to take it for their own. But they didn't.

She wants me to suffer, I'm sure of it. I'm not going to give her the pleasure.

I storm into the control room, to the screens, and I flick through them, trying to find out where they've gone. Jonah stands behind me as I touch the screens, as I make them turn to other views of the ship. I need to find them. No choice.

'Chan,' Jonah says, and he reaches for me again. I swat his hand away from my arm.

'Don't,' I tell him.

'She's in trouble,' he says, and then – realising he needs to clarify – 'Agatha.'

'She'll be fine,' I tell him. 'She's always fine.'

'Not this time,' he says to me, and I hit the screen I'm cycling through harder, faster, smacking it with the palm of my hand so hard that the glass breaks, and the picture behind it disappears

My hand bleeds. On the cracked screen, there's a black background, and three words at the top, blinking in white. *Rebooting, Please Wait*, it says. *Please Wait*, like this is any time for patience.

'You need to go to her,' he tells me.

'Then you find them,' I say, pointing at the screens. 'Please.' He nods, and I go out, through the kitchen. Everybody's waiting there, quiet as they've ever been. Rex escaped; the Lows will know where we are, and they will come for us, for this place.

But first there's Agatha, and I only have to take one look at her, lying on the bed in her berth, to know that she's dying, and that there's nothing I can do to save her.

AGATHA

Your mother and I stopped talking for a while. That didn't just happen once, of course. We argued; everybody argues. We always forgave each other. There were only two times that I didn't think that we would.

The first was shortly after I killed the guards. I killed them all, even the older one that I spared at first. But there's something else you don't know about what I found down here, Chan. The guards got women from the ship pregnant, and they took their babies. I don't know how long they had been doing it for, but I knew that they would never do it again.

There was another baby down there, older than you, by maybe a year or so. He – it was a boy, bruised and clearly not cared for, not in the right ways – was so quiet he barely made a sound when I picked him up. I couldn't leave him to die. I didn't know where he came from, whose child he was, and that didn't matter. He needed help, and I could give it to him. I could find somewhere for him to be, so I took him back to your mother. I fought my way through the Pit with him, and I felt sick, climbing up the ship, trying to protect this one who was alive, when the last time I had done the trip it had been with the corpse of the poor child we used to fool your father. It's hard to travel Australia with a baby. Your mother didn't really leave her berth, not for the first year or so you were alive; and then you were strapped to her back, clinging onto her clothes and hair for dear life. But she was a natural with babies. I wasn't. I never have been.

I thought, for a second, of keeping him for myself, but I knew that I couldn't care for him, not in the way that your mother cared for you. I watched her, when I finally reached the floor she lived on: feeding you, making faces at you. The love that she felt, Chan. It was so obvious, so evident. I didn't feel that for this baby.

I thought that I would resent him. This little thing that would take my time, my strength. And I wanted to protect your mother, and you. He would stop that. And if I gave him to your mother . . . Well, that was another mouth to feed. Another body to defend.

So I climbed again. I went up further, up to the highest points of the ship. To the Pale Women—

Wait. Let me finish.

They took some persuading, let me tell you. It was not easy for them, to accept that taking him was for the best. But I persuaded them: that he was pure, that he could be shaped. There, at least, he would be safe.

You know the rest of that story, and how it goes.

I didn't tell your mother, not at first. She was so busy with you. Later, when I told her what I had done – that the boy had gone to them – we argued more fiercely than we ever *would again. (At least, until the day that she told me that she was dying, and what she wanted you to do.) She told me that I was irresponsible, that I had cursed the baby to a life of abnormality, an upbringing that couldn't be predicted. She told me that I should have given him to her. She was a mother, she would have brought him up. I had never been a mother, she told me. She used it like a weapon, that I didn't have those feelings, so I couldn't possibly understand. But looking at you, I'm not sure that she was right. I could feel that love. I did feel it, for your mother and for you: only for you two.*

So I left. For weeks, I was alone.

One day, she came to find me.

'You did what you thought was right,' she said. 'That's true, isn't it?' And it was true, Chan. I thought that it was right: for me, for her, for you. And she wept, and I wept, and we were friends again, closer than ever before.

Years later, she told me that she was dying: that the coughing, the blood, that was all leading her towards a single end. There was no chance to change that. She told me her plan, that you would be the one to kill her. That, by doing it, she might be able to create a new story: using the smoke pellets that we had, the belief that the people here have in ghosts and nightmares. She might be able to make them stay away from you. She could use her final moments to keep you safe forever.

I loved her, and that was what she wanted from me. It was the final act of looking after her, as I had been doing her entire life. So I agreed, and I helped you.

And now she's gone, and you're left. You're all that's left of her; and I love you, just as I loved her.

TEN

Agatha coughs. Australia is full of truths, and this is one of them: an injury like hers can't be recovered from. Her breathing drops away in stages: first quieter, then drawn, scratching her throat like a Low.

Then it stops. *She* stops.

The door opens and Jonah comes in. He's still covered in her blood, his hands stained. He hasn't cleaned them, and I don't know that he's even noticed. 'I've watched the screens,' he says, 'and I can't find them.' He looks at Agatha, and his face changes. I can see that he doesn't want to ask.

'She's gone,' I say, and I stand up and push past him. There's no time for mourning. 'We need to find Mae,' I say.

I pull my suit on while he flicks through the screens, touching them almost too gently. The one that I broke has come back, a pretty background there now instead of the video feed: a mountain, grass, a lake. It's almost ridiculous, this beautiful image. But it's not here. It's got nothing to do with us.

'She's nowhere,' he says, 'or there's something missing.

Some parts we can't see.' He points to sections where the view of the ship is totally blank, where there's nothing but darkness. Maybe some day I'll tell him his story. When we're quite past this. When he can be distracted. That day isn't today.

Our stories are something we make for ourselves, not something we're born into. 'The broken screen,' I say, 'Is it working again? We need to find them.'

'I don't know.' He reaches for it and touches it, but nothing happens. There are three smaller symbols on the screen, at the base of the mountain: a light bulb, a black circle and a white circle. I point to the first: the light bulb. 'Try that,' I say, and he presses it.

The lights flick off down here, all along the corridor, in the kitchen, in every berth. The children scream. We're only lit by the screen, the two of us. I reach out and press it again, and everything comes right back. The screaming stops.

'Try the next one,' I tell him. He presses the black circle and the screen instantly changes. The mountain scene is replaced by a list. Reading it, it looks as though every part of the ship is named: Sections I through to VI; floors 1 to 91. Other parts are listed too: *Base, Arboretum, Exterior.*

And then one final one, at the bottom of the list: *Earth.*

I press the button.

The planet clicks into view. I've never seen a planet before. There are no windows on Australia, no view of the stars. We know that they're out there, because we were told. We know that we're travelling from system to system, searching for a new home, because that's what they told us. Those are the oldest stories.

We were lied to; I know that now. This is a prison. There was no flood. Earth is the same as it ever was. They just put our ancestors on this ship and sent us into space.

The planet on the screen is a sphere of green and blue and white, so close that it's almost touchable. It's so clear.

I press the button for the exterior, and I see it, what I know to be Australia herself: a lumpen metal mass in a muddy red-brown colour, covered in white rungs – like ladders – around the outside. And behind the ship is that same planet, white swirls over all the other colours.

I look closely. It must be a picture, I tell myself, to remind the guards where they came from. But it's not. As we stand there watching, I realise that I can see movement. Stars, winking into life as the planet moves across space, as the bulk of the ship moves across the screen: in the distance, the blinking of other distant objects in the sky. And further away, the sun. I've never seen it, but I've had it described to me. This isn't a picture.

We're seeing the outside of the ship.

The ship is outside Earth, right there, right next to it.

And we've been here the whole time.

Beneath it all, underneath the image, there's a new button on the screen. Another button, featuring a single word, a word that we've been looking for the whole time: but here it's not just a definition, not just a location, but also an instruction. I know that pressing it will do something.

Home, it says.

PART

THREE

ELEVEN

I don't bother trying to keep my movements hidden as I push my way out of the Pit. Being up and out here will be easier, I decide, than trying to decipher those screens. This is how it would have been for me before I knew about what was below the Pit; how it's always been here for us. Somebody wrongs you, and you find them in the darkness; and then you deal with them.

The ship feels empty, even though there are still people living. So many abandoned berths, or people hiding to make them look abandoned. The Bells, the Pale Women, all dead. The Lows are all in the arboretum, Rex with them. And Mae. Jonah finally found them on the screens while I stared at the Earth, absorbing that last horrible truth. I saw Mae, Bess clinging to her. They were out in the open. There were torches all around. They wanted me to find them. I don't know how many of the Lows are waiting for me. I never knew. Rex built an army, and she took what she wanted. The ship is hers. Even when I took her prisoner, they didn't believe that she was dead.

I'll worry about her later. For now, I have to focus on Mae.

I wonder, as I climb up to the arboretum, how they would react if they knew about the lie. If they knew how close to home – a real home – they actually are. I wonder what they would do then.

I crouch on the edge of the gantry and look over into the arboretum. They're crowded inside, nestled amongst the burnt trees and blackened remains of the bushes. The Lows are cheering and jeering and calling out in angry voices. Their breathing seems to happen as one: this long, gravelly inhale; then the same sound pushing back out again. Rex stands in the middle of them all, her one hand raised up, rallying them. She shouts something that I can't hear. I don't need to.

Mae is there, next to Bess. It's hard to make her out at first, and then I see her outline through the goggles: a small glow of green, held tight, Bess's hands on her shoulders. She must be terrified. It makes my heart hurt to imagine how scared she must be.

I start to creep along one of the gantries that leads to the arboretum, taking it slowly. None of them are looking towards me, which is good. If they saw me, if they attacked now, I'm not sure I'd survive. All the other Lows want me dead. But Rex wants something else. She didn't kill me down below. She wanted me to know that she escaped; to see what she had done to Agatha. But that can't be all. She could have held my head while it happened, made me watch Agatha die.

As I get closer, I see that she's sent Lows up onto the bracers at the top of the arboretum. I can't see what they're doing, but it can't be good.

Then Rex screams, and the Lows disperse. They run in every direction, towards me, across the gantries, towards all the other parts of the ship. I'm quick, faster than I knew I could be, and I leap over the edge of the gantry I'm on and swing down underneath it, using every muscle in my arms to hold on. They won't look for me under the gantry; they can't see me here, I know. They thunder across, shaking the bridge. I hold on. I wrap my arms through the metal, hook my feet in. I'm not going anywhere, not without Mae. As soon as the noise stops I'm back up, back to my feet, and running.

Mae is there, and Bess, and Rex. Rex doesn't see me, not until I'm on top of them; not until I've got Mae in my hands, until I've slammed a fist into Bess's face, until I'm running as fast as I can, Mae clinging onto me. But holding her slows me down.

I can't worry about that. I keep running.

I feel something slam into my back. Rex has caught me, but all I can feel is her blade: it's sharp, hard, digging in; and then I'm falling, face first, right down into the soil. I can't breathe, and I can't see, and I can't move. Mae screams, and I let her go, because I can't hold her any more. And then Rex is in front of me, and she plants her feet into the soil near my face. She treads onto my shoulder, and the pain isn't like anything I've known. It's roaring inside my flesh and bones, hot and cold at the same time, stinging and yet strangely dulled. She pulls something out of me: my mother's knife, still stuck fast into what's left of her arm; the same knife that, I know, took Agatha's life. That same knife has taken the life of two of the most important people in my world. Only Mae and Jonah have been spared so far.

'I knew that you would come,' she says, pushing her foot down on the wound. I struggle, trying to fight back. She kicks me over, presses down on my chest, grinding the hole in my back into the ground. From here, I can only see upwards. My vision swims, but I can make out the top of the arboretum, where it's connected to the roof of Australia: the fixtures that it's hanging from, the bits where it's plugged in and fastened to the rest of the ship. From here, it's so delicate. And even in the dark, I can see some Lows hanging from the metal that keeps it up. They have equipment, welding tools, taken from the weapon makers and the Shopkeepers. They clamber, like spiders, moving around, putting their tools to use. The sparks fly, lighting their faces in the darkness. That's how I see them.

I know what they're doing.

The arboretum could have grown back. We could have cared for it, nurtured it, fixed the lights and brought it back. But they won't let that happen.

Instead, they'll use it as a weapon; something to beat down the door of our new home. I watch them as they work on the girders, on the joists, taking their blowtorches and saws and weapons. And the arboretum creaks. It shakes beneath me. Cutting through the supports will take them a while, I know – the metal is thick and strong, designed to withstand far more than a few Lows with basic tools – but they'll get there. What Rex wants, she gets, and she wants the arboretum to fall. What happens when it reaches the bottom of the ship, I don't know. It will slam into the Pit. It will crash through, most likely. Maybe it will kill everybody I've saved, everyone down below, by crushing them. Or maybe worse. Maybe it will punch through the hull of the ship itself.

I don't know what happens if the ship is torn apart.

I'm guessing that it's nothing good.

Rex kicks my shoulder again, and the pain brings tears to my eyes. I choke them back. I watch as she reaches down to pick up Mae, who struggles as much as she can. Rex is too strong. She squeezes her arm, and Mae squeals. 'She comes with me,' Rex says. 'How about I don't kill her? How about I bring her up, just like me.' She says that, but there's no bite to it. In that moment, it's almost sadness, I think. She aims the knife directly over me, pointed right at my face. 'This went into the old woman so easily,' she says, 'and it only took one try to finish her. But she was soft. You? You're harder. I wonder how many times I'll have to use it on *you*.'

She pulls her arm back, ready to strike. I shut my eyes, expecting blackness; the nothing that comes after. I want to make it come easier.

I expect, for just a moment, a fraction of a moment, to see my mother. Like the Pale Women said, when you die, you go to somewhere else and see everyone you loved in life.

Instead, I hear Mae cry. I open my eyes, and she's pulling at Rex's arm, holding onto it, to stop the attack. Rex turns, slaps Mae with her good hand. The little girl falls backwards, but it's worked. Rex is distracted.

'Maybe first you should watch me kill everything you care about,' she says. She's hesitating; something's made her rethink this. She grabs me by my head, her hand trying to get purchase on my hair, but she can't quite take hold. She kicks me to the side, booting at my shoulder over and over, making me howl. I try to crawl away from her, towards the edge, and she grabs Mae from the ground and pulls her close. 'Watch her!' she screams to someone else, but I can barely even hear her over Mae's howling. I'm barely awake, the pain is so intense. Bess rushes to Rex, pleads with her.

'Don't,' she says, 'don't, don't.' Rex pushes her backwards and she falls, then scrabbles forward, begging, pawing at Mae, at Rex's legs.

'No,' I say. I push myself to my knees. Rex is wheezing. She's still hurting from before, from being in the freezer.

She bends down and slashes at me, Mae's face close to mine. The knife cuts my cheek and I feel warm blood running down the side of my face.

Don't die.

I see the blood drop down onto the charred ground. I hear the arboretum creaking. She'll kill everybody, condemn us all, pass a death sentence without even knowing the truth about our lives, all because of what? Because she can?

But then, I think, why do we do anything? I thought I knew, but I don't.

Then I see him. Jonah. Jonah's here.

He runs for us all, leaps, throws something down. A smoke pellet. It engulfs us, and I hear him struggle with Bess. I don't see what happens through the grey, but then she's running, away from us, back to the main part of the ship. He could have killed her, and he didn't. He spared her.

Rex struggles through the smoke. I see her flailing limbs pushing it away, as she backs away to get out of it. But

Jonah's fast, and he can see where she can't; and he snatches Mae away from her; and then he's gone, back into the smoke, and she screams again.

This is my chance. I push myself to my feet with my good arm, leaving the injured shoulder to recover as much as it can, and I throw myself into Rex's back, all my weight onto her. She's physically stronger than I am, but it surprises her, and I wrap my arm around her face, tightening it as much as I can.

'Get Mae out of here!' I scream, wrestling with Rex. I shift my arm, down to her throat. Her breathing is worse now, choking out of her in hard gasps. She kicks back at me. My mother's knife, where her hand once was, flails, trying to find a part of me to cut. She can't. I watch Jonah scoop up Mae, and I pull harder at her throat.

She's seconds away. I just have to keep holding on, then she'll be gone.

Jonah is watching, waiting for me; and so is Mae. I can't let her see me kill Rex. I need her to believe that life isn't just death and revenge. I would let Rex go, but I can't. The war would end another way if I did. She's ceaseless, and she's had too many chances. I have to end it, I know that, but it doesn't mean I want Mae to see it.

'Go!' I shout, and Jonah nods. He knows what I have to do. I wait until they're gone, down the gantry. The Lows above us are still working on loosing the arboretum, too high up to know that we're fighting to end it all. I just need to be faster than them. I'll deal with Rex, and then we'll leave. We'll get below the Pit and hit the home button before they cut the arboretum down. *Home.*

247

Then she gets me, catches me with the edge of the blade, scraping it along my arm. It cuts through the fabric, down to the skin. It hurts, but not enough to stop me, not now. Still, I flinch, and my grip loosens, and she wriggles away. She's breathing badly, heaving in air that she can't quite seem to hold, and coughing as it leaves her. But she's on her feet, and she's staggering backwards.

'You can't kill me,' she says.

'I can try,' I tell her.

We're both too tired to keep fighting, but that doesn't matter. She swings at me and I dodge her. She kicks out and I slam my striker – I was able to find it, in the moment she was gasping for breath – into her leg. Her blade clashes with my striker over and over, as I try to get close enough to her to inflict the necessary damage.

We've both been doing this – *surviving* – for too long. We're both pretending that we have more left to give than we do. I scrape her with the stick, and she flinches as the blue flames rip across her skin. She cuts me with her blade, tearing through the outer layer of my suit. She kicks me in the shins; as I falter, I whip back and smash the point of my good elbow into the side of her head. I move back towards a burnt-out tree, then pull myself up it and leap over her head, landing a few feet away with a jar that makes my shoulder ache, my scratches sting and my wounds bleed; and then I run, to get some distance between us. Breathing room.

'Why can't you kill me?' she asks, as if she wants that; as if she's daring me to, taunting me. 'Little girl, why can't you kill me?' She is hardly older than me, and yet this is how she sees me: as a child. She sucks in air, wheezes and then runs towards me. We go at each other again, slashing and bashing and bruising. I notice that, every time she connects with her hand-blade, she winces. Her stump must be infected. And I know that it's the blade; one final way that my mother is somehow managing to help me. Thanks to the infection, it hurts her to hurt me. The pain doesn't stop her, not yet, but I can use it against her. My bad arm doesn't work as I want it to. I can move it, but only barely. The blood has spread, I know, and I can feel its dampness soaking my suit, pressed against my skin.

She pushes forwards, jabbing the knife out, and I dodge; but she's expecting that. She swipes the knife back the other way as fast as she can, slamming it into my shoulder, right where she stabbed me before; another hole, widening the first.

I've never felt pain like it. She pulls herself closer to me, right up next to me.

'You have ruined everything,' she whispers, and her voice, her manner, is so cold. I see her hatred in her eyes, and in the honesty of her words. She wriggles her blade-hand, drives it deeper into my flesh. I scream. 'But you couldn't kill me.'

I drop suddenly to my knees, the knife still deep in my shoulder, wrenching her wrist down and pulling her off balance. I sense my advantage and snap left, bending her wrist with me. She tries to brace, to regain her balance, but she can't. I feel the snap of her wrist breaking as the knife is wrenched in my shoulder. The pain is nearly unbearable. She howls, and I lurch to my feet. I kick back at her, and she falls away. The blade pulls out of my body; I can barely feel the pain now. After that sharp spike, it's fading.

I turn to face her, my striker held aloft. She lies on the ground, clutching her arm. White bone is protruding through her thin skin. I stagger over to her. She turns and starts to crawl, pulling herself away from me. I bend down and take her ruined arm, the stump, my mother's blade, and I grab the hilt of it in my hand. 'This is going to hurt,' I say, and I pull the blade out, yanking it from the wound, from the bindings that hold it in place. Black blood spurts out onto my hands, onto the knife. Beneath, I can see that the flesh is blackened with rot, and the smell of it rises, hitting my nostrils like the worst stench of the Pit. The infection will take her whole arm; probably, at this point, her life. The fact that she's going to die is pretty much inevitable. If I don't kill her, the rot will.

I take my mother's knife and I kneel down, ready. Prepared. One short, sharp push, up into her skull. That's the fastest, cleanest way. Agatha told me that once.

I press the blade against her skin. She keeps her head perfectly steady.

'Now kill me,' she snarls. 'Show me that you can. Kill me.' She wants me to, and too much. It's all that she's got, now: being defeated.

'No,' I say. 'You're already done.' She is in so much pain. She's devastated, ruined. I do not need to lower myself to murder.

Agatha was right, in the end. You can make your own story. And this is my story. You can be better than them.

I stand and throw the knife away, and walk off.

'I know where you are!' she screams. 'I will come and find you, and I will kill you! I will heal, and I will come for you, Chan, daughter of Riadne!'

'You can try,' I say. But I'll be somewhere else. I hear her screaming my name as I walk away, but I know that the war is over.

It has to be over.

Looking up, as I get to the gantry, away from the remains of the arboretum – where I spent some of my happiest moments, the only place of tranquility on this whole ship – I see that Rex's Lows are nearly done. They don't know what's happened, and they're too far in to stop. The orange sparks of their work fly off around them, and I can see the metal splitting: giant jaws of jagged iron starting to tear themselves wide. I can hear the metal groaning, and feel the ship shaking. Won't be long, and we can't be here when it happens.

I'm running to the gantry when suddenly something gives. The arboretum shifts, tilts. I slip, falling backwards, land on my shoulder, howl, cry out. I start sliding, going down. The gantry wrenches away from the fixtures that hold it in place on the berth floors, a scream of metal as it tugs itself apart. The whole arboretum is shifting, pulling away from the sections of the ship. I fall, slip, slide; managing to hook my fingers into the grated iron of the floor at the edge of the arboretum, my good arm holding me as the whole thing tilts.

I look up. One of the Lows made it through their support, splitting apart the metal, and the other bracing struts have buckled. They creak and moan, the same moans that Australia has always made, but a million times louder. The Lows fall, colliding with the floor of the arboretum, bouncing off the slope and tumbling down into the Pit below.

I watch them go. I can't see Rex, but I know that she'll be taken along with all the other detritus. I can't worry about her.

The whole thing shifts slightly, dropping a foot, creaking and moaning. I need to move, I know, and fast.

It must have seemed like such a good idea to give us all of this: these trees, these plants, this water. I can imagine the creators of this prison, thinking that this was in some way being kindly. A garden is a simulation of nature. They were giving us something that we would miss from our lives. But it's never been that. It was always just another story. And now? Now, it's collapsing, tearing itself down. The trees are uprooting themselves; the water is spilling from the river, rushing over the dead ground, washing away the burnt remains of the plants and fruit and crops that we were growing; and the earth is falling out in clumps of sodden char.

And me. I'm there, hanging on to the edge as the arboretum starts to fall apart. Chunks of earth, water and plants fly down, tumble off, nearly hitting me. I have to get off this, I know, or something will take me, and I'll be done. I watch the detritus fall down, past me, into the Pit. It suddenly doesn't seem as far to fall as it once did before.

I look behind me, and I can see the creaking remains of

the part where the gantry once fitted on section IV. It's far, but I might be able to reach it. If I swing out enough, if I can get enough force when I push off.

I've never jumped that far before; but I guess I've never had to.

Three. Two. One.

I push off, kicking away, forcing myself into the air, letting go of the edge as I reach for the other side.

It's only when I'm in the air that I realise I don't know if I can make it. And I think, then this is it. This is how I break the promise that I made to my mother.

Then my arm hits something, and I hook it as well as I can. It's the forty-sixth floor, the railing along the edge of the gantry. I feel my shoulder – my good shoulder – pop, the bone slipping from the socket. The noise is almost as powerful as the pain. But I can't stop to think about it. As I haul myself up and over, suddenly safe – as safe as you can be, here – I look back, and I see that the water is hurling itself down now, pouring off and down into the Pit. It isn't stopping. I don't know how much water there is in the systems, but it's not done yet. Australia is flooding.

I start to move, heading to a stairwell. Fastest route down, no stopping. I can't afford to. My shoulder is dislocated, but I can fix that; Agatha taught me how, back when I was a kid. I take a run at a wall, hurling myself at it to try and fix it; to get enough force to pop my shoulder back into place.

The first attempt burns with pain, worse even than the knife hole in my other shoulder.

The second time – when I open my mouth, and scream as

I do it, because that feels like it'll give me some extra burst of strength, maybe, just enough – it works. Thud, clunk: this shoulder feels like it's going to burst, but it works again.

One day I won't be in perpetual pain, I tell myself. One day soon, all of this – the fighting, the hurt, the ship – will all be over.

I start to climb down, faster than I think I've ever climbed before. I hope that Jonah and Mae made it down before the water started. I hope that they're safe inside the ship. I picture the button on that screen: the temptation of our destination; and that pushes me, faster and faster. The arboretum tears itself apart, the pieces falling as the structure rocks and creaks. I can hear the Pit filling.

So I begin dropping floors as much as possible, covering as much ground as I can without killing myself each floor I go down. I can't use my arms properly – my bleeding shoulder is nearly useless, and the other hurts when I do too much – but I know that I have to get to the bottom of the ship before it's too flooded for me to make my way to the hatch; and then back, to Jonah, to Mae, and to that big button that is going to take us home.

By the time that I get down to the Pit, it's a mess: bits of the arboretum piled up, water that's run down making the level of the mulch rise to nearly lap up against the first floor. And it's getting deeper. It's too deep to wade through easily now, that much is clear. I run to the edge of the gantry and look out, over the flooded Pit. Anybody left – Lows, free people, whoever – they're panicking. People are swarming up the stairwells even as I climb down, and there are fresh bodies in the water: Lows fallen from the higher levels and lost to it.

But this is just the start. Sooner or later, the parts of the arboretum will stop falling, and then it's only a matter of time before the rest of the structure follows. Above, I can see it creaking, swinging, shaking on its moorings.

Even if it doesn't break the ship in two, the loss of the arboretum would be fatal to whoever's left on the ship. No fresh food, no fresh water, only this bloody diseased mess in the Pit to drink. Being here, without those things . . . That's a death sentence. Even the people who sent our ancestors into space weren't that cruel.

I look up at the ship that is my home, all I've ever known, and see that everybody around me on these floors – whoever they are, Frees and Lows alike – is looking down at me. They don't want to die.

They watch me. Faces, all the way up the ship, as far as I can see. Fires burn in every section, seemingly on every floor. We're lit up again, as bright as we've ever been.

I stand on the edge of the gantry, and I let them watch me. I shout, because I have to, because I can't just leave this be.

'There's a way off this ship,' I yell, 'a way to get somewhere safe. Follow me.' I let my voice echo up, the flood making it sound like it's spoken from underwater somewhere. But it carries. It reaches a few of them, and they spread the word. They start coming, then, another flood, this time of people.

And then it all gets so much worse.

*   *   *

The arboretum squeals, a terrible noise of metal grinding against itself, and it shifts again. Another support strut gone, and now the arboretum is hanging almost vertically, a plate balancing on its side. There's a creak, and then something else in the air above me: darker, heavier, solid, coming right down.

It's a tree, bigger than anything that's fallen before. This is one of the hard-rooted trees, the bigger ones. Maybe you would survive a smaller one colliding with you. This one? Not a chance.

It falls faster than I can see, and it smacks into the surface of the Pit, creating waves that crash across the gantry where I'm standing. The roots jut upwards, like fingers reaching out.

After that, everything is chaos: every other bit of the arboretum follows it, everything that used to be fixed in and secure, spilling into the dirty black water of what used to be the Pit.

No time. No time. I slip into the water, grabbing the side. It's high enough that it's over my head, and I have to paddle my arms and stand on sunken debris and crane my neck to even hope to keep my face above it. I don't know what I'm doing. I pull my mask onto my face and put my head under-water, and I can see almost perfectly. I try and push myself down, deeper, pulling myself with my hands. It's hard, the water denser than I thought it could be, and I can't get any-where; so I go back, and I use the sides.

Something grabs me, and I panic, looking up. I see them, through the water: a person. I don't know from here if they're a Low or not, and I don't care. They grab my ankle, and I reach up, and I take their hand. They pull on me, tugging my bad arm, because they're scared of the water. But I see them take another hand, forming a chain of people, and I tell them to take a breath if they're too short to stand, to cling onto others to help them, to pass the message along. I heave myself face-first into the water, down to the bottom; and then I find the floor, and I do exactly the same, treating it like rungs. I've climbed this ship my entire life, and I've gotten good at this: hauling my weight on hand and footholds. I go for the middle, for the hatch. I can see the lever.

More. More. I worry that the people behind me will get swallowed; that they won't hold their breath properly when they need to dive down to get out of here. The Lows, especially, can't breathe well as it is. But they have to manage. This can't all be on me.

The ship is useless, I tell myself. If they stay here, they'll die.

So I do what I can.

I push down, to the hatch. I struggle. It's chaos here, worse than it's ever been. We could die in this. We could drown. This could be our ending; but I won't let it be. Not now, not after all we've been through.

I find the lever, and I pull it as hard as I can, and I wait. There's no vibration, no rumble of it working, of the hatch opening.

It's as dead as everything else on this ship

It must be the water. The flooding. I don't know what to do. I'm stuck. I can breathe but they can't. These people are stuck. I try to not panic, because then they'll all panic.

I pull myself back to the surface and look around, and I see a chain of desperate faces, leading up and out of the water, all holding onto each other in desperation and terror.

For this moment we're unified.

I take the hand of the man behind me. 'You have to help me,' I say, 'we've got to pull this open. Take a deep breath.' I drag him underwater and guide his hands to the door in the floor, and I put his fingers around it. I do the same for the next man, and the woman behind him. We crowd around, all of us, as many as can fit, and we pull. I don't have to tell them to do it, they just know.

It starts to give.

The water will flood down if this works. It'll pour into the area down below. But if I'm fast, I can . . . *We* can stop it. Maybe it won't flood. Maybe it won't . . . Maybe there are sluices, something like that. There must be measures.

If I've called this wrong, I'm not just killing us. I'm killing Mae, and Jonah, and everybody else that I saved.

Don't die.

I've called this wrong.

I wave my hand for the people to stop, but they don't. It's too late. The hatch is nearly up, more metal being torn apart.

It opens, and still they don't stop. They're going to drown, struggling under this water, and desperate. They all know how bad it is. The door is wrenched off, tossed aside.

Underwater, everything moves like it's been slowed down. The chamber, big enough for one, a squeeze for two, fills immediately, and they start going to work on the bit below, wrenching that second door open as well; kicking it in, forcing their way. Suddenly I'm being sucked in, pulled along with the water as it goes. We're all dragged in; everything flows downwards.

The water rushes through the corridor, and makes it hard to run. I see Jonah in the kitchen as the mulch burbles around our feet. He's holding Mae, and she lights up when she sees me, grinning. He notices my shoulder.

'You're hurt,' he says, before saying anything about the flood, or asking about Rex. Noticing that before anything else.

'It'll keep,' I say. 'We need to do something.' I wade through to the control room. 'People are coming down,' I say, 'you'll have to help them.'

'Who?'

'Whoever. Australia's finished. They need somewhere to go.' He turns back and looks down the corridor. 'The water's coming. Find a way to stop it,' I tell him, and he nods. He's about to go when he stops. He turns and looks at me, right into my eyes. He's so different from when I met him. I can see all of him now; every part of who he is. Or, who he wants to be. I don't know.

'You did the right thing,' he says, and then he's gone. I realise that I didn't tell him that I didn't kill her. He thinks that I would kill her, that I wouldn't have spared her life. He thinks that's who I am.

But then I see the screens, and that he's got the arboretum camera up on one of them. It's tilted and broken, at an angle that I have to bend my neck to understand, but then I see that it's pointed right at where we were; right to where I spared Rex's life.

He saw me let her live, and dear gods – if there are such things – that's a relief.

On the other screens, I can see the people trying to get into the water, to get into the ship. The water down here beats around my waist, higher by the second. Bloody water, infiltrating this place that was meant to be safe, that was meant to be secure. Somewhere different, not quite ruined yet by the rest of Australia. And now it is. Now, we're nearly ready to leave. The people outside get into the water still, and they flail and froth the surface, and they avoid the still-falling debris from up above them. They dive down, trying to find a way to get away; to get home.

'Come on,' I say, 'come on.' I stride out and grab Mae from the kitchen counter, hauling her up onto me. She touches my wound and I don't flinch.

'It doesn't hurt?' she asks.

'It will,' I say. 'But not yet.' Time for that when we're out of here: when we're safe. We watch the screens together, as the water rises higher, up to my chest, and they're still coming; and then to my neck, and still, more and more of them. There are so many people here, and I know that I'm going to have to make a decision. I crane my neck, tilting my chin up. People are still climbing into the water, bodies floating. Not everybody making it. They can't.

Don't die.

I look at the screen that shows Earth. It's so perfect, such a perfect sphere.

Home.

I press the button, and I wait to see what it will do.

TWELVE

Nothing happens. Nothing happens. This is like with the hatch, I think: the water has broken whatever was meant to come next. We're all here now, stuck here, and we're going to die in this place.

I shut my eyes. The water creeps higher. It laps against my chest, a wave splashing onto my chin.

I wonder how long my breathing mask will last. I hike Mae up higher and press it against her face.

'Take this,' I say, 'put it into your mouth and breath normally. You have to do this.' I'll be keeping her alive for a little while longer, I think; for all the good that it will do.

And then the noise comes. There is a grinding at first, and then a lower rumble through us all, and we all shake. Then, the blare of some alarm that rings through everything, loud and sharp enough to make us all clutch our hands to our heads, fighting against the water, trying to stay on top of it. I look into the kitchen, now crowded with people, Lows and frees and Shopkeepers and weapon-makers and maybe even surviving Bells and Pale Women and anybody else, everybody who has ever lived here.

Somebody screams. I look at the screens, the ones still showing the rest of Australia. We didn't get everybody. People are still up there, panicking, floundering in the water. Here, the people that I've saved scream and cry, afraid of what's happening. I shout for them all to calm down, but it's pointless, and I get the horrible dark water in my mouth. The children will cry; the adults will be terrified. This only gets better when it's over.

And then the entire room starts to shake, like nothing that I have ever felt, even when the arboretum tipped. It's like the rumbling of the engines, of the whole ship, only closer than ever before, more powerful. It's brutal, shaking my teeth, making the water crash around us. I try to find something to hold onto for support, clutching Mae to keep her head above water. The water splashes up, over our heads, and Mae screams, and the mask falls from her face, into the mess. I lose it, and all I can do now is tell her not to open her mouth.

'It's okay,' I say. 'Don't swallow this water, okay? Just keep your face looking up there.' And I point at the ceiling, and I realise that I can see it vibrating.

'What's happening?' Mae cries. I'm clutching her to my chest. She's heavier than I would like, even though she's light in the water, and my bad arm struggles to hold her. But this is more important than my pain, I think. Giving her comfort now, letting her know that it's going to be alright; even if that's just another story.

'We're leaving here,' I say to her.

'Where are we going?'

I don't get the chance to give her an answer. There's

another rumble, and a creaking; and then we drop, falling slightly, and judder to a halt again. I can't see the screen and have no idea what's happening. The ship could be falling apart. It gets worse, and worse: the rumble, the screaming of the engines. We quake. We thrash in the water, trying to find a way to stay steady, but the waves knock us left and right. The lights go dim and flicker off, leaving only the pale light of the screens to illuminate us. The children are all screaming, their mouths wide in the same terrified O. The floor lurches, and there's a terrible noise, of something uncoupling; like the noise of the arboretum falling, a thud, a crack.

And I know, I just know – in my bones – that we have left the spaceship Australia.

We are thrown around, all of us. I lose my grip on Mae for a second, just a moment, and she tumbles to one side, out of my hands, beating the water desperately. I heave her back, and she's hit her head on something, and there's blood on her face, being washed off almost as soon as I notice it. That's the last time I'll see Australia, I think. All of the things that happened to me there, and as suddenly as a click of the fingers, a spark on a match, we're off, away from that place. We're going somewhere new; and I notice that the water is going down, that there's a wind. No: more than a wind. It's like standing by the turbines, the air generators, at the bits where they suck in the bad air before making it slightly less bad. It sucks, and the water starts going that way.

The wind pulls more, and I panic, because I don't know

what is happening. On the screens, I can see the ship, as this smaller part leaves. I can see the Pit; and I can see where the hatch must have been, the water in the Pit emptied out through where we wrenched the door loose, leaving a hole into nothing. All the mess in there, all the people that are left, they're all being sucked towards it. The picture on the screen is crackly, grainy, harder to see than it once was. But I can't worry about that, not now. There's a hole in our new ship as well. It's tugging at us, too.

In here, the water gushes out, and everybody is still screaming. We're carried along with it. We're pulled out of the room, out of the kitchen, and I desperately throw my arms out, trying to grab hold of anything that'll stay still, that I can use to stop myself. It isn't until we're in the hallways that I manage to grab a doorway, dragged off my feet, holding on with my fingertips, clutching Mae, and she clutches right back. I scream at her to hold on to me, to not let go, whatever happens; and I shout Jonah's name, but I can't see him anywhere, and he wouldn't be able to hear me anyway, not over the noise of everything. Mae is making a noise, but I can barely hear it; it isn't until I look at her face that I see she's screaming, her face buried in my chest. She sounds so far away.

I look down the passage, and I see people being sucked out through the hole where the hatch door was. I don't know how many we'll lose, or what happens when they're out there.

Perhaps this is what the Pale Women meant, when they spoke about ascending.

And then I realise that this isn't where my duty stops. It

doesn't end with my clinging on as the people that I've saved are lost.

I struggle to push Mae up and around the corner of the doorway, into the room, and I scream at her to stay. Here, the pull seems slightly lesser, and I wrench the door – she screams right back, begging me not to leave her, but I have no choice, not now, not after all that's happened – and I tug it shut. I pray that she'll be safe.

Down the passage, people try and block the hole, but they're failing. They're using bodies, I think. It's hard to see, hard to tell exactly what's going on, but there's something happening at the door. So many people there, all trying to stay alive. We need something bigger, something that can cover the hole.

I touch the door that I've trapped Mae behind, and I get an idea.

I let go, and it's like I'm dropping down a level in the ship all over again; clinging to the side of the gantry, doing this for the first time. Crossing my fingers.

I grab the next doorway down the hall. My shoulders – which have taken more than their fair share of pain, these past days – sting, but I work through it. I grab the door, pull myself around. I take my knife from the sheath and start hammering at the hinges with the hilt, smacking them until they buckle and the door starts to shake. I hit them harder and harder, over and over. The first breaks, snapping away from the wall. I start kicking the second, the one lower down, and then bend down. I lose my grip, and I swing around, and I cling to the door.

I am not even close to done yet. When you need it, you get

strength. You find a way to get things done. I press my legs against the frame, and I wrestle with the door, and I wrench it away, pulling the last hinge clean off the wall. It jams in the doorway, being sucked by the hole in the hatch.

'Move!' I scream, down the passageway. 'Move!' But nobody can hear me, so I do what I can. I hold on to the door, and I kick backwards, and I let the air carry us down towards the hole.

I shut my eyes and cross my fingers, and I pray.

Then all is calm. There's no wind, no noise. I wonder, for a second, if I have died, and if I'm going to open my eyes to see somewhere else: somewhere that's like a dream I've never had. But no, I'm still here, in this passageway, in this ship. Around me, people lie, collapsed on the floor. The door that I broke loose is jammed against the hole, juddering slightly, but covering it entirely. It's stopped the wind.

It's not perfect, but it'll do. I rush back down the corridor, treading over struggling and unconscious survivors, and I push open the door to the room that I put Mae in, and I drag her up from the floor, telling her that it's okay, that we're past the worst. I shout Jonah's name, and I look for him, but he's nowhere to be seen.

The floor shakes. I cling to the side, pushing through to the screen room, to see what I can see, if anything.

They all show the same thing: there, in the distance, a red shape, six metal sides. Behind it, space: a blackness punctured with glimmering holes. I know, I just know, that the metal box is Australia. That place was my home. And now? Now it's not.

Then everything rocks. Everything shakes, and the ship we're in starts howling, the engines doing something else. Through the screens, I see something else fill the view: the black fades, replaced by a layer of beautiful pure blue, and then white; and then we're past that. I tell Mae to look at it, to look at the screens.

'Clouds,' I say, something about a story I was told when I was little about what Earth used to be like. I know that these are clouds. The screens are showing us what we've passed, what we've left, not what we're heading towards.

I can feel the ship slowing. We level out, and we all find our feet. We stop having to cling on. 'Wait,' I say, but I don't know who I'm speaking to. Mae stares at the screen with me. She's even more astonished than I am. I wonder, for a second, what we'll see when we get out of this ship: if the stories were somehow true anyway, that Earth is gone and destroyed. Or if the people that abandoned us have carried on just like before, doing whatever it was that they used to do. Living, as we've been deprived of it.

Then I hear the same hiss that we heard when we left Australia. A hiss and a clunk and then grinding, and the craft rocks once more. There's a scream from the children, no doubt thinking that we're starting to fall again, but we don't. We stop.

Down the passageway, the door that I used to block the hole in the hatch falls to the ground.

'We've landed,' I say. My voice cracks, and I can barely find it, but I say it as loudly as I can, to try to reassure those people who are here, who survived. 'We're home.'

* * *

We all swarm the corridor, soaking wet and dripping, though no more than the corridor itself. There's a rush and a push as everybody tries to get close to the hole, to see what happens next. This is all we have ever dreamed of. The story we were told, that we would drift until we found a home: we're now at the end of that.

'It's okay,' I tell Mae, and I shout Jonah's name. I look for him, for that flash of red hair, but I can't see it. I'll find him soon, I tell myself. When we're on land, out of this place, he'll be easy to spot.

He'll be here, and he'll be safe, I'm sure of it. He has to be.

I think that I should say something to everyone: tell them all that we're back on Earth, that the myth was a lie. They don't give me a chance. They struggle through, trying to get to the hatch, to climb the ladder. I stand back. There's time. The Lows in here, the free people, everybody is suddenly united: we're all just people. I don't know how the people out there will take to us: to our group of people who had been stranded, who had been forgotten about. Maybe somebody will remember us.

And I look into the room that was mine once, my new home for such a short time; a new home that everything since spun out of. On the floor, by my bed, I see Jonah's collar: the soft black leather now soaking wet, stretched and pulled, the spikes that hurt him. My gut aches, and I call his name again. I take it, turn it inside out so that the spikes don't jab me, wrap it around my wrist and tie it up. He can't be lost. I know that.

I pull Mae close to me. We look up at the hole where the

hatch was, and see the sky up there: bright blue, lumps of white inside it. The yellow of a sun, brighter than anything I've ever seen, and when I look away from it, my eyes sting, and there are dark spots around everything.

A ladder drops through, made of metal and rope. I stand at the bottom of it and I breathe in, and I taste the air, clean and crisp and so cold that it makes me cough, and I can almost taste it. It's almost so good it's hard to breathe it in.

I put Mae's hands on the rungs of the ladder.

'Go on,' I say.

The air is thin, and it's hard to breathe. Around us, shiny metal structures tower high, reflecting everything in their glass. Reflecting the sun from above us. There are spires and adornments across the top of some of the other buildings; some are blunt. I can see figures on some, the outlines of people watching us. I heave myself up and onto the top of our ship, and I see that we've landed in the middle of a grey area, cold and stark and ugly. And more than that: we're not alone.

Seven figures stand in front of us, on the ground. Their clothes are like nothing we had on Australia: harsh clean white fabric that clings to their bodies. Their faces are shrouded in masks. Their eyes shine through visors. In their hands, they have weapons. I shouldn't be surprised. They didn't know what they would find with us, I suppose.

One of them steps forward. 'Line up,' he says. His voice is clunky, his speech different from ours; like the difference between the Lows and the rest of the ship. 'All of you, line up.' One of the Lows who travelled down with us snarls

269

and rushes towards him. Idiot. The man in the mask flicks his wrist out, a small black pole in it. It looks like the strikers, I think; and then it extends, a bar coming out of the end, unfolding to click into place, and it wraps around the Low's neck like a whip, expertly handled. The Low screams and chokes and falls to her knees, and gasps and beats at herself and the whip, but can't get free. I watch the whip tighten, and then she's unconscious or dead.

'I said to line up,' the man says.

'Do as he says,' I say, hoping that the others hear me. They don't know who we are, I'm sure. We have to explain.

'You should listen to that one,' the man says, pointing at me. He motions to the others to move forward. I try to count us all: fifty, maybe. Sixty. I look for Jonah again, as we're out here in the light. I still can't see him, but there are so many of us, and I'm short. The crowd makes this hard, and I'm lost in them slightly.

These new people take the children, shoving them into different lines. The kids cry when they're taken from their parents, or from whoever held them as we travelled down here. 'Scan them,' the man says. The others walk up to the adults standing on the front row, and they pull their arms roughly forward and hold machines over their wrists.

'No ID,' another of the masked men says. 'But . . .' He whispers something to his colleague, their backs turned. We can't hear them. They both nod, and then the first man turns back to face us. He paces, waiting for us all to come out.

'Stop it!' one of the women at the front screams as her child is pulled away from her, fighting back, beating at the man who's taking her. I remember saving them both. I brought them both down below the Pit. This new guard – because that's surely what these people are – raises his hand, his black weapon primed for her. Other parents hold their children back. We've come too far to let them go now. The guard shrugs. He must be their leader. They listen to him, as do we. He addresses us all. 'All of you, eyes to me,' he says. And then he brings his stick out, twists it in his hand. He holds it upright. 'Look at me.'

So we do. The stick flashes, a bright orange light, and it takes a second, but then I have never felt pain like it. We all collapse, falling to the floor. I can still see, even through the pain. I grit my teeth and I try to call for Mae, but my mouth doesn't work. I can't turn my head. We're all paralysed.

I watch them walk through us, picking up the rest of the children. One by one they take them in their arms like useless limp dolls, and they carry them away. When they reach Mae, I can only watch as they haul her into the air, away from me. She drops her own doll, and they leave it lying on the ground. She can't react to its loss. She can't cry, but she stares at me as she goes, and I stare back at her. She has to know that I will save her. Whatever they're going to do to her, I won't allow it.

When the children are gone, I watch as the guards climb into the ship and begin to pull the bodies out. Those who drowned; who died fighting; who didn't survive the fall. Everything starts to fade. The pain becomes too much. My eyes sting, and they water, and my vision blurs. I try to focus. Jonah, Mae: I need them. This isn't what was meant to happen. Jonah: please be alive, I think.

Please.

'One of them's breathing!' one of the guards shouts, and they drag the body out, just as my eyes close. I look for the hair, for the skin, for the eyes, because I know that it must be Jonah: it can't not be him. He and I: maybe there's something. He's a person I can rely on, who knows me. I've always needed that. But now my mother's gone, Agatha's gone, even Mae's gone. I've always had somebody who knows me, supporting me, I think. I can't not have that – can't not have *him* – now. They put the body down in front of the lead guard, and he peers down at it. I can't stay conscious any longer. I'm fading.

'Welcome home,' the guard says, inspecting the body, laughing. It's not Jonah. It's not dressed the same. I see muscles, and I see scars, and I see the body twitch; the stump of where a hand should be, ragged and bloody from where I pulled my mother's blade loose.

Then everything goes black.

EPILOGUE

I try to move, but I'm strapped to something: a table, maybe. I open my eyes, and I see that I'm upright. It's not just me: it's everybody from the ship who survived, and others I don't recognise. I feel groggy, like I've been asleep for too long. I can move my hands and legs, but only a little. My muscles feel as if they are tired; as if they never want to move again. I am not strong enough to sit up, because I try, and my back and stomach rally against me. I'm suddenly aware of how much every part of my body hurts; the dull aches, the sharp stings. No adrenalin to stop me being in pain any more. Still, I can open and close my hands, and I can move my feet. I feel myself slowly coming back into my body.

I manage to turn my head enough to look around. We're not where we landed any more. We're inside a building, all of us heads and bodies and feet bound, attached to a wall. People – guards, whatever they are – patrol the room, coming up to us, pulling on the straps to check that they're secure. I play dead. No sense in letting them know I've come around.

'What did they do?' asks one, as they tighten straps.

'They're from the Australia.'

'Can't be.'

'Like cockroaches.'

'They should all be dead by now.'

'Like I say, they're roaches. Somebody must have been watching them, just not telling the rest of us.'

'Jesus. So they've been up there this whole time?'

'Yeah. No wonder they're monsters.' Their voices are stilted, not quite pronouncing the words in ways that I understand easily. They come to me and check my straps, tightening them, step close enough that I can feel their breath on my skin, and then walk on. I flex my hands once they're gone. They don't see.

I look for Mae, but she's not here. There are no children here. I flex my hands again. My strength is returning and it feels good. I flex because I can. Why do we do anything? I know now: *Because we can.*

A guard stands at the front and shouts to the others. 'Ready for transport?' They shout their replies, and he looks down the rows of us all. 'You lucky lot,' he says. He laughs. 'You're headed for The Firmament.' And then he turns and leaves. I watch him, heading down a ramp, through a door, back into the city. I can see that it's raining out there; real rain.

I flex my hands, opening and closing them. I am trying to move my arm at the wrist, the elbow. I can feel it coming. I just need to work it more. I thought that I was saving everyone, but I didn't. So now I have a second chance. I tell myself that, and I feel the blood running through my body

– strong, healthy blood – and I feel my ankles start to twinge. It's like pins and needles: when you have been sitting on your leg, and then you stand and it falls apart, and you can't walk for a few minutes; and then it comes back. That is how this feels.

I can move my neck, so I do. I move my hips. I crick my back. I don't know how many of my muscles work, and I don't have time to find out. I know that I only have one chance to escape.

I cough. I cough, and I make out that I'm choking, that the bracer on my neck is too tight. I'm dying, I pretend. I've heard dying sounds enough to do a pretty good impression of them, and the guards who checked me have run over, and they're loosening the straps, to make sure that I'm alright. They're not inhuman.

While one unties the bindings around my wrists, the other removes the collar on my neck. This is my chance. I open my mouth, snap my head down, and I bite down as hard as I can on the guard's hand. He takes a second to work out what's going on, and then screams, falls backwards. I can taste his blood.

My hands are free. I lash out with them, getting the other guard in the face, and then they're both on the floor, panicking. I reach down and yank the bindings on my ankles free.

'Lock her down!' the guard I punched shouts, so I kick him in the face as I climb off the table. That shuts him up. I step over to the other guard, who's cradling his hand, sobbing beneath his helmet.

'Where are the children?' I ask. My mouth hurts to speak,

my throat burning. 'Where did they go?' He doesn't answer, and looks away from me. I slam my forearm into his throat and he gurgles. I haven't done any real damage; I've hurt him just enough. 'Where?' I ask again.

'The Services!' he says. 'The bloody Services took them!'

He's panicking. I don't know if this is true, or what the Services are, but I'll find out. I stand up and he tries to scream, so I drive my knee down and into the side of his head, knocking him out.

An alarm sounds. The exit starts to close, the ramp pulling upwards. The lights dim. There are more guards coming; I can see them in the distance, rushing towards the transport. I don't have any weapons – they've taken everything – but my body is feeling better. Every moment I'm moving, it feels better.

I run to the ramp, reaching the door the first guard passed through just before it closes, and I drop and roll through the space, tumbling out onto the ground below. Behind me, the door slams shut. No changing my mind now.

I face the guards who have come toward me, weapons out. They slow down, taking stances that I recognise, that show they're gearing up for a fight. One of them fires something into the sky, a glowing red light that arcs up into the clouds. In the distance, an alarm sounds, a shrill scream of a noise. These guards walk towards me, all barking orders, telling me to come quietly, to lie down, to put my hands on my head; to give up.

But Mae is still alive. I promised her that I would keep her safe, and I haven't broken a promise yet.

'Surrender!' I hear one of the guards say, as he steps forward, his striker extending into that whip, ready to attack me. Ready to take me down.

'No,' I say.

ACKNOWLEDGEMENTS

My agent, Sam Copeland, and all at RCW; my amazing and insightful and just thoroughly brilliant editor Anne Perry, along with the similarly skilled wider team at Hodder; my wonderful friends who read this and told me where it was very likely broken and where maybe it possibly wasn't; everybody who has worked so hard on getting my books into the hands of readers – booksellers and reviewers and bloggers alike; and then the readers themselves, without who I am basically nothing.

Enormous thanks to you all, and I hope you had as much fun reading this as I did writing it.

WANT MORE?

If you enjoyed this and would like to find out about similar books we publish, we'd love you to join our online SF, Fantasy and Horror community, Hodderscape.

Visit our blog site
www.hodderscape.co.uk

Follow us on Twitter
🐦 @hodderscape

Like our Facebook page
f Hodderscape

You'll find exclusive content from our authors, news, competitions and general musings, so feel free to comment, contribute or just keep an eye on what we are up to. See you there!